A LIFE LESS DAMNABLE

JACK ROBERTS

©2013 AMERICANA eBooks, Szeged

Jack Roberts: *A Life Less Damnable*

ISBN: 978-615-5423-00-0

AMERICANA eBooks is a division of *AMERICANA –
E-Journal of American Studies in Hungary*, published by the
Department of American Studies, University of Szeged,
Hungary.
ebooks.americanaejournal.hu

Cover image by János Kozma
Author's photograph by György Novák

A LIFE LESS DAMNABLE

JACK ROBERTS

I FOR AN I: A PARTIAL PREFACE TO *A LIFE LESS DAMNABLE*

Jack Roberts's detective novel is set in Szeged, in the South of Hungary in 2000 and it represents the symbiosis of political and personal life in post-Communist Hungary in a university context. In a nutshell, when the retired professor of history dies, the question of motive is this: was the crime committed because of political or personal reasons, and the reconstruction of the crime (not the task for the preface) follows up both agendas in minute detail. To be more observant of the stylistic merits of the text, one also has to assert at the very beginning that the text relies on the framework of the hard-boiled detective novel to expose a difficult moral dilemma of manipulation and being manipulated through tightly composed psychological close-ups worthy of a Modernist novel. This mix of features results in a very much regional but at the same time philosophical novel that needs an introduction mostly because of its 'local color' aspects.

The political context of life in Szeged in 2000 offers the threat of shifting to the right of the political compass, even of fascisation. One thread of the narrative is concerned with the popularity of the right-wing Party of Truth and Life—which was an existing Hungarian party in 2000 with István Csurka in the lead—, and the violent actions of skinheads against anything they consider to be the legacy of the Communist era and anything they consider Jewish. Another thread of the narrative is the issue of how the Communist legacy of the country and the anti-Communist legacy of the 1956 Hungarian Revolution are actually present in post-communist Hungary, in the life of intellectual workers at the Faculty of Arts. The point where the old professor is killed is exactly the time he intends to publish his memoirs and through confession cleanse himself of his Communist past—an act that exposes him both to right-wing activists and to fellow ex-Communists who do not wish to come out just yet. The intermingling of political and personal lives provides the central theme of the story.

The personal lives represented in the text are connected through the figure of the protagonist, Pál Berkesi (named after a successful Communist-era Hungarian detective story writer), 51 year old associate professor of history at the Department of American Studies. He is involved in the case in more than one way: the old professor had been his old-time mentor, he has to postpone his well-deserved last minute Croatian holiday with his young girlfriend because of the funeral, and as he is the ex-brother-in-law of the inspector in charge, he will eventually perform the roles of the hard-boiled dick in the final resolution scene, etc. Most importantly, he is the composite ghost of his alter-egos: he could have been the head of the Department of Slavic Studies had he got on well with the old Professor, he could have become a member of the Party in 1968 and then necessarily an informant as well, he could have been a happy father and family man—but is lost for all these causes. Also, he is comically full of phobias of impossible things. In a very down-to-earth sense, he has little to show of what people would normally consider success—but his life, as it is, is perhaps less damnable than the life of those whose roles he did not take up.

The deceased Professor's life was full of moral choices. He had been a leader of the '56 Revolution, not executed but imprisoned, then allowed to take on his university position again. This story of success had a price, as he had to agree with the Party to serve them illicitly. The arch betrayal was the result of a decision: the Professor died as a moral individual at the moment of the betrayal of his former self, yet in his new position he could shelter his family and *protégés*, minimize the harm politics could do to institutes of intellectual work. Part of his new role was to supervise the hiring of young faculty members, and he chose persons he saw fit for work in the Communist context. That is why he fired Berkesi while he was still a brilliant student—he was not good enough for the roles of assistant professor and Party member and informant the Professor was casting for. After the manipulation of his own life, the Professor began to manipulate the lives of others to an extent readers will find thrilling.

The narrative takes the form of a detective story, in which a classical detective story evolves into a climactic hard-boiled ending. Mickey Spillane's name is constantly referenced: Berkesi adopts his voice in the opening scene already, his books are packed as part of the vacation luggage, and Berkesi eventually acts out the role of Mike Hammer, Spillane's detective hero, in the final resolution scene. The eye for an eye principle prevails when, at the risk of his life, he facilitates the elimination of the culprit. Moreover, the masculine perspective is palpably present in the text, for example in the numerous erotic scenes—with one exception when the nymphomaniac sees the neo-nazi body—and we witness one bright woman landing in a secretarial job, while others are cheated, divorced, raped, picked up, mounted, or saved. The final chapter, besides being bombastic, is also visionary *à la* Hammett. Yet, all this comes with a touch of ridicule.

So it is not surprising to notice that there are many elements of the narrative that transgress the boundaries of the detective framework. For one, the university context resonates with the legacy of the comic university novel. Secondly, there is a touch of political satire in the representation of the political extremes. Thirdly, one can find the 'local color' element, Ferenc Temesi's dusty Szeged functioning, ironically, as Spillane's New York City. Last but not least, this is also a morally oriented realist novel with the central theme of manipulation: the Professor, giving up his revolutionary '56 principles and his own self, manipulating the lives of those around him at the same time. I think the extra twist is produced by the fact that it is a mocking style that cradles the central moral issue of manipulation. The psychological and moral interest of the text reminds one of Henry James's comic sense of duplicity. For instance, in *The Golden Bowl*, the Ververs' (the father and his daughter Maggie) cast the role of the husband on the Prince with full knowledge of the fact that he will cheat on Maggie—then who is responsible for the adultery and the emotional cost? There is no answer and all involved look morally dubious from an external comic perspective. This is exactly the moral problem of manipulation you will find in the case of the Professor.

4

So if one still wants to label the novel as a detective story, I think one needs to add that it is at least meta-fictional, strongly parodic, and possibly philosophical.

You will encounter a wealth of contextual references in the text: minute, exact, informed, putting on the insider's perspective about Szeged and the region. You will find out a lot about streets, buildings, restaurants in Szeged as the possible world of the story. The representation of the issues of Jewishness in Hungary in general and Jewish Szeged in particular is a gem of local color in the text. In this context, detection becomes metaphoric, as the ignorant detective fulfills the role of the uninformed American who comes from the outside and reveals the details of local relations, up to a depth that has never been explicit for locals. To put it in another way, detection actually becomes a metaphor for the experience of cultural exchange represented in the book. The Hungarian-American cultural exchange represented here extends from political to geographical, social, psychological, and moral aspects.

Ágnes Zsófia Kovács

PROLOGUE

Tuesday, 23 October 1956

By late afternoon, students from Budapest Technical University begin to mass at the statue of General József Bem, hero of the 1848 Polish revolution. Their number swells to tens of thousands as workers and residents of Buda join their ranks. Against orders, recruits scramble onto the roof of their barracks and hoist the national colors. With great gasps of joy the marchers raise their own flags, each with a hole through the center where the hammer and sickle emblem of the People's Republic has been cut out.

Monday, 16 June 1958

After a secret trial, Prime Minister Imre Nagy, Defense Minister Pál Maléter, and journalist Miklós Gyimes, members of the reform-minded leadership that came to power during the October uprising, are sentenced to death and hanged. Police commissioner József Szilágyi, another Nagy supporter, is tried separately and hanged. Minister of State Géza Losonczy dies in prison. Their bodies are dumped into a mass grave in Plot 301 of Rákoskeresztúr cemetery where hundreds of martyrs of the Revolution already lay. Neither headstones nor anonymous markers grace the site.

Friday, 16 June 1989

In Heroes' Square, five coffins enclosing the remains of Nagy, Maléter, Gyimes, Szilágyi, and Losonczy lie in state awaiting ceremonial reinterment, at the request of their families, in the now sacred earth of Plot 301. An empty sixth coffin honors the unknown freedom fighter. Beside the caskets, which rest on the steps of the Palace of Art, ritual flames burn. Loudspeakers broadcast Nagy's last words to his executioners. Several hundred thousands chant patriotic verses: "We shall never be slaves again!" From colonnades hang revolutionary flags, each with a hole cut through the center.

Wednesday, 16 June 1999

In the provincial city of Szolnok, police charge two members of the ultra-nationalist Szálasi Guards with the fatal beating of a former communist official. Detectives arrive at the murder scene to find the corpse beneath a blood-soaked Hungarian flag with a hole through the center.

Thursday, 15 June 2000

CHAPTER ONE

You'd think that a personal-injury lawyer with so un-canny a knack for predicting accidents that ambulanc-es chased *him* might be more attentive; that an attor-ney who never crossed dust-choked paths with any of Szeged's one-hundred-sixty-five-thousand inhabitants without picturing even the most hale of them in whiplash collar and body cast might take greater pains to spare a prospective client even greater pains. You'd think.

But then you wouldn't be the one on the verge of a major panic, the one around whose throat and chest fear was about to lock steel bands or down whose back dread was about to loose an icy cataract of sweat, all because a downpour was about to wash away, fittingly in this city of floods, months of plan-ning and, with them, one's dreams of someday being *Führer*.

On a warm June evening, Mr. Viktor Uborka, Esq., Szeged chapter vice president of the Law and Freedom Party padlocked the door of his airless sec-ond-floor office, barreled down stairs whose wooden treads had been rendered positively spongy by innu-merable thunderous descents, hurtled through the open doorway at the bottom—though, given Uborka's girth, not without considerable insult to the jamb—and bam! knocked a scruffy-bearded pedestrian sprawling onto the cobblestones. In the pet-shop window across the way, screeching parakeets the color of unripe bananas and whistling zebra finches formed a mocking chorus as they hopped and flitted from perch to perch.

"My apologies, sir," the well-fed attorney shouted into the fine-grained cloud that had engulfed the aggrieved party as the seat of his trousers made rude acquaintance with Oroszlán Street. Through swirls and eddies of dust, neither man could see the outbound Number One tram tottering across the intersection half a block away.

The air began to clear and the tousled gentleman, disheveled now beyond recognition, struggled to rise from the gutter, out of the cellar-reek that blew onto the pavement from broken street-level windows and filled his nostrils with the stench of rotting spuds, mildew, rat turds, and paraffin.

Bruised and half-destroyed, he wore his life on his face and just now his face was a badly creased study of pained surprise about to give way to pained acceptance. His nut-brown eyes sat deeper in their orbits than usual. His cropped dark hair, flecked with dust-enhanced gray, made his face look round. A salt-and-pepper beard concealed pale lips and a prominent mouth. With his vaulted chest and short bowed legs, he resembled an undersized circus bear.

Stately, plump Uborka, hands in pockets, looked on.

"I never saw you." He lifted his anxious gaze skyward to scan the dark clouds brooding over the city.

For his part, the man who a moment earlier had stopped at the window of the first-floor travel agency and lifted *his* anxious gaze to scan the last-minute vacation offers, never saw Uborka.

Now, on his feet again, he was still doing his best to make good the poet's claim that the life of the Magyar was "gray, the color of dust."

"You must send me the cleaner's invoice." Uborka pressed his card into the man's free hand, the other one busy exploring a wide rent in the elbow of his cast-off tweed. "And the tailor's," he added, confident that on hearing this addendum the poor soul would at once perceive his incredible good fortune at having been flattened by an Uborka.

From under a fine layer of dirt, the rumpled jury of one, regarded the beefy counselor with sensitive eyes full of—Uborka was sure of it—admiration and gratitude.

Uborka began his summation—"I can't tell you how sorry I am."—but the portly attorney must have pressed an invisible button unlike the leather one that the pavement had torn from his victim's coat sleeve or struck a chord *not* unlike the fugitive diminished seventh that broke out of the piano school to dally among the parakeets and finches before sinking its talonlike quarter notes into the risen man's crumpled shoulder. Either way, pallid acceptance now reddened into rage.

"Don't give me that, chum," the man sneered in perfect hard-boiled American.

Uborka bristled.

"And if you ever try anything funny again, I'll beat the living daylights out of you." The stranger lit a bent cigarette. "Get me, fat boy?"

Uborka's piglet-pink face turned eggshell. Umbrage mingled with alarm. Had this unkempt gnome with an accent out of a Hollywood gangster flick really just threatened him with grievous bodily harm? Why else would he stare at Uborka as if he wanted the lawyer's guts in a shopping bag? Uborka ran fingers like fat homemade sausages through sparse hair and resumed in shaky English: "Admit my apology, sir. I am sorry, Mr. ... I am afraid I do not..."

"Hammer. Mike Hammer."

A smoke ring broke across Uborka's porcine cheeks.

"Mr. Hammer, allow me to—"

"Beat it, four eyes."

Uborka froze.

"I said scram!"

Uborka started and took off like a deranged ox.

Pál Berkesi flicked his cigarette into the air, caught it on the tip of his boot, and launched it, still smoldering, after the fleeing attorney like an avenging angel after fiendish Pride.

CHAPTER TWO

Outside the weather was holding. The smell of rain filled the city and blended with the breath of blossoming linden trees along the quieter streets and leafier boulevards, a mingling of scents heady enough to stagger an old man and make him feel as if his youth had been stolen a second time.

So István Borsódy had felt earlier this evening as he'd passed out of the city center with its Habsburg-yellow stuccoed facades and their cornices and friezes and flowering wrought-iron vines, as he'd passed beyond the inner ring road with its bright shop windows flaunting children's shoes and office furniture, discount CDs and designer jeans, and, finally, into the shadowy peace of Szeged's old Jewish quarter. Of all the downtown neighborhoods, he'd thought, only this one, which mutely, in mushroom hues, surrounded the secluded synagogue, which even on bright days seemed shrouded in permanent dusk, always evoked pangs of loss and withdrawal not blunted by time.

But here in the high-ceilinged front room of László Kellner's flat, István didn't feel so old. That he and László could still quarrel like their younger selves cheered him. At least when István was winning the quarrel. He wasn't winning now. István ran his fingertips over the faded lemon sofa searching for the silken thread of an argument. His tatty mackintosh draped one scrolled arm, an arthritic elbow eased itself onto the other.

"In little countries with terrible pasts like ours," he said, "the line of guilt never runs between *them* and *us*. It runs through the middle of each of us."

László Kellner was brooding about the flat; in his wake trailed the desiccated sweetness of bay rum, talc, and age. His faintly striped charcoal suit was freshly brushed; his trousers held their crease, his black oxfords their shine. Even the room seemed well tailored to fit his tall, shambling frame. He kept his hair cropped close, and, except for the full mustache he'd worn since his release from prison thirty-seven years earlier, he was clean-shaven. He came to a halt as if István's words had finally reached him. Turning to face his oldest friend, László arched an eyebrow and said, "What's bothering you, István?"

"I just don't see how you can blame some and not others?" István said, tensing slightly as if he'd tossed a lit match into a pan of alcohol.

"So everyone's a victim. Is that it?" László's slate gray eyes flashed. "No matter how much he complied with the regime?"

"Compliance was the price our consciences paid to keep others from harm," István said, fumbling about in mental darkness for a key that might release László from his guilt-forged manacles.

"Soon you'll tell me the only reason we never had to endure another brutal repression was because sensible people like us complied with the regime," László said, still in shackles.

István tried another key. "A second revolt would have invited another round of reprisals. We did what we could to soften the Central Committee's directives."

István wiped his lenses with a threadbare handkerchief, revealing bright and sympathetic if worried blue eyes. In the nearly four decades since his incarceration for his role in the October uprising, László had cultivated, perhaps too successfully, a reputation for party discipline, less to protect himself, than his colleagues and students at university. Even now, many remembered him as a hard-liner. Others accused him of having made a devil's bargain with the former regime, since of all the academics who'd backed the losing side in '56 and had been severely punished for it, only László Kellner had been restored to a university post after completing his prison sentence. Whether or not they were mistaken on both counts in no way weakened László's desire for atonement.

István slid his bifocals back onto the high bridge of his nose and tried to squint the rangy figure near the bookshelf into focus. But László remained a blur, an image that refused to resolve either in the near distance or, as István sensed darkly, in the present. Not until László spoke did he seem real again.

"Why is it so hard for you to accept that we historians, while serving the old regime, committed sins against the truth?" László said, leafing through a broken-spined tome with the apparent interest of one reading an instruction manual.

"What I find so hard to accept is your willingness to spend the rest of your life scolding us all for past transgressions," István said. He ran his fingers through his long silver locks like a distraught poet.

"For transgressions against the past." László slammed the book shut. "What we did can't be excused so casually."

István watched his friend fiddle with the front door's lock. He wasn't afraid of losing the point. It was László himself he feared losing. Beside the entrance on a teak jardinière, a large green pitcher held purple-white lilacs. A big black ant reconnoitered across the emerald glaze.

István drained off the last of the Theodora, the sparkling water bubbling against his lips and tongue, and plunked the tumbler down atop a mahogany coffee table barely visible under a week's issues of *Népszabadság*, the former Party broadsheet, a dozen or so back numbers of *Élet és Irodalom*, the most interesting of the literary weeklies, and dusty piles of scholarly journals with Hungarian, Russian, and French titles. He checked his light gray vest and black and red monkey-striped shirt for water stains, and, finding none, fumbled with his collar button before letting his bird-like hands flutter gracelessly to his lap.

László trudged across the room again and out of István's sight to a large window looking out on Hajnóczy Street, trying perhaps to place himself beyond the range of his friend's good sense.

Soon both men were gazing across the street at the "new" synagogue completed a quarter century before either had drawn his first breath. Over its cupolaed dome, the clouds that threatened rain parted. The last of the sun's rays bathed the synagogue and its austere grounds in ghostly light. Cypresses in the temple yard stood in silhouette against lavender dusk. Spikes atop the yard's scrolled-iron fence shone as if illuminated from within.

"You can't go to press with this book," István said, coming to the point. "You've been a target of neo-fascist diatribes for ten years."

For every column that appeared in the nationalist press denouncing him, László received a dozen or more pieces of hate mail. Wild prayers for his death outnumbered death threats three to one. He particularly seemed to enjoy the curses of a Transylvanian cleric who signed his red-ink maledictions: *Your brother in Christ, Father Ágoston.*

In his latest invective, the good priest had, as always, damned László's Red soul, before relating, in menu prose, the culinary fate that each of László organs would meet in the devil's kitchen: *May your liver be marinated in pig's blood, dredged lightly in bone meal made from your femur, blackened over an infinitely high heat, and served in a molten pool of basaltic vinegar and gall reduction.*

"I don't pay attention to those lunatics," László said.

"Go and confess publicly to crimes of intellect and spirit and *those lunatics* will take your confession as an acknowledgment of graver offenses," István said. "They'll come after you."

László's back stiffened, raising ripples on dark worsted. "You're crazy, István. That sort of vengeance ceased forty years ago."

"So you've already forgotten Szolnok?" István said. "Why can't you see, László, that we only forgive our own sins when we confess them to others, that the others neither forgive nor forget them?"

László spoke with the thin voice of a ghost: "I want to come clean."

"If you publish this book, you'll put others in danger as well," István said, shaking his head and limping over to the carved desk that filled one corner of the room. If István could make László fearful for others' safety, he might withdraw the book and save himself. Opening the binder at random, he read aloud: "*The mendacity that plagued our profession under the dictatorship afflicts it still.* Is this what you mean by coming clean? You're damning the whole profession, László."

"Perhaps *troubled* and *affects* would be better," László said.

István turned the page and began reading again: *Regrettably, academic politics did not change when the regime changed. There is little difference between today's university department and that of thirty years ago.*

Fixing his sternest gaze on László, who still refused to face him, István reread the statements as questions. László listened blankly. "Don't you find that to be so?" he said, "I'm sorry, István. I cannot feel remorse for the bad choices others made."

István closed the binder in frustration. "*Jaj*! We're talking about your choices, László! Choices that you can still reverse! The publisher doesn't have the manuscript yet."

"Such people implicate themselves," László said, sounding as distant as if he were speaking from another room.

"But we're talking about you, László!" István squeezed between his friend and the window and, looking straight into his vacant eyes, said: "I'm trying to protect you! If you publish this book, you'll be delivering yourself into the hands—"

"No one compelled him to inform," László said, still staring blankly ahead as if István was not there.

"—of some of the worst people," István continued, before breaking off, stunned. "Who said anything about informers? Who are you talking about?"

László winced as if he'd turned an ankle on wet pavement. "You didn't allow me to finish," he hedged.

"You said that no one forced him into informing." István said.

"As I was saying when you interrupted me: no one compelled anyone else to inform, to promote the official version, to spread lies and call it scholarship, all these—"

"Who are you talking about, László?"

CHAPTER THREE

"This is the worst part," Gabi Varga whimpered, waking from her post-coital nap. The "afterwards" was always the worst part. Not the right "afterwards," which could be nice and snuggly, assuming the guy with whom you'd just coupled wasn't a rotten bastard. She meant the much "afterwards," when the love chemicals that flooded your brains and bodies before, during, and right after sex stopped flowing and the two of you no longer felt the need to be so close that your arms and legs would have to be in knots before either of you would feel even a smidge closer to being as close as both of you wanted to be.

"This is the worst part," Gabi whined into her pillow. She no longer felt his body against hers or his breath on her cheek or on her neck or in her hair.

In the bathroom, pipes began to cough and sputter. A broken spray pattered the tub. Along its rod, the shower curtain whooshed, its rings clattered. So he hadn't left.

"This isn't so bad," Gabi said. There hadn't been enough plum brandy left in the green bottle he'd handed her on the train to do any real damage and they'd polished that off in two good pulls apiece. Still, she kept her eyes shut. She knew what she would see. Beginning at the door, a trail of shed clothing would lead to the narrow bed hardly big enough for one prone female, who lay half-covered by a sheet still translucent with their sweat, to say nothing of the swiving lovers who had strained the already weakened frame to its limits a half hour earlier.

Approaching climax, Gabi had expected another kind of culmination, that moment when her little bed's brittle pine slats would snap and the thin mattress would gobble them up like a giant clam engulfing two exhausted swimmers, thrashing and gasping for air. She'd laughed out loud at the image of four naked feet trying to kick their way free from the mattress turned mollusk-of-prey. Thrown off by her sudden mirth, he had halted mid-thrust and raised an eyebrow before finding his rhythm again.

Bleary-eyed, Gabi now caught sight of his leather jacket on a sunlit patch of floor beside the bed. Her studded denim jacket, her pink tee and short black skirt must have come off first, followed by his white tee, her pink plastic shoes, his Doc Martens, his socks, her bra, his blue jeans, and her thong, this last article hanging like a tiny tea rose garland over the mittened leaves of a fig tree the previous tenant had left behind.

Naked, she must have pranced to the front door so he could better admire her cute little *segg*—she din't attend aerobics class twice a week for nothing. Turning to face him, she must have wrapped his leather jacket around herself in an attitude of false modesty before goose-stepping across the wooden floor, doubling over in laughter at least once because she'd tried too hard to keep a straight face, and back into the tattooed arms of her skinhead lover.

The faucets squeaked shut and the shower curtain rings jangled. Gabi buried an expectant smile in her pillow.

She must have thrown her legs around his waist and drawn her face level with his to kiss him hard on the mouth. She must have shaken off the jacket and let it drop to where it now lay like the blackened carcass of some thick-skinned sea creature stumbled upon during a search for shells.

CHAPTER FOUR

Chunky dusk-tinged pigeons fretted atop Klauzál Square's neo-classical facades. Lajos Kossuth's statue, one palm opened skyward as if testing for rain, raised or lowered his brazen cap in the equivocal manner of one unsure about the weather. Steeling himself against the pastry-fragrant invitations issuing forth into the square from rival confectionaries, Viktor Uborka shouldered his wide way through columns of Magyars armed with ice cream cones.

A squad of pigeons descended on black-banded wings, putting down at Kossuth's feet. Uborka glanced at his wrist. Nine minutes to seven. His fellow L&Fers would soon converge on Bartók Square. And, in less than an hour, the principals would arrive from Kecskemét.

At least the episode with the elfin mobster hadn't cost him much time. He still had plenty to worry about. For instance, he hoped that gypsy halfwit Jóska had enough sense to staple the red, white and green bunting to the dais that carpenters had erected earlier this afternoon at the southwest corner of the square. Yesterday, he'd paid a dreadful man reeking of onions and bacon fat 30,000 forints in cash—10,000 for the rental, 20,000 for the security deposit—to deliver a dozen flags and assorted decorations by half-past six.

Their little corner of Bartók Square must be awash in the national colors by now. At a quarter to eight, when the chapter president emerged from the limousine with party leader Ferenc Gyufa, an appreciative throng would greet them.

Uborka ticked off the last items on his list of things to do. He needed only to drop by a cheerless little bakery off Tisza Lajos Boulevard to pick up gâteaux for the dignitaries. The selection and quality were better at the upscale Kálvária cake shop where he went every Sunday for *dobostorta*, but the baker and his wife were L&F Party members in good standing and party loyalty took precedence over pastry.

Impulsively, he thrust a hand into his breast pocket to make sure the recorded music for tonight was still there. He adored polkas. "The happiest music in the world," he would say should anyone ask him why. He recalled the planning committee's resistance when he suggested that the music for the rally be polkas rather than the fusty Magyar folksongs they always played.

"Everyone enjoys a merry polka or even a saucy little mazurka now and then," a kindly but dim electrician called Villám said. "But, Viktor Uborka, surely you agree these dances come from Poland. We are Magyars."

"May I humbly submit," Uborka said, "that one reason the Law and Freedom Party has so hard a time attracting new members is the current membership's reluctance to look beyond our borders. How many *gulyás* parties have we given, ladling out bowl after bowl of steaming, paprika-stained soup from big, black cauldrons?"

Committee members smiled and nodded indecipherably at each other.

"But," Uborka continued, "have we even once considered hosting a spaghetti-and-meatball dinner or a Swedish smorgasbord or a Hawaiian luau? The time has come, ladies and gentlemen, to strike out for new worlds. The day of the *csárdás* is rapidly passing. To-day, the polka. Tomorrow, the limbo, the tarantella, and the Virginia reel." Uborka pounded the table with his fist.

A rental agent called Gólya woke up and applauded.

Miss Mogorva, a schoolmistress, spoke next. She wore the expression of an addle-brained cat that had lapped from a saucer of sour milk. "Do you not think, Viktor Uborka, that it will be difficult for the boys and girls of the folk dancing troupe to adapt their native steps to an alien mode on such short notice?"

"Would the lady please explain how she is using 'short notice'?" Uborka said. "We cannot begin to know her intentions until we reach consensus on the meaning of this slippery phrase."

"I assure you, Viktor Uborka," Miss Mogorva said, her thin lips trembling, "I have no intentions—"

Uborka was steadfast: "Would the lady please—"

"Two days!" Miss Mogorva confessed.

"Exactly!" Uborka beamed. "O, it may take the little ones a moment or two to adjust, but they'll soon be twirling to the gay polka beat."

Uborka defended the accordion's nationalist credentials and all residual opposition melted away. He had never been surer of his powers of persuasion.

Now, crossing Feketesas Street, Uborka felt confident again, composed, poised to buy a bunch of posies from the first old hag he saw and toss her twenty forints.

CHAPTER FIVE

László turned on the spigot marked "H" for *hideg* to run cold water for the kettle. The pipes were old and the water from the spout ran murky brown. At least István hadn't followed him to the kitchen.

Refuge was temporary: István would seek him out here and ask him again who the informer was. Should he counter that he'd spoken hypothetically, István would insist they forgive the hypothetical informer. László bristled.

Whether or not István wanted to admit it, László reflected, preemptive forgiveness, hypothetical or real, was just another term for looking the other way. A Pole had written: *Do not forgive for you have no power to forgive in the name of those betrayed at dawn.* Only the victims could forgive. Of course, István might point out that they'd both been victims once themselves. Though István, unlike László, had not been a member of Nagy's inner circle in '56, his public support for the revolutionary government during the uprising, though it didn't earn him time in a prison camp, deprived him of his university post for several years.

At least, László told himself, he'd won the argument. István had wanted him, for reasons even László understood, to protect himself from his enemies by softening the book's tone and drop the self-criticism and the polemics about how little everything had changed since 1989.

The water was beginning to clear. László filled the kettle and lit the burner with a match.

For a decade, he'd grown surer each year that the old regime's anti-democratic character had survived the transition. He wondered how much his sense of things owed to his reaction to the events whose eleventh anniversary was tomorrow. He recalled his outrage upon learning, only days before the reburials of Imre Nagy and the other martyrs, that the Committee for Historical Justice had invited Party leaders to stand ceremonial guard beside the coffins. So, he'd thought at the time, the Party has finally succeeded in making the October uprising its own. The kettle whistled.

Then his own invitation arrived with the force of an accusation, charging him, or so it had seemed to his guilt-ridden mind, with having made a remarkable career for himself by serving the regime. Until that moment, he believed his reputation for getting as close to the historical truth as possible was deserved, especially given the obstacles the regime placed in the scholar's path. From that moment, he began to question whether he'd only gotten as close as his ambition would allow him to get. From that moment, he'd been overcome by the desire to make amends.

The synagogue melted into the purple evening. If this were tomorrow night, the great doors would swing open and yellow light from the sanctuary would flow through the iron gates into the street. The aged congregants would greet each other in the yard before advancing unsteadily, assisted by one another, toward the glowing entrance. Before the war, several thousand Jews made their living in Szeged, married, trysted, divorced, raised their children, buried their parents, died. It had taken only a few mild days in the spring of 1944 to gather the whole community inside the sanctuary—the synagogue had been generously designed to accommodate the entire congregation—and load it into cattle cars bound for Auschwitz. Less than a third came back. How many Jews lived in Szeged now? A thousand? Five hundred?

István had come here tonight certain that László intended to publish his memoirs and, for reasons even István understood, that László refused to consider the damage, to others and himself, their publication would cause. Did he have any right to be surprised that all his best arguments had failed to change László's mind?

Yet he'd finally found an opening in László's slip of the tongue. Did László intend to accuse some colleague or former student of betrayals even more grave and destructive than intellectual dishonesty and collusion with a corrupt authority? István had read the manuscript in the binder carefully—he'd only returned it to László earlier this evening—and while he'd encountered allegations of fraud and connivance in chapter after chapter, he couldn't recall having tasted the bitterness ordinarily directed at informers. You tended to recall the accused's name. It became a hated word, a fetish to be secreted away in the folds of one's brain as in a kid pouch, to be fished out when only the most powerful charm would do.

István understood the common demand that those who did the most harm to their fellows under the regime pay for their actions even this late in the day. Still, no good could ever come of it. Retroactive justice was merely another name for score-settling.

When István wedged himself into the tiny kitchen's doorway, László was measuring spoonfuls of black leaves into a green teapot with a broken spout. The lid, which looked as if it had been repaired more than once, lay beside it. László dropped the spoon on the counter top as if remembering a missed appointment and slapped his forehead with an open palm. "I probably should have added the tea *before* I poured the water," László said. Then, sheepishly: "Do you think it matters?"

István pretended to think about the question and stroked his stubbled chin. "I think it probably does," he said.

"Let me get rid of this muddle," László said.

"László, you spoke of an informer a little while ago," István said.

"I merely spoke hypothetically." László put the kettle on again and spooned tea leaves into the pot. He sliced some lemon and reached for the sugar bowl. He placed a teaspoon and a lemon slice on each saucer and another spoon in the sugar bowl. He turned off the gas jet and poured boiling water over the leaves. He gingerly lowered the cracked lid onto the pot and let the tea steep. "And no. You didn't miss anything. There's no mention of informers in what you read."

László poured the steaming tea into two china cups. He dribbled rum into his cup from a small aquamarine bottle on whose label's palm-lined sea a great-sailed ship floated. He tipped the mouth toward István's and waited. István nodded. István waited.

CHAPTER SIX

Jaj!, what horrible lyrics, Gabi winced. He was sing-ing—well, screaming anyway—in the shower:

> We'll do away with every bad thing,
> everything evil will disappear.
> Our only weapon, a roaring gun,
> we'll shoot every gypsy, young and old
> And when the job is finally done,
> we'll hang a sign: Gypsy-Free Zone.

Then again, she hadn't invited—what did he say his name was? Zoli?—she hadn't invited Zoli back to her flat to discuss his ethnic views. At least he'd be leav-ing soon.

Five hours earlier, she'd boarded the Szeged train at Kecskemét where she'd spent the morning and part of the afternoon in her hometown running errands for her ailing mother. Mr. Takács, her boss at the Vo-dafone store, had given her the day off. When the train pulled out at three minutes to two, the sun was still shining and the day was warm. She entertained thoughts of sunbathing at the municipal pool in Újszeged by late afternoon. At a quarter to three, the train stalled outside of Kiskunfélegyháza.

The sky turned dark over the Alföld. A lone hawk hovered and circled and hovered again over the great grassy plain spreading out on either side of the railroad tracks, featureless but for the occasional stand of yellow acacia trees. At half-past three, a straw-haired drunk, who had passed out next to Gabi just as the formerly running train pulled out from Kecskemét, stirred and straight away ran one deft hand under her skirt. The other, as nimble, grabbed a breast.

Her resistance drew the attention of the taller of two skinheads seated a few rows back. Zoli lifted her admirer out his seat, his hand a vise on the man's neck. To the stranded passengers' hoots and whistles, he frog-marched the reprobate off the train. The unfortunate drunk soon found himself upside-down and unregarded in a green dumpster overflowing with lard and rotting cabbages. Back on the train, which resumed its timid progress toward Szeged, Zoli found himself rightside-up and highly regarded by Gabi, who found herself inside out with desire and without regard for any but her blue-eyed hero.

Now Zoli stood in the bathroom doorway, tall, muscled, and very white, drying himself with a washcloth.

"I'll get you a towel." She started to rise. The sheet slipped from her and she let it fall. Her honey blonde hair was disarmingly tousled. She blew a lazy strand from almond hazel eyes.

"I'll be late." He leaned over to kiss her. She wanted to pull him down onto her, but his kiss said he was going. He gently took her hands from around his neck and loped across the room to the bookshelf where his boxers perched. Her gaze traced the curve of his spine up to the base of his powerful neck before fixing itself on the death's head tattooed below his right shoulder blade. The grinning skull, like its bearer, fascinated but did not frighten her. She did not know why. She only knew she wanted Zoli to stay. She remembered lines by a much-loved poet,

> *Within your arms you enfold me*
> *when I'm frightened.*
> *Within my arms I enfold you*
> *and I'm not frightened.*
> *In your arms, the great silence of death*
> *frightens me no longer.*

And she knew why.

CHAPTER SEVEN

The baker's wife, a she-bear of a woman with a kindly growl of a voice, waved goodbye. Uborka dangled a small white box tied with red and green twine from his pinkie as he drifted toward Bartók Square.

Even from a block away, Uborka's untutored ears registered the nuanced clash of chords and crash of drums resolving into a heavy metallic din just as the lyrics began: "*Sharpen your knife on the sidewalk. Let it glide into the kike's heart.*" Hurling awful curses at an imaginary Jóska until the real Jóska appeared, he broke into a trot.

"Turn off that devil music, you beastly little toad," Uborka screamed. "You've fucked up everything!"

"I sorry, Uborka," Jóska said. "They show up nasty and rude and what have you. Next thing they blow speakers up with noise. I try stop them but one wave knife and say fuck off. I fuck off."

Jóska cast sad brown eyes toward a reporter, a cameraman, and a soundman forming a little arc around two leather-jacketed skinheads in blue jeans and Doc Martens. The thugs were at ease, joking with the crew. Before his rage flared again, Uborka noted how reflective their shaven skulls made them seem. He charged the bald intruders.

"I'm afraid you'll have to leave," Uborka said to the hooligans, who were too busy mugging for the viewers at home to acknowledge him. "And take your ghastly music with you."

"Isn't this a public park?" the shorter, more crazed-looking of the two said.

Uborka pondered why a skinhead's eyes—blue and clear but unfocused like a newborn's—always looked that way. He spotted the Arrow-Cross tattoo on the taller one's neck: four perpendicular rays like the points of a compass guiding him back to the short one's hostile question. Uborka heard himself saying, "This assembly's by invitation only."

"Invite us," the taller one said, pulling himself out of a slouch.

Uborka mustered the last of his nerve. "Look, we're a peaceful organization. We just don't do the brown shirt thing very well and we're not sure we'd want to even if we could. Perhaps another party will go in for your brand of violence. We're going for a more positive image, see, and what you boys project, while I'm sure it suits your purposes nicely—"

He never got to finish. The shorter one punched him so hard in the throat that he barely regained his voice in time to greet the venerable Ferenc Gyufa twenty minutes later.

At eight o'clock, the great man himself mounted the platform to address the tiny assembly. Gyufa counted the flags that lined his route to the podium. An even number of flags promised a successful event. An old habit, he told himself, silly really, mere superstition. His tally reached eleven and ended. He recounted to be sure. Eleven. The empty flagpole didn't figure in his tabulations. He winced inwardly. At least it wasn't raining. An inane polka played. The huge croaking man who'd greeted him began to clap to the music.

Gyufa raised his palms over the little assembly as if trying to hush a cheering multitude. A few supporters at the foot of the platform took the benediction as a cue for applause, which commenced at once, though unevenly. Others set their flickering candles on the ground and joined the tiny ovation.

The benign Gyufa smiled, his blue eyes twinkling behind steel rims, and, as if awaiting inspiration, lifted his gaze over the heads of his admirers to glimpse two shaved heads bobbing across the square in time with the polka beat. He followed the jogging skulls as far as the square's perimeter where they dissolved in the dying light. A moment before they vanished, Gyufa thought he saw the national colors floating on the evening air, the red, white, and green all running, promiscuous, bleeding into the browns and plums and blacks of the fast-approaching night.

CHAPTER EIGHT

Oszkár Neumann couldn't complain.

First, his teeth didn't hurt. Dr. Gyula Halász at the dental clinic had seen to that this morning. The man handled the tools of his trade as Kreisler once handled his bow.

Second, his Sári had called from New Jersey to tell him she'd be coming to Hungary with Tammy and Stevie, Jr., his American grandchildren, for two weeks in July. He wondered if Sári still spoke Hungarian to them at home. Bence and Eszter Lang's granddaughter from Los Angeles visited last month but all they could do was smile at each other.

It had been three years since he'd seen Tammy and little Stevie. They'd been too young to understand the rules for *ulti*. Still, the thirty-two card Hungarian deck delighted them with its brilliantly colored suits of hearts, bells, acorns, and leaves, with its charming aces, each card heralding one of the four seasons, with its picture cards showing the heroes and villains of the William Tell legend, which he'd reenacted for them again and again.

Nearly as pleasant was the news that Stevie, Sr., the *putz* who happened to be married to his daughter, would not be able to join them. Oszkár had been so happy to hear about *die kinder* that he'd even tried to sound disappointed when Sári explained why Stevie, Sr. couldn't leave his swimming-pool-cleaning business at the height of the summer season.

Third, his sister Ella had invited him over for the evening meal and surprised him with his favorite dish: Szeged-style fish soup. He ate two steaming bowls of the rich red broth, occasionally stuffing his mouth with hunks of fresh white bread to quell the heat from the fiery paprika, before he attacked the tender filets. Bless his sister. She'd boned the carp, so worried was she about his teeth. Even his brother-in-law Móri had been in a good mood, for a change.

Crossing Mikszáth Kálmán Street, Oszkár heard a polka coming from the far side of Bartók Square. Was there folk dancing tonight? What he most wanted to do right now was to get home and make himself some bodza tea. Then, he would tune in the BBC World Service in Hungarian on the Grundig shortwave Sári bought for him when his Judit died. After the funeral, Sári pleaded with him to come back to America with her, to live there in his own sunny room in her New Jersey home.

He hadn't kept her waiting for an answer. He couldn't leave Jutka here alone. Who would weed around her grave and water the ivy? Who would place a pebble on her headstone each week? Who would read her the detective stories from *Zsaru Magazin*, a favorite pastime, while she lived, when they weren't gathering bodza blooms for tea from the bushes beside the railroad tracks? Who would say the mourner's Kaddish for her? Of her large family, only Jutka and her sister Hanna survived the deportation orders and the camps. Hanna, never healthy, died of stomach cancer fifteen years ago. He could never leave Szeged or Jutka. On the morning she returned to America, Sári stopped by the little radio shop on Mérey Street and returned with the Grundig.

Oszkár considered his chances for a good night's sleep. Tonight, he'd open his windows wide and let the fragrance of the lindens fill the flat. It had been a good day. And now, with bodza tea, the BBC, and decent prospects for a sound rest, it occurred to Oszkár that it might end well too.

So he wasn't concerned when he heard them approaching. In fact, he wasn't even concerned when he felt them closing in. Just kids, he told himself. One seized him by the shoulder and spun him around. Oszkár saw their shaved heads and struggled, in spite of the fear that clawed at his bowels and wrung the air from his lungs, to suppress a grim smile. He should have known.

CHAPTER NINE

"Ha! I'd almost forgotten," László said. No sooner had István set down his empty tea cup than László produced, from inside his jacket, two Churchillian cigars. "Sándor brought me these from Budapest the other day. You know the little tobacconist's on Márvány Street?"

"Do you mean that ancient shop behind Castle Hill?" István said. He knew it well. You could buy anything there: bicycle tire repair kits, egg timers, transistor radios, fountain pens, tea strainers, sewing machine parts, fine camel-hair brushes, wax fruit, shoelaces should yours break mid-cigar.

László had planned to surprise István with the cigars anyway, but since Éva would arrive in the next half hour, he needed only one more pretext for putting off the subject of informers for the evening, and the cigars would serve nicely. A man with a cigar has an advantage, he told himself. It's harder to figure out what he's thinking. Of course, István would be smoking too, but László already knew what *he* thought.

"Care for a smoke?" László asked in heavily accented English, offering István a fat *Corona*.

István's father had been the aficionado, at least when he could still get cigars, which meant before the Second World War; he'd died in a Siberian labor camp in 1947. But István knew his father's ritual by heart. He passed the length of the cigar beneath his nose— no mustiness here—before holding the Connecticut wrapper to his ear and rolling it gently between thumb and forefinger. Perfect. Barely a crinkle. He clipped a small disk from its tapered end and held the leafy cylinder to his mouth to await the spark, flash, and flame of the brass lighter neatly enclosed within László's grip.

"What are we celebrating?" István said. The rich winy smoke enfolded his tongue and spilled from his lips. László's dodge seemed to have worked.

"Tomorrow is the 16th of June," László said through a swirling cloud as every note of contentment left his voice.

"Can you believe I'd forgotten? It's been eleven years."

"It's been forty two years, István."

"Why must you insist we look only at the bad times?"

"Why must you insist we look away from them."

"Beyond them."

Smoke coiled and rolled in the lamplight.

"How many more of these terrible anniversaries must I celebrate?" László had never made it a secret that the agonizing conflicts he'd spent the last decade trying to resolve could be traced to that extraordinary scene eleven years ago when the hundred thousands had massed at Heroes' Square.

István said: "Why can't you be happy for the rest of us?"

He remembered how a raven-haired law student in jeans addressed the crowd that day not as *comrades*, in the usual fashion, but as *citizens*. The courageous youth was now a conservative MP of the populist ilk. Of late, he'd been busy making a second name for himself by preying on the frail hopes of ethnic Magyars for dual citizenship, at least until someone told him that Magyars living in neighboring states were not yet eligible to vote in Hungary. Still, on that brilliant spring morning, he'd addressed his compatriots with a word that some had waited a generation to hear, that more had never heard.

"I'm tired of remembering," László's said, in an almost self-pitying tone unusual tone. "Why shouldn't those of us crushed by evil, whether it took the form of Soviet tanks or secret trials and death sentences, carried out or commuted, be spared the shame of having to relive our worst days?" He nearly stubbed out his cigar, thought better of it, and took it to his lips again.

István couldn't share László's sense of humiliation. He'd not been in Budapest during the uprising. He'd not heard the swiftly-turning treads of Khrushchev's T-54s churn streets to rubble or the blasts of shells and rockets raining down upon the city from the big gun emplacements high on Gellért Hill or low-flying Russian jets. And afterward, with the fighting over, the sentences handed down, he hadn't suffered what beatings, what deprivations at prison camp.

"No one's forcing us to do that, László."

"Don't you ever think about it, István?"

"We were rehabilitated. We resumed our careers. Nearly everything we lost was returned to us."

"Have you ever asked yourself what we gave up in exchange?"

"Why don't you tell me, László?" István took another puff of his *Corona*. "Better yet. Tell me who that informer was?"

CHAPTER TEN

"Don't look so scared, *Fater*," the shorter one said. "We're not going to hurt you. We just want to know where Hajnóczy is. Is that the street, Zoli?"

"That's easy, boys. It's straight ahead. Just keep walking the way you were walking." Oszkár said, relieved.

"And how were we walking, *Fater*? You don't like the way we walk?"

"I didn't mean the way you walk...," Oszkár said, growing confused. "I meant how you were walking. Wait. I don't mean how..."

"Again he says he doesn't like how we walk," Zoli said. "Are you trying to insult us, *Fater*? You think we're too stupid to find our way?"

"Not in the least." Oszkár's hands began to shake.

"Stand up straight when we talk to you. Show some respect, *büdös zsidó*."

Oszkár tried to straighten up. "I'm sorry, boys," he heard himself say. He didn't recognize his tone: not defiant, but not timid either. "This is as straight as I am going to get. Forty years I've been bending over my work table."

"Tell us, *Fater*, what's in the bag?"

"It's only fish soup, boys."

He clutched the paper bag tightly with both hands, felt the still warm *halászlé* inside its container.

"Let's have a look."

Oszkár drew the bag closer to his body.

An arm like a steel bar came down hard on his wrists. He lost his grip on the bag and recoiled in pain, raising both arms to protect his face. Two hands grabbed him by the wrists from behind and jerked them down, held them at his sides. Another hand forced his head forward until his chin touched his chest. "Look what you've done. Your supper's in the street."

The dark broth trickled out of the sodden bag into the gutter.

"Are you going to do as you're told from now on, *Fater*?"

He tried to answer, but fear had him by the larynx. He tried to nod, but the hand still clasped the back of his skull. The hand let go, but before Oszkár could raise his chin, the same hand grabbed a shock of white hair above his forehead and tugged Oszkár's head back, exposing his throat to the knife whose point rested against his gullet.

"Are you going to do as you're told?"

"Yes."

The other skinhead released Oszkár's arms and stepped into view, a Hungarian flag draped around his shoulders like a swimmer's towel.

"Do you recognize this flag, *Fater*?" Clutching a corner of the flag with one hand, Zoli raised a swastika-tattooed fist in an arc to display the colors as if he were opening a fan. He repeated this motion with his other hand until both arms were fully extended. In his black leather jacket, he resembled nothing so much as a vulture with striped wings of red, white, and green.

"It's our flag," Oszkár said.

"What do you mean by that, Jew?" The pressure from the knifepoint grew. "This flag belongs to the Magyar nation. What nation are *you* talking about?"

Oszkár was trapped. He had been a Magyar, a Hungarian national from birth. But he knew they would never accept that answer. At the same time, he couldn't bring himself, scared as he was, to say what they wanted to hear. That he was a Jew, that he was of an alien nation, that his whole life he'd been a guest in theirs—as if one had to choose between one's country and one's faith.

He tried to force the answer they wanted past his quavering lips, but something inside wouldn't let him. The knife's argument couldn't be any more persuasive: Just say what they want you to say and you'll live to enjoy another bowl of fish soup. Again, Oszkár tried to force himself to speak. Still no words came.

Now you get courage? he chided himself. But, it wasn't courage exactly. It was his recognition, as his life teetered on a knifepoint, that his predicament could not be any more absurd. After everything this little country of theirs had gone through, after everything her people had suffered, if someone wanted to call himself a Magyar, what right had anyone else to question his worthiness? For who in his right mind would choose to cast his lot with a nation whose past appeared to be little more than one nightmare after another?

He heard himself begin to sing, softly at first, barely above a whisper, audible nonetheless: *"Isten, áldd meg a Magyart…"* God, bless the Magyar people...

"What are you croaking, *Fater*? Is that the national hymn?"

He closed his eyes and waited for the knifepoint to pierce his throat. Still, he kept on singing, Kölcsey's words flowing from his lips. He knew he was provoking them but he couldn't stop singing. He could hear his own heart beating out the anthem's stately tempo. He could feel the warm night air on his forehead and cheeks dampened by sweat and tears of angst and fear and stress and, yes, rage too.

"Do you want to die, *bibsi*?"

"*...megbűnhődte már e nép a múltat s jövendőt.*" *All our past and future sins atoned through our suffering.* He could see and hear his poor mother, deported sixty years ago, singing, her eyes shining with generous tears for the nation she'd loved, for the nation that had been unable to save her from a horrible death in a foreign land. At least he would die at home.

He heard footsteps approaching. They stopped meters away. A woman's voice: "I'm calling the police. It's ringing..."

The knife slipped from its mark. Oszkár opened his eyes to see the owner of the voice, an attractive woman whose soft eyes were hardened with resolve. She was keeping her distance from the skinheads who, surprised by the warning, turned to her. The shorter one said, "You don't have to call the police, ma'am. We were merely asking the gentleman for directions."

She pressed the phone closer to her ear, burying the device in wavy red hair. "Hello? I wish to report an assault. On Jósika near the corner of Hajnóczy..." The woman's voice was firm and calm and loud enough to be heard by several pedestrians. Three rushed to her aid.

The skinheads deserted their victim, dashed back toward Attila Street, and disappeared around a corner. As he ran, the taller one made a lopsided ball of the flag he'd unwrapped from around his neck and tossed it to his partner, who stuffed as much of it as he could under his jacket. The remnant trailed behind him in the night.

CHAPTER ELEVEN

The Virág's glass doors squealed as if for joy and the little flowerpots that lined the great windows tapped and pattered as Kati drifted into the café in a white sundress, her strawberry blonde mane brushing porcelain shoulders. She spotted Pál at once and flashed her brightest smile. He signaled for the waiter and rose to kiss Kati. Her lipstick colored his mouth dreamy tangerine.

"*Mit parancsol?*" the waiter said, trying not to snicker at Pál's freakish chops. Kati sighed apologetically, pulled a small mirror from her red vinyl purse, and held it up to Pál's face. He saw the sad eyes of a silent-movie clown; and, raising his chin a bit, the Creamsicle lips.

"Tell laughing boy here another *kávé* for me," Pál said through a napkin. "You have whatever you like."

When he returned from the washroom, Kati started to giggle, her oxheart cherry eyes filled with mirth.

"Seems I haven't rinsed away my knack for inspiring laughter," Pál said.

"What have you done to your sleeve, Pál?" Kati said, hooking a finger through the hole in his coat and tickling his elbow.

"I was trod upon by an unhinged buffalo."

Kati skeptically fluttered her lashes.

Pál was too preoccupied to notice. He needed to prepare her for the news about the last-minute travel offer he'd spied a few hours earlier. It was good news after all, the stuff he feared and loathed more than surprises, which he merely loathed. Bad news he could take and give. Bad news arrived with all the boring frequency and dull regularity of the mail. *Bad news flies, good news barely toddles*, the saying went. And so, it was good news for which the receiver must be readied if the bearer hoped to lessen the damaging effects of an unexpected boon to the central nervous system.

But the strong black *kávé*, topped with a stiff-crested though swiftly liquefying hillock of whipped cream, and two pieces of oven-warm poppy-seed *rétes*, which he'd as good as inhaled while waiting for Kati, had infused Pál with unusual optimism. The Virág's satin upholstery had caressed Kati's plush bottom for all of five minutes when he proposed that she might begin to pack cautiously later this evening.

Fearing that he might have raised her hopes too high before he had the tickets, he added: "I'll probably be struck by a tram on my way to the travel agency."

"You won't let a few smashed vertebrae and mangled limbs stop you."

"Absolutely not."

She mined another forkful of custard from between paper-thin sheets of sugar-dusted pastry and held it to the tip of her tongue, her big sea-blue eyes dancing like a child's.

"Eat your cake," Pál said. For all his nonchalance, he had to admit that finding a vacation package for the two of them had not been easy. His professor's salary had obliged him, each evening for the last week, to meander home past the flyer-filled windows of every travel agency in Szeged's downtown—ten of them stood within a five minute walk from Kossuth's statue, four on Oroszlán Street alone—in hopes of spotting among all of those last-minute offers a Day-Glo green or orange or blue ad for "the perfect Croatian getaway."

He'd finally caught sight of one this afternoon—the flyer was yellow—in the window of the third of four agencies on Oroszlán Street. True, he'd been clobbered by a self-important oaf charging out of the adjoining doorway. But the thrill of discovery survived even that.

He and Kati had been planning this trip since that Sunday in March when good weather arriving from the south had finally persuaded a timid spring to stay awhile. Together they'd walked north along the Tisza embankment from the flood memorial as far as Stefánia Park, their arms entwined as they watched the melting river ice glide south toward Serbia. When they reached Maria Theresa's gate, sole remains of an imperial fortress, Pál declared: "I'm taking you to the seaside as soon as this awful semester is over." The adoring Kati had turned to face him, cradled his bearded cheeks in her hands and drew his lips to hers. Pál lived for such moments.

But he could do nothing to shield Kati from the disenchantment that would surely come. Even if the four-color brochure depicting a marine paradise was not an unfaithful rendering of their actual destination: he imagined they would end up at some fleabag hostel conveniently located an hour's cramped tram-ride from the briefest stretch of tar-stained beach; even if the tour bus was not turned back at the frontier by surly border guards; even if some beefy Serbs were not determined to aim their mortars seaward and begin shelling the coastal resorts for kicks as they had a decade earlier. Even if none of these delightful scenarios materialized, disappointment would still find them.

But wait. He regarded the unsuspecting Kati beaming at him from across the table. Disappointment would never find her. She could be happy in a leaky shoebox as long as the two of them were together. What was wrong with her anyway?

No, it was Pál whom disappointment would hunt down and thrash within a millimeter of his fillér's-worth life. He'd never been able to ward off the dejection that fell over him like a net even in the sunniest climes. Wherever he went, however attractive, alluring and affectionate his lady friend, however lovely the view of the harbor from the balcony, however soft the pillows, however mellow the wine, however brilliant the Adriatic sunset, at some point he would discover that he had accidentally brought himself along.

CHAPTER TWELVE

Éva had climbed the stairs to László Kellner's second-floor flat so many times to she no longer took notice of her ascent. She was still thinking about the old man who had just escaped a terrible beating or worse.

"I live just around the corner," he'd said. He was badly shaken but lucid.

"I'll wait with you for the police," Éva had said.

As he lowered himself into the back seat of the police cruiser, Mr. Neumann had taken her hand and kissed it. She had found herself unusually touched by the old manners.

At László'sfront door, she smoothed her light blue summer dress over slender hips and checked her lipstick and mascara in the mirror she carried in her purse. Her copper-brown eyes were clearer now, but the tip of her high, straight nose and its gently flared nostrils was still red from crying.

The door yielded before her knock, swinging open to reveal two old men standing in a billowing cloud of smoke.

László hadn't warned her that István might be here.

"*Jó estét kívánok*, Professor Borsódy," she said, her voice clipped and chalky. "*Jó estét kívánok*, Professor Kellner."

"*Kezét csókolom.*" Both men replied, bowing slightly. István tried to smile but could not bring himself to look at her.

"I've come at a bad time," she said and made as if to leave. Something like relief passed over István's face.

"Not at all, Éva." László waved her inside. István withdrew to the sofa, opened a journal and pretended to read.

She hoped they wouldn't be able to tell that she'd been weeping almost steadily for the last forty-eight hours. She'd done her best to conceal the evidence of her tears from her friends and co-workers with makeup and references to spring allergies. The first time she hadn't felt like crying was half an hour ago when she'd come to the aid of Mr. Neumann.

"Here are the pages you wanted typed, Professor Kellner," Éva said and handed him a brown envelope. "Would you like me to put them in the binder?" Of the two people in the world she hoped would never read them, one was sitting just meters away. Had István read them in draft already?

"Why do you assume they're intended for the manuscript?"

"It just occurred to me—"

"How is that your concern, Éva?"

A green wave of panic rolled over her. She waited for her breathing and pulse to return to normal.

"I've made some more corrections." László handed her the binder. "As to whether I'm going to include the new pages in the final manuscript or not, I haven't made up my mind yet. Clearly, you have some reservations. But you must keep them to yourself, Éva. I don't solicit editorial advice from typists and I certainly don't encourage them to offer their opinions of my work."

He had spoken to her this way before but it always offended and saddened her when he did. Even so, she might have borne the humiliation had István not heard the unkind remarks. He stirred uneasily, struggling to appear as if he was absorbed in the journal he wasn't reading.

"I'll go now," she said.

László looked at Éva contritely. She sought István's gaze and, for the first time this evening, she found it, his eyes showing none of the hurt she'd seen in them so often. But if it was a glimmer of love or forgiveness that she saw in them now, she couldn't bring herself to admit it. Her throat constricted. Pressure built in the corners of her eyes. She hurried out the door.

She nearly reached the bottom of the stairs before she sat down on the third from last step, clutched the railing with both hands, and wept out of hurt and remorse, out of love and hate, for herself, for István.

She did not weep for László. She would not weep for him. Something black and violent and hobbled with pain stopped her. She had only just begun to understand—or thought she had, for even now she wasn't sure—why László had told her what he'd told her one March morning over twenty years ago when he found her standing, wracked with guilt, on the Tisza embankment.

She didn't know how long she'd been there. She had propped herself against a stone rampart and was thinking how much better it would be to let the river carry her away. László offered her his handkerchief and, after she told him what she'd done, his strong counsel.

"You must go away at once, Éva." László said in his seminar voice: even, grave, and soft. She watched the blonde Tisza's imperturbable surface. He took her hands and turned her around to face him. "You must go away."

"But I can't leave him, Professor," she said avoiding his gaze. Her voice was high and weak like a sick child's. She started to cry again.

"Éva?" László said.

"Yes, Professor."

"Where do your parents live, Éva?" László said.

All sounds, all voices were melting into her tears now.

"Please, Professor, don't make me go."

László placed a gloved fist under her chin and gently raised it until her eyes met his. She couldn't speak or cry or breathe. He pressed some forint notes into her palm.

"Éva, I promise he will never learn the truth."

At that moment, László's voice was the only sound in the world.

Later that day she collected her things from the Batthyány Street flat while István was at work teaching and took the 4:10 bus to Karcag. She not only followed László's instructions, but, ever the respectful student, she never questioned them. Never in all these years. Never until she read what he'd given her to type two days ago. He must keep his promise.

Éva cast the binder away. It struck a wall hard and sprang open. Pages flew in every direction, before drifting down to cover the black-and-white tile floor. Fearing discovery, she collected herself, the scattered pages, and the black binder. She pushed with all her strength against the front door's heavy glass and felt the night air on her burning cheeks and forced her way onto the sidewalk and set off toward home.

CHAPTER THIRTEEN

"What can I get you boys?" Géza Eperjesi, the proprietor of the Kéknyelű Wine Tavern, was almost certain when they walked through the door. He finished refilling an empty *Kékoporto* bottle from a watering can of after-wine and waited to make sure.

Not many skinheads came in here. Once in a great while, a couple might drop in for a glass before catching a bus across the street at the Mars Square station. They favored beer halls and dance clubs. He'd heard about their various haunts: the Viking and the Fekete Lyuk in Budapest, Taverna and Expressz in Eger. When in Szeged, they frequented the Steffl beer pub on József Attila Avenue.

"Two *VBK*s" came the reply. Red wine and cola, a cut-rate muddle popular among indigent students and the perpetually broke. It was also the signal he'd been waiting for. He checked that his regulars' glasses were filled and waved for the skinheads to follow him to the back office.

The three of them stood around a metal desk buried beneath delivery invoices, a black ledger, a rotary phone, and a layer of cigarette ash from an overflowing ashtray. A fluorescent lamp buzzed and flickered overhead. More than once, Géza spied his visitors sneaking peeks at *Miss December* smiling at them out of a centerfold of Christmas past. Wearing only knee-high black vinyl boots and a fur-trimmed and tasseled red hat, she of rosy cheeks, improbable breasts, and manifold gifts abounding, winked merrily and spread more than good cheer. Géza motioned for the skinhead nearest the door to shut it and waited for another sign.

The shorter one unfurled the national colors and laid them on the desk. Géza opened the ledger to reveal a fat brown envelope on which someone had written a phone number in a small neat hand. The taller one slipped his blade beneath the sealed flap and pulled. He counted out ten fresh 10,000 forint notes, rolled them up, and stuffed the wad into his jeans. His partner reached for the phone, but Géza caught him by the wrist and shook his head no.

Unfazed, the skinhead pulled out his cell phone, flipped it open, and poked at the keypad. He waited, mumbled something, and listened for a reply before snapping the phone shut and slipping it back into his jacket. He fired the envelope with a lighter he'd picked up off the desk and lay the burning paper down atop the heap of butts in the ashtray.

Géza escorted them out the back door and returned to his stool. He wondered if the stiffs pickling themselves at the bar had even noticed his absence. He lit a cigarette, poured himself a glass of good *kadarka*, and tuned in the Fradi-MTK match on the black-and-white set. He had no interest in *futball* but he liked the sound of a roaring crowd.

CHAPTER FOURTEEN

Professor Sándor Petri, the other person Éva hoped would never read the disturbing pages, waved Csaba goodnight before he noticed the porter wasn't inside his office. At twenty or so to nine, Sándor passed through the Ady Square building's great doors into the night and set off for his house on Mátyás Square. He was walking tonight because Anna had bundled the children into the minivan this afternoon and driven to her parents' Lake Balaton home for the weekend.

For days, he'd waffled about going with them. Then, late last night he'd told Anna that the Ministry of Education's announcement of a reduced allocation for the University had forced him to scrap next year's departmental budget and start over, a chore that might take all weekend. It wasn't the first lie he'd told her in twenty odd years of marriage and she'd probably guessed that by Saturday afternoon he'd be grunting atop a buxom graduate student whose ascending staccato cries, even half-muffled in eiderdown, would set the inn-yard's host of blackbirds atwitter.

Sándor had taken his evening meal alone at Cathedra, half a block from the Calvinist Church with its strait-laced bell tower. His *paprikás* had gone down well with a half-carafe of good Szekszárd *kékfrankos*. He'd even treated himself to two *deci*s of golden *tokaji* before returning to the department offices to review the budget and check his appointment calendar on

Éva's pc. He'd been all ready to leave for the night, when the phone rang. A wrong number, someone wishing to speak to Adolf.

Halfway home, he ducked inside a small *cukrász-da* near the train station where he bought two *pogácsa* for breakfast and flirted over the counter with a doe-eyed girl with violet spikes for hair—she blushed like a farmer's daughter when he admired her nose-ring. Soon he was wending down Szent Ferenc Street, wait-ing for the illuminated white walls of the Franciscan church and cloister to appear through the tulip trees. The house he and Anna had built together stood on the other side of Mátyás Square. The sight of his own roof with its chimney pots and red clay shingles al-ways filled Sándor with pride. He had everything he wanted. The secret was to hold onto it all.

The front gate, a wooden door set in the stuc-coed wall that enclosed the property, swung open as Sándor's key hit the lock. Anna had forgotten to bolt it again. He imagined her entreating the children and their mutt, *Füles*, to stay in the minivan as she loaded the last of the luggage this afternoon. In this neigh-borhood, an open gate was no cause for concern. But the large Arrow Cross painted on his front door was. Below the symbol, in red letters: SZOLNOK.

CHAPTER FIFTEEN

If a heart slow-to-heal had once made István uneasy around her, now it was his compassion for Éva that made seeing her so hard. He'd read somewhere that no pain, even one's own, could outweigh that felt for another, *with* another, and, though he remembered doubting that compassion could weigh heavier than a broken heart, he now thought he'd been wrong.

"You shouldn't have spoken to Éva that way," István said.

László slouched on the sofa, his chin resting on his chest.

"No." He sat up a little, seemed to think about rising, and sank back down into the cushions. "She was a brilliant student. And, later, as department secretary…well, I don't know what I would've done without her."

László would surely ask for Éva's forgiveness the next time he saw her. All the same, the rebuke troubled István. As steely as it had sounded, it had also seemed put on. But why would László say such hurtful things for István's sake?

"I want to read the pages Éva dropped off," István said, gazing at the brown envelope, which lay unopened on László's desk.

László stared at the ceiling, his head resting on the sofa's rosewood crest rail, his hands clasped behind his head.

István balanced himself on the edge of an arm-chair, leaned over, and placed a hand on László's knee. He said: "Your tone with Éva, this shadowy business about informers… I want to read those pages, László."

"It's late, István. We can talk tomorrow."

"Do you want me to go?" István said.

"Don't you want to finish your cigar?" he said, seemingly distressed at the prospect of being left alone.

"No, László. You're right." István ignored the long ash, the pale ghost of the leaf, at the end of his cigar and smudged out the glowing coal. He stood to leave. "It's late. I should go."

László caught István by the cuff of his jacket. "Stay a little longer," he said, gesturing for István to sit down. László opened his eyes wide and raised both eyebrows to show he understood the conditions upon which István's lingering depended. He began: "You know that I was granted access to secret police files after the Interior Ministry started accepting inquiries from scholars. I've been weighing whether I should include some of my findings in the manuscript."

"You're worried that some lives and careers would be ruined if you publish your findings?" István said.

"Not exactly," László said. "Those who spied for the regime weren't concerned about ruining the lives and careers of their colleagues or teachers or students."

"Even so, it's hard to be sure that those listed as informers in secret police files were actually informers," István said. "The incompetence of our secret policemen at keeping records used to be a point of pride among us. Didn't they often put down the names of guiltless persons as informers to make their recruitment quotas?"

"The informers themselves weren't very meticulous about their lists of potential informers either," László said. "They made up names or borrowed them from minor characters in old novels. One informer had a predilection for names belonging to stable boys and elderly footmen."

"So, at worst, they're guilty of plagiarism."

"The presence of so many real names won't permit such charity."

István lowered his head and closed his eyes to gather his thoughts.

"László," he said without looking up, "what does Éva know?"

"I named no names in the pages she brought by."

"You didn't need to. Who is she protecting?"

"One of our own, no doubt."

István lifted his eyes, catching László in his gaze.

"Of whom are you speaking, László?"

"Don't you know, István?"

István surprised himself by saying: "I think I do."

"To be fair," László said, staring back at István blankly, "we were the ones who taught him how to kidnap the truth and leave a base fiction in its place."

István waited as a dike-watcher waits for the river to rise.

"It wasn't enough for him to disfigure the past." The charge that must have been droning angrily in László's mind all this time attacked: "He had to mark his fellows for ruin."

The accusation stung and as its venom spread it was not the smart of betrayal István felt but the barb of self-doubt. So many times, both before and after the changes, he'd been troubled by misgivings about certain friends and colleagues. He'd refused to delve into their cause, preferring instead to bury them with all of his other doubts in some remote and unmarked corner of his mind.

"Are you sure he's the one?"

László nodded with more humility than satisfaction. "There may be others I don't know about. I'm working through a file dated February 1981, a typical month for him. There are twenty-two reports for the month. An average report runs ten to fifteen single-spaced typewritten pages. Some reports treat an individual's activities, others the participants in a class or a seminar, still others contain photographs shot with a concealed camera. The more delicate the information—I have in mind reports detailing afternoon trysts or weekend assignations—the more photographs the report is likely to contain."

"You don't have to go on." István threw himself back into the chair's sheltering arms. Once again, he'd failed to persuade László to let go of the past.

Why were we so in love with the past, with all that's dead and dying, anyway? He asked himself. Last Monday, in the cemetery, he'd bumped into Pál Berkesi, a former student. They'd grinned at each other a little shamefacedly, as if to ask: why do we, you and I and the whole damn populace spend so much time wandering among the ghosts, among the graves of old lies?

Was there no limit to a nation's mourning? The country was one big bone yard—so many dead, a mere ten million Magyar souls to mourn them—but did that mean the living must ever tremble graveside like so many Hamlets, waiting for the moment when we might each our quietus make? With nothing left to say, István stood up to leave.

"Tomorrow?" László took István's hand and smiled warmly. István nodded, thinking how funny it was that on parting they always seemed sure that neither of them would turn corpse overnight, that the next time they were together one would not find the other laid out in his best suit, unable to tease, chide, divert, cajole, or comfort the other.

CHAPTER SIXTEEN

Sándor was waiting for them when the white Astra pulled into his drive. They hadn't wasted any time getting there. The authorities took politically inspired acts of criminal mischief seriously these days, especially when they smacked of extreme nationalism.

"When did you get home tonight, Professor?"

Officer Horváth was in her twenties and unexpectedly pretty. Her hand—she wore no wedding ring—was poised over the notepad she'd drawn from the breast pocket of her starched blouse. Officer Dániel, her partner, was examining the Arrow Cross on the front door. As if on cue, they clicked their ballpoints and started taking notes.

"When did I call you?" Sándor said, trying to imagine what she would look like with her ash-blond hair down.

She flipped back a few pages. "9:13," she said.

"No later than ten after then." Sándor said.

"Did you notice anything unusual upon entering your property?" she said, scanning the perimeter.

"I'd just assumed my wife had forgotten to lock the gate," Sándor said, scanning her toned calves and thighs, though the latter were all but hidden beneath loose-fitting navy shorts hemmed just above the knee. Undeterred, Sándor tried to imagine what she would look like out of that prim blouse and those obstructing shorts.

"The wall would have made it hard to see them."
She called to her partner, "Find anything, Ernő?"

"Nothing," he said. He might have been her twin.

Sándor wondered if they were sleeping together. Young fellows such as Ernő rarely went in for an unadorned Magyar beauty like his lanky, green-eyed partner. He most likely dreamed of an exotic lovely with dark eyes lolling about in black brassière and sheer silk slip.

Csilla went on: "…assaulted an elderly man downtown an hour ago. Before that, they caused a disturbance at Bartók Square. Maybe they were here before that."

"I can't imagine why," Sándor said.

"Were you ever involved with the Magyar Socialist Worker's Party in any capacity?" Like so many of the generation that came of age after '89, Csilla seemed uncomfortable talking about politics.

"Involved? In any capacity?" He had to smile. "Are you asking me if I was a member of the Party?"

"Below the Arrow Cross, they sprayed SZOLNOK. They seem to think you're a former communist or…." Csilla paused as if she was looking for the right noun.

"Or still a communist?" Sándor said. "I'm not one anymore."

"I didn't mean to—"

"There *were* a few of us before the changes, you know," Sándor said. "But what does any of this have to do with Szolnok?"

"A year ago in Szolnok two members of the Szálasi Guards, an extremist group linked to the Skinhead International, murdered a former Party official."

"And you think they may be responsible for painting my front door?" Sándor said. "Isn't this small potatoes by comparison?"

"That's why I suspect another skinhead group did this," Csilla said. "More and more of the Budapest skins are falling under the spell of an old sculptor called Csorba, founder of the *Anti-Bolshevik League*. This job matches the League's m.o. nicely."

Sándor listened to this last remark with an interest that nearly eclipsed his attraction to Officer Csilla of the Csongrád County Police's Division of Pretty Cops. Csilla must have taken this attentiveness for dread because her earnest tone turned tender.

"I'm not suggesting you did anything to provoke them, Professor," Csilla said. "The skinheads get things wrong sometimes."

"Really?" Sándor said, stuffing as much hope and fear as he could into that *really* now that Csilla's pity had begun to flow.

"Last month in Eger they attacked a man they thought was Jewish. The victim turned out to be the anti-Semitic uncle of a fellow skin."

Ernő stepped out of the darkness and switched off his flashlight.

"Very clean job," Ernő said. "They usually leave something behind. An empty spray can. A boot print. I didn't find anything."

Csilla gave Sándor her card. Sándor smiled weakly and extended a hand to thank her. She took it, but his gesture was empty of charm and he knew it. Still, he was sure that she hesitated before letting go.

CHAPTER SEVENTEEN

Éva's swift departure from László's flat had put István in mind, as he walked home, of her swift departure from his own life.

They'd lived together, happily, he had thought, for three years until the day she left. The letters he'd sent afterward to her parents' in Karcag had gone unanswered. When she returned to accept a position as László's secretary two years later, he could no longer bring himself to ask for an explanation. A veil of academic protocol had mercifully descended between them and their exchanges assumed the character of office routine.

He'd never been sure whether László had encouraged Éva to leave him or, if he had, why he had done so. At first, he'd half-believed that Éva left him because of László, even for László. After a few months, he'd concluded that László and Éva shared a secret that would hurt him if he found out what it was. Though they sometimes spoke of Éva, he'd always been so afraid of what he might learn that he never asked László what he knew about her decision to run off.

And so he'd lived with his conclusion, until tonight when he'd started tugging at a thread he was sure he'd clipped from his coat of sad experience years ago. What, if anything, he now asked himself, had the talk of informing, or even László's counterfeit response to Éva's inquiry, to do with her going?

István was halfway home when he remembered he'd left his raincoat at László's. He paused near the musical fountain at Dugonics Square—its dancing waters had shed their crystal slippers for the night— and thought about turning back. The sky was clear and the stars were shining, it wouldn't rain tomorrow. He started for home again.

László had never fully grasped the depth of István's sense of loss when Éva had gone away. Perhaps László's unorthodox married life had made him insensitive not only to the pain that his affairs had caused others, but also to the heartache that ordinary people felt. With the exception of their first years together, he and Zsuzsa had never been faithful to each other. Many believed László had driven her mad with jealousy. A blurred image surfaced in István's mind.

Yet it wasn't her knowledge of László's extramarital pursuits that had shattered Zsuzsa's mind. Zsuzsa, after all, had taken her share of lovers. The source of her madness lay not in family unhappiness but in family history. Her father died by his own hand while she was still at University and two uncles and a brother perished in the same institution that Zsuzsa herself had been in and out of for the last twenty-two years of her life.

Two blocks from his Batthyány Street flat, the image cleared. István saw or thought he saw a grainy photograph of Éva, at twenty perhaps, in bed. Her cheek was pressed against a pillow, her hair matted on her forehead as by fever. Her wild, frightened eyes explored the middle distance. Here, flickering upon his mind's screen was the image of a young Éva touched with Zsuzsa's madness.

Yet he soon sensed that she was neither sick nor mad. A white sheet hid a shoulder and a breast. Her other breast was half-concealed beneath a lover's hand. The shadow of his torso fell across her chest, across the bed on which she lay. As if loath to watch her lover watching her, she was looking into the lens of a camera she could not see, a lens that might have been the lens of István's mind, which he now drew back to reveal more photographs, a dozen more perhaps, each almost the same but slightly different from the first. In each shot, Éva was looking at the camera, looking away from the man bearing down on her. He envisioned the photographs spread atop a file with shoelace-like ties and a broken seal of wax.

A block from home, a gust of murderous feeling nearly sent István reeling to the sidewalk. His right foot refused to take another step. His left foot joined the protest. Something so improbable—for several moments his mind had been foiled in its efforts to make it known to him—now seemed possible. Before tonight, István would have rejected any link between Éva's disappearance from his life two decades ago and the vile maneuverings of the former secret police. But Éva's tense query about the final shape of the manuscript and László's cool description of secret-police files detailing betrayals, both professional and personal, had struck home. Even before István could put the two together, his mind had revealed Éva in the embrace of a shadow lover and taken pictures of them with a hidden camera.

His forward progress blocked, he considered going back to László's. The raincoat would serve as pretext. Only an hour ago, when he'd proposed that Éva was trying to protect someone, László had tried to distract him from the most likely conclusion: that the someone she was trying to protect was István himself. Even though László hadn't named names, Éva must have believed that whatever was written in the pages she'd returned tonight would hurt István.

Had she merely betrayed him with another man so many years ago, had that been the only reason for her leaving? She must have known by now that such a possibility had long since presented itself to him. Belated proof of her infidelity would cause him pain, but not enough to justify her distress. Besides, why would László waste ink on a sexual liaison that occurred years ago if he hadn't meant to show that behind this infidelity lay another more profound and far more destructive betrayal?

All the dikes now broke at once and dismal understanding flooded István's brain. He knew why Éva had left him and why she hadn't told him she was leaving. He knew whose shadow it was that hovered over her in the images that surfaced out of his mind's dark. He knew that László knew everything. He knew what he must do. He began to walk again, with the slow, deliberate steps of a judge to a sentencing.

CHAPTER EIGHTEEN

Abandoned by its owner, István's raincoat clung dejectedly to the sofa's arm. After so many hours of point and counterpoint, László half-expected the garment to take up István's part and set the argument going again. So grateful was he when it did not that he thanked the threadbare article for its forbearance.

Five minutes earlier, Sándor had called with news that skinheads had painted an Arrow Cross on his front door. Anxious that someone might have similarly decorated the door to László's flat, Sándor had insisted that László check before he would consider saying goodbye. Finding nothing, he'd left the door unlocked should István return for his raincoat, and reported back to the holding Sándor, who, even then, wanted to come over. László put him off with the sharpest words he could muster and hung up.

He switched on the old Supraphon, waited a moment while the turntable came up to speed, and gently lowered the stylus onto a Deutsche Grammophon disk smuggled out of Germany forty years earlier. Under Fricsay's baton, the strings of the Berlin Radio Symphony Orchestra stirred with nocturnal longing in the *adagio* of Bartók's third piano concerto. Anda's piano answered them with a stately progression of chords befitting an ancient holy rite, haunting chords that grew more dissonant and more plaintive as the strings wandered through the nightwood, occasionally rising as far as the lower branches to sing and call in the dark before drifting back down to the forest floor.

László returned to his desk and began to turn over an old Magyar saying in his mind: *Temetni tudunk.* At least we know how to bury folks. He had never questioned it before. He and his fellow Magyars had buried so many in so short a time in the earth of this dingy little country. Behind the saying lurked the bitterest irony, the darkest pessimism cherished by every Magyar. And, by the god of the Hungarians, wasn't nurturing so bleak an outlook the nation's second favorite pastime, behind trailing hearses and before medalling in the Suicide Olympics?

Of course, just as in Olympic *futball*, Hungary never won the thing outright anymore. Still, they were happy to take an occasional silver or bronze. For the last three years, the Finns had edged them out for the European division title. What was the Finnish secret anyway? Alcohol? Snow and ice? Clinical depression? An unspeakably difficult non-European language? Then again, who were we Magyars to call Finnish difficult when many Magyars themselves never got the hang of their own native tongue?

László recalled dinner with an American scholar who'd visited Hungary last summer to attend a conference. He'd taken Professor James Middleton to an inn in the Buda hills. Its garden overlooked the Duna and, on the other side of the river, Pest spread out over the lowlands like a vast Persian or Ottoman rug, the latter designation more fitting, given Hungary's one-hundred-fifty-year occupation by the armies of Suleiman the Magnificent and his heirs. The Ottoman conquest, however disastrous for the Magyar nation, could not have been all bad for the old town's residents since the invaders brought coffee, paprika, Turkish baths, and even the roses that bloomed on the terrace the *Arany Horog*. Nearby, the tomb of the dervish Gül Baba, "father of roses," stood serene within its walled garden as it had for more than four centuries.

"Why do they do say you Magyars are born with a desire to off yourselves?" the American had asked, over the last generous spoonful of *somlói galuska*. Over the years, he'd met enough Magyar exiles and ex-pats living in the U.S. to know that the Magyar penchant for self-slaughter was a dark joke among the members of that community.

"Do they say that?" László, in a playful mood, turned to the tavern's other patrons for an answer.

"Tell me, *uram*," he said. "If you had to choose one of the metropolis's lovely bridges from which to throw yourself into the Duna for the purpose of ending it all, which would you choose?"

Three times László posed the question. Three times he received a gracious reply from his respondent.

A balding man with large incisors and a glass eye that didn't match his good one explained that for its historical value alone, the Chain Bridge was the only choice.

A bearded iconoclast, whose whiskers advertised the some of the best fish soup in Buda, insisted that Freedom Bridge was a better option since its mythic turul-bird-crested towers loomed high enough over the current to insure demise. Besides, what earnest suicide would not aspire to cut his life short in accordance with its designers' guiding principles: beauty. simplicity, economy.

An outlandishly attired gentleman—cowboy shirt, bolo tie, red rodeo boots with silver stitching—who, with a turn-of-the-*last*-century elegance rarely encountered these days even among the Pest literati, protested that only the fierce flow under Erzsébet Bridge would guarantee a quick end to life's miseries. No, he insisted, it was dear old Erzsébet or nothing. Or, as László reflected at the time, it was dear old Erzsébet *and* nothing.

The American was bewildered by the range of answers and the seriousness with which they'd been framed, so bewildered, in fact, that after one look at the professor's bemused expression their pony-tailed waiter had rushed over to find out what was wrong. László recounted the exchange and the waiter's concern gave way to a raised eyebrow and a knowing smile.

"That's ridiculous!" he said and switching to English: "You'll convince our American guest that we Magyars are congenitally mad…"

"Not at all," the American said. "I'm just glad there's at least one person present who hasn't considered throwing himself off a bridge."

"…because," the waiter continued, "every Magyar knows that throwing oneself off one of Budapest's bridges is no way to kill oneself. I've given much thought to this. The quickest possible exit is to be had by walking off the highest platform of the lookout tower on Jánoshegy. You can see it from here." The waiter pointed up and to the right. The three patrons who'd answered László's query nodded in admiration. The American professor barely spoke for the rest of the evening.

Did we bury well? The saying had it wrong. After they'd hanged Nagy and the others, they buried them without coffins, face-down in the earth. For sober-minded socialists, this was an oddly superstitious gesture. Peasants in remotest villages sometimes buried a corpse face-down when they held it to be dangerous, but Party elites? *Let the dead sink down into the earth. Bury them skyward and they might rise from the grave.* Still, for thirty years, Nagy's and the others' remains hadn't risen, at least under their own power. When they were exhumed, the neck bones of a giraffe from the zoo were found scattered among the remains.

No, we're much better at burying our dead a second time. *Let the dead rebury their dead.* The list of the twice-interred read like a textbook of Hungarian history: Rákóczi, Batthyány, the martyrs of Arad, Kossuth, Horthy, Rajk, and, of course, Nagy.

Not so long ago, an eccentric furnace tycoon had tried to convince the nation that he'd recovered, at great personal expense, the remains of the poet Petőfi from Siberia. Archaeologists determined the skeleton was that of a young Jewess and the dejected entrepreneur buried the bird-like bones without ceremony in his own garden.

Even old Bartók found his way back to Hungary from America fifty years after his death. His sons had hoped the publicity occasioned by the reburial might spark one last run on their father's scores before the copyright expired.

But why, László wondered, were such thoughts foremost in his mind? István had called justice another name for score-settling. Was there another justice to be had in digging up and reburying the dead? To confess one's own sins, to expose the sins of others, weren't these ways of joining past to present, of spanning the wide, dark gulf between the first hasty interment and the ritual reburial? What happened to all those years wasted in the service of the god that failed? Forty years of repression could hardly be erased. But hadn't they been redeemed?

László heard someone in the hallway outside. Could it be Éva? He hoped Sándor hadn't defied his express wishes. Perhaps István had returned for his coat after all.

CHAPTER NINETEEN

The job was nearly finished. Fifteen minutes earlier, they'd received the signal: Kellner was alone. Now this last bit fell to Zsolt as the artist of the two. Zoli was the poet. Well, he was good at song lyrics anyway. Zsolt couldn't see the door in the dark. But he'd found the doorjamb easily enough, and confidence gained from having done this many times before assured him all was well.

The secret was to keep your strokes fluid. Nice, steady strokes. There. So much for the vertical. Go ahead. Pass that horizontal right through the center. Zsolt knew just how much pressure to apply to the nozzle, how to angle the spray to prevent runs, how to end with a flourish or an interrupted stroke. Just keep the marble rolling. And...release. The Arrow Cross, symbol of the Aryan Brotherhood of Hungary, was finished. He waited.

No signal from downstairs. No sound from within Kellner's flat. What had he expected to hear?

Only the tag remained. The nozzle hissed again. *S.* Keep it smooth. Now the *Z.* Pressure steady. Marble rolling. *N.* The second *O.* Finally the hardest of the letters to paint blind. *K.* Done. Well, they'd certainly earned their evening's wages. Bit more violent than most. An honest night's work all the same. Now to find the stairs and tread lightly all the way down.

Zoli still stood watch in the vestibule.

"Some stinking drunk got in my face," he said. "Lit a match, I'd have blown up the whole block."

"What'd he want?"

"Should've seen him. Staggering about, reeking of bad booze. Insisting he was the manager, that I should leave."

"Where's he now?"

"I let the fucker in. Better that than flash the blade again. No point in bringing the cops all the way back over here."

"What's with these old guys anyway? That's the second time tonight."

"If you hadn't popped that fruity *dagi* at the rally, we might be in danger of losing our reputation."

"I don't think we need to worry about that." Zsolt lifted his gaze toward the ceiling. "Given any thought to leaving town?"

"If you're worried that the cops are waiting for us at the train and bus stations, we could stay at Gabi's tonight. Set out early."

"Let's borrow a ride. We can take it all the way to Pest or ditch it and catch the train somewhere up the line."

Three minutes later and one street away, Zoli hotwired an Audi. Zsolt crushed the mobile phone under his heel and scraped the fragments into a sewer. They followed back streets north and west past the city limits until they found the Budapesti Road.

CHAPTER TWENTY

Officer Rudi Szim of the Kiskunfélegyháza police hated his job. His uniform was confining, his hours bad, and he had never been able to figure how to use the two-way radio on the dashboard. Worst of all, firearms made him nervous. Whenever he was sure he would not encounter another police officer, he would remove his loaded revolver from its holster and lock it in the trunk. At the moment, the gun was safely stored between two wool blankets he kept in the trunk for those cold, clear Alföld nights that some-times continued long into the spring.

Yet Officer Szim was nothing if not conscien-tious and he had long ago perfected a system by which he could extract his pudgy frame from the front seat, detach the keys from his belt, unlock the trunk, and retrieve the revolver all in under two minutes and ten seconds. While he was sure he could complete the procedure in less than two minutes, the proper execution of each step required total concen-tration. What point was there in trading attention to detail for speed?

The sad-eyed Szim sat glumly over a tin of stuffed cabbage, sipping tea from his thermos. He'd parked behind bushes near the railroad platform, the better to intercept two skinheads who, it was believed, might try to board the Budapest-bound train at Kiskunfélegyháza. They had already bypassed the po-lice officers posted at Szeged's train and bus stations.

It seemed unlikely to Szim that the suspects, having gone to the trouble to steal a car, would abandon it before reaching the outskirts of the capital.

The two-way radio squawked: they'd ditched the stolen vehicle three kilometers from the railway station. Szim tried to copy. He only succeeded in producing an eardrum-piercing screech. Defeated, he listened helplessly as the dispatcher called all cars to burn rubber to the station, not without frequent mention of an elaborate maneuver by which he would rip Szim a new one.

The skinheads appeared on the platform when the Budapest train was four minutes away. But Szim had the advantage of surprise. He leaped from the car and ran a short distance toward the culprits.

"Excuse me, please. I am Szim of the Kiskunfélegyháza Police Department. I place the two of you under arrest for... for.... We will sort it out down at the station. If you will kindly follow me, please."

"Where's your gun, officer?"

"Excuse me, please. Would the two of you please wait here? I'll be right back."

The skinheads were still laughing as the train pulled into the station. Szim fumbled with his keys, struggling to unlock the trunk while trying to keep an eye on the suspects. They edged toward the braking locomotive. The trunk sprang open. Szim pulled his revolver out from between the blankets and hurried to the platform. He reached it just as the skinheads jumped aboard the still-moving train.

Szim lowered his eyes. He expected the skinheads would be hanging from an open window, taunting him. Instead, through the windows of the carriage nearest him, he watched several officers converge on them. Within moments, they were cuffed and led off the train into a waiting van, blue lights flashing, siren silent.

The year's excitement over, Szim locked his revolver away and went back to his cabbage and tea. Offended that not one of his big-city counterparts had acknowledged his role in the arrest, he added the ingratitude of his fellow officers to a growing list of reasons why he hated his job. If only he'd listened to his uncle and gone to barber college.

FRIDAY, 16 JUNE

CHAPTER TWENTY-ONE

Pál arrived safely at the travel office early the next morning. Cash in hand, he waited three quarters of an hour until a tall blonde—slender, fortyish, smartly attired—opened the agency's doors. From the way her every hair lay in place, from her graceful movements, from the tilt of her head as she nodded welcome, Pál deduced that she'd once been a stewardess. In reassuring tones perfectly suited for calming uneasy passengers and mental patients, she invited him in. He looked warily up the adjoining stairwell for charging attorneys before following her inside.

He'd traveled by air only once—to America, thirty years ago. But to this day whenever he recalled the long uneventful flight over the Atlantic, he conjured up those exceptionally pretty air hostesses who'd passed him tiny paper cups of tepid Coca-Cola for his nausea while patting his other hand, which was cemented to the armrest of his aisle seat.

Pál emerged from his queasy reverie to find the sympathetic gaze of the gently smiling travel agent upon him. He relaxed his death grip on the seat cushion beneath him and said: "I would like to book an excursion"—spinning around in the chair to point to the yellow sign in the window—"for two." As one long accustomed to negotiating narrow aisles, the air hostess glided to the window and retrieved the flyer. Alternately glancing at the offer and the blue screen's winking prompt, she began to play her laptop's keyboard with elegant fingers. In seconds, she confirmed that Pál might yet purchase the last two seats on the evening bus to Dalmatia. He reached for his wallet.

Pál was out the door by 8:07. Even before the echo of the travel agent's cheery *"Jó utat!"* left his ears, he had convinced himself that the journey would end miserably.

In spite of such dreary presentiments, Pál's long-buried hopes of earthly fulfillment, however short-lived, had nevertheless begun to revive and color his careworn features. His permanent squint began to ease, his tired, kind eyes, though weakly at first, to shine, his brow to unfurrow in anticipation of the bright pleasures of the coming week. At least, he reasoned, at least what had seemed like an endless term was nearly over.

CHAPTER TWENTY-TWO

At half-past eight, István stepped through the doors of the Ady Square building, which housed the Faculty of Arts, and began to climb the foot-hollowed stone steps leading to the second floor, where Sándor would be waiting for him in the Slavic Studies Department offices. He'd only paused at the entrance to look at the makeshift shrine to one side of the entrance. Beneath the colors and the bronze plaque commemorating the '56 uprising someone had laid a homemade wreath of yew across which had been stretched a red, white, and green ribbon bearing the dedication: "16 June 1958: IN, PM, MG, JSz & GL."

Sándor greeted István in the outer office. "Éva called to say she wouldn't be in," he said. "She didn't sound well. I'm manning the phones until Henrik arrives."

Despite his relaxed tone, Sándor's usually benign countenance had given way to one that mixed goodwill, weariness, and apprehension verging on distress. Dark arcs shadowed his eyes. His mouth looked weak, his lips pale. In spite of the signs of fatigue, Sándor's curly brown hair and clean features gave the impression of youth, albeit of one that had lasted ten, even fifteen years longer than one might expect youth to last.

The well-scrubbed student assistant appeared, removed his bicycle clips, and stationed himself at Éva's desk. Sándor asked Henrik to make coffee and

guided István into the inner office, a spare and masculine chamber with a polished floor and dark-grained
wood paneling. He closed the heavy door behind
them.

The office had been László's before it had been
Sándor's, and the present chairman seemed smaller
having entered the former chairman's space in the
same way that a tall and slender boy seems smaller
having donned his hulking older brother's hand-me-
down suit. The two men sat down at the long, high-
finish conference table László had installed during his
tenure. A great Dagestani rug of intricate design hid
the floor.

Outside, the coffee machine began to cough and
groan.

"I see you haven't slept, Sándor," István said.

"Some neo-Nazis left their calling card on my
front door last night."

"Why didn't you say anything when you called?"

"I didn't want to alarm you. Besides, I'd just finished with the police."

"Well, if it makes you feel any better," István
said, "you weren't the only one whose door got a new
coat of paint last night."

Sándor's weary eyes widened.

"You mean they painted an Arrow Cross on your
front door too?" he asked.

"Mine was spared," István said. "But someone
painted one on the front steps of a former dean of
the law school."

The shadow of something like anger passed over
Sándor's face.

"He lives a few doors down," István continued.

"The poor man only discovered the fascist efforts at home beautification last night when he and his wife returned from a law conference."

"Where's that coffee?" Sándor drummed his fingers on the table.

"Thing is" István said, "he's strictly FIDESZ. That hardly makes him a nationalist, but it does make him an odd target for persecution by neo-Nazis."

"And as targets go, I'm not so odd?" Sándor said. "Is that it, István?"

"You know that isn't what I meant, Sándor," István said. "Still, had the dean been a Party member, the choice of his front steps would make more sense."

Henrik knocked. Sándor raised a finger to his lips, an ancient habit.

"*Tessék*," Sándor said. Henrik set the tray down.

István waited for the young man to leave before speaking again. "You may as well know, Sándor," he said, changing the subject. "László's determined to publish his memoirs without further revision. He says he wants to come clean."

"But he hasn't anything to come clean about." Sándor raised his coffee to his lips and drained off half the steaming cup.

"He thinks he does. And he's written a piece of self-criticism that he knows will leave him open to more vitriol from the nationalists."

"It's not the polemics that worry me, István." Sándor set his cup down on its saucer. "The extremists raised the stakes last year at Szolnok. Let's just hope the neo-Nazis don't want to turn what happened there into an annual rite."

István was thinking about Éva again. Had she known he was coming to see Sándor this morning? Perhaps that was why she'd called in sick. Perhaps she'd been unable face him now that he knew what she and László had kept from him all these years. But did he really know what she and László had kept from him? He thought so. László had seen to that. Sándor was talking again and István, grown sullen, found it hard to pay attention.

"...think it's a good idea, I'll pay László a visit. I told him I might come by this morning."

István thought it best not to mention either the new pages or Éva's exchange with László. If Sándor should find out about the pages later, István would say he hadn't read them. "You go ahead, Sándor. I just don't think...well, there's no changing László's mind now."

CHAPTER TWENTY-THREE

"A one-night reign of terror!" Colonel Jenő Krebán's slammed his fist down on Major Balogh's report. "Where the fuck were our guys?"

If Krebán's gestures, like the man himself, tended toward the pugilistic, his diction tended toward the gutter. Small and fiery like Szeged's famous export, he had once challenged Ercole "The Duke" Ferrara for the European bantamweight crown. "Kid Paprika" had rarely lost a fight, never taken an eight-count, and always given better than he'd gotten.

"You can't defeat the bad guys by letting them take it to you again after they strike the first blow."

Even after a decade as Szeged's top cop, Krebán hadn't lost the lean and hungry look that had so unnerved his predecessor. Krebán wouldn't settle for a draw when it came to fighting crime. He couldn't stomach talk about modest advances against wickedness. He spun around and faced the back wall, on which hung a glossy of a young Krebán pretending to land a murderous right cross on the jaw of a beaming Laci Papp, the three-time Olympic champ.

"You have to take it to them. You have to keep the bastards backing up."

A ruffled Krebán cursed like a brushmaker drank. Unruffled, he cursed like a brushmaker's wife. His grin was terrifying and a half-minute's silence among the most garrulous officers would begin whenever he showed up at briefings or department gatherings. Rookies dove into the nearest broom closet when they heard him coming and hardened veterans thought twice before knocking on his office door.

The Colonel's penchant for throwing things more than justified the latter's trepidation. Krebán never actually aimed his ad hoc missiles *at* his officers. He merely launched them in the entering party's direction. Occasionally, one found a human mark. Krebán would apologize and, then, with utter courtesy, ask the unlucky officer what possible fucking business had he showing up at so inopportune a moment.

To enhance the confusion of those who dared cross his threshold, the Colonel spoke even to his solitary visitors as if he was addressing a roomful of people and God have mercy on the unfortunate constable who failed to answer one of his rhetorical questions. He spun around again. "How could two bald-headed pricks cause this much havoc in one night? Would someone kindly tell me that?" Krebán bellowed.

Major Balogh, chief detective of the criminal investigation unit of the Csongrád County Police and the only other person in the office, replied at once. "The skinheads are rather skilled at that sort of thing, sir."

"We better not have another rash of hate-crimes on our hands. I don't want those university-educated pheasant-fuckers from Budapest turning our headquarters upside-down and filling our ears with their egghead nonsense about evolving class relations in post-fucking-communist Hungary or the social psychology of race hatred." Krebán winced. After some letdown years ago in Budapest, he hated anything having to do with the capital, especially the police. "The last time the political section sent those pricks down here, they put our best guys on coffee detail."

Balogh reserved comment. He'd long ago discovered that it was best to let the Colonel's roaring river of words run its course. Either that or risk being swept away in its raging torrents.

"Betcha the pricks aren't even allowed to piss without written permission up in Budapest. Here, they expect the royal treatment. I could have paid four rookie salaries with the money we shelled out each week for Gerbeaud slices and Esterházy fucking gâteaux. I half-expected the head prick-in-charge to order pedicures for himself and all the little..."

Krebán broke off, mid-sentence, as if he'd heard a round-ending bell. His thoughts stumbled back to the report on his desk like an exhausted boxer retreating to his corner.

"Would someone kindly explain to me why the fuck we didn't collar them before they got to—what's the second victim's name?"

"Mr. Oszkár Neumann, sir."

"...before they got to Mr. Oszkár Neumann?" The Colonel didn't wait for an answer. "Because if the first assault occurred at half-past seven, that left us plenty of time—*three quarters of an hour* by my watch—to track them down before the second attack."

Balogh only nodded.

"And if one considers that the suspects couldn't have strayed far from the scene of the first assault—you say that they were spotted at the other end of Bartók Square with the missing flag shortly after eight o'clock?"

"Yes, sir."

"And that the two assaults took place less than a block apart?"

"Yes, sir."

"One would have to conclude that the police performed miserably last night. Am I right, Balogh?"

"You are correct, sir," Balogh said, sounding more like a talk-show-host's sidekick than an officer of the law.

"One might even conclude that one would have to be a fucking idiot not to arrive at this conclusion." Krebán's color turned three shades of red before settling on primrose. "Does anyone here think that one is a fucking idiot?"

"Which one, sir?"

"What do you mean 'which one, sir'? It's the same fucking one. There's only *one* one. Answer the fucking question!"

"In that case, sir, I think one would be justified in both conclusions." Balogh leaned back in his chair and waited for the deluge.

"You're fucking right one would be." Nearly all passion spent, Krebán's color began to lighten. "You're all just lucky these pricks didn't do any lasting harm to the people of this city or to their property."

On behalf of everyone present, Balogh nodded.

"But tell me, Balogh, when were you sure the same pair of thugs carried out both attacks? Did it ever strike you that the similarities between the assaults might have been coincidental?"

He'd never treated the attacks as isolated incidents. The crime scenes were so near one another, and when Balogh learned from Mr. Neumann's statement that a Hungarian flag had shown up at the scene of the second assault, well, that settled the question for him. He was merely waiting for the results of the line-ups later this morning to confirm what he already knew.

"The longer I'm at this job, sir," Balogh said, "the more I appreciate how events, and the evidence of their occurrence, arrange themselves into patterns without any help from coincidence or fate or any other mysterious agency."

Yet even as he spoke, Balogh sensed that coincidence had everything to do with a hunch that had been trying to break into his consciousness all morning as he studied the incident reports and victims' statements. While he hadn't seriously considered the possibility that the similarities between the attacks might be accidental, he had considered the alternative: that everything had been planned; that, despite the appearance of random violence, neither the assaults nor any of the lesser offenses had been haphazard.

In his mind, Balogh felt something like the triumphant splashing that attends a float held under water and released. He thought he glimpsed, however dimly, a pattern, a watery and far from clear one, in the sea of calm that bathed the city once last night's torrents of hate had ceased to flow. That glimpse, brief as it was, led him to doubt whether the suspects had acted wholly on their own.

CHAPTER TWENTY-FOUR

Pál Berkesi sat alone in the alley of an office he shared with Kálmán Révai at the Department of American Studies, which fifteen years earlier had brashly declared its independence from its Anglocentric origins in the University's English Department. For the first time in a very long while, Pál allowed himself to feel...well, not content exactly. The examination period was almost over. Increasingly long intervals of uninterrupted silence had begun to settle in the corridor outside, which just yesterday had echoed with the nervous laughter and prattle of students waiting to be called for the last of their exams.

He heard the occasional footfall, the hushed hallway conversation, the soft squeak of doors opening and closing, but within a few hours most of the Institute's students would be on their way out of Szeged if they hadn't left town already. From his window, Pál, had he cared to look, would not have seen a soul along the length of Egyetem Street. The only sound that passed through the casement was that of the old "Red, White, and Green" snapping to attention in light wind or furling itself around the flagpole mounted on the front wall of the mammoth Faculty of Art building across the way.

Only the stragglers remained. The dreary triple failures who hoped only for a "pass." The overly prepared, overly anxious, and overly earnest but quick bright young things who'd convinced themselves that the difference between a "*jó*" and a "*jeles*," between a "4" and a "5," between a "good" and a "first-rate" hinged on perusing one more seldom-cited predestinarian tract, on memorizing the terms of one more royal charter, on evaluating the class dynamics of one more bewitched New England hamlet. The indefatigable correspondence students who twice a year juggled work and bus and train schedules and made their solitary ways here from remote villages and far parishes, even crossing borders when necessary, to be put through their paces by a band of dyspeptic scholars who, for the most part, would be far too preoccupied with visions of lunch or of their own or their spouses' imminent infidelities to appreciate the enthusiasm and unapologetic idealism of those who still believed the promise of higher education. These and others had been drifting into the Institute's offices, one by one, since eight o'clock. Soon, they too would be gone.

Pál was not content. Not yet anyway. He felt the warmish glow of limited possibility, the only slightly trammeled hope of stumbling upon a mood that bordered on pleasure on the Adriatic coast with Kati. Katalin. She had been so happy when, moments earlier, he'd called to tell her they would set off tonight for Dalmatia.

CHAPTER TWENTY-FIVE

"Frankly, Balogh, I've not much faith in coincidence either," Krebán said, his skin's hue comfortably established at the cooler end of the pink-red spectrum. "It's just that I'd love to be able to tell the press that it's too early to assume last night's events mark the start of a new 'hate offensive.'"

"You'd be telling them the truth, sir." Balogh said. "Especially since we've turned up no evidence of coordination."

Krebán went on as if he hadn't heard Balogh's encouraging words: "Because as soon as the headlines proclaim that a carefully-planned campaign of neo-Nazi terror has begun in our fair city, we can kiss any hope of conducting a proper investigation goodbye. There'll be so much pressure from Budapest to nail these boys that justice won't have time to cover her tits or even to adjust her blindfold."

Though Balogh seldom gave the Colonel enough credit for subtlety, the man frequently surprised him. It had taken him this long, for instance, to realize that Krebán's questions had been part of an effort to anticipate those that the reporters would pose later today. For good or ill, the Colonel had already resolved not to withhold anything from the press. He couldn't risk negative publicity for the department by doing otherwise.

In recent months, editorial after editorial had charged Hungary's police forces with taking a soft stance on skinhead violence, with looking the other way when it came to assaults on Jews, Roma, and foreign students. One commentator had even suggested that a majority of police officers quietly supported the skinhead platform. Making the most of this allegation, the skinheads at once adopted a friendlier public stance toward the police.

"Do you think we might, Balogh?"

"Might what, sir?"

"Turn up that evidence of coordination."

The Colonel had been listening after all.

"Hard to say, sir."

"Why, Balogh?"

"I wouldn't rule it out, sir."

"Let me to rephrase the question. Why, Balogh?"

"It's the skinhead m.o. to terrorize Jews. But before that, they bashed a local nationalist."

"You know, Balogh, the only reason that their pummeling the nationalist bothers you is because you've never met Mr. Viktor Uborka. A minute with that fat prick would lead anyone to punch his lights out."

"And before that," Balogh continued, "they took questions from a news crew. It doesn't add up. It's as if they wanted to make our job easy."

"Magyar genius aside, these Arrow Cross pricks don't win many Nobel Prizes, Balogh." Krebán's volume was rising again. Maybe he was trying to hide his disappointment at not getting from his detective all he needed to silence press jabber about neo-Nazi conspiracies.

"I'm merely wondering, sir, why they would've planned and carried out a series of random-looking incidents to draw attention to themselves."

"I suppose you have your reasons for not shutting down any possibilities at this point. Fuck you very much, Major. What else have you got for me?"

"We've been able to work out a rough itinerary for the suspects' adventures in Szeged yesterday. Shall I run through it, sir?" Balogh blandly offered.

"Go ahead, Major." Krebán waved a largish, bubble-gum-colored trapezoid at Balogh. "But I think it only fair to warn you that Terézia overlooked this India-rubber eraser during her morning sweep."

Of late, Krebán's fondness for letting everyday office supplies fly had become so pronounced that his beleaguered secretary had resolved to keep all sharp objects out of reach and to serve the Colonel his coffee—black, no sugar—at sub-scalding temperatures in paper cups.

"We learned from a conductor on the Budapest-Szeged run that the suspects arrived on a delayed express from Budapest shortly after four o'clock yesterday afternoon. A local girl was with them. The conductor said she regularly takes the train back and forth to Kecskemét."

"Other local girls take the train back and forth to Kecskemét, Balogh."

"Apparently, sir, the girl in question is a looker."

"In that case, I insist you bring her down here for questioning at once. You do have a name, an address for the young woman?"

"We're working on it, sir."

"When were the suspects next seen, Major?"

"When they were interviewed by the news crew from Szeged TV. We've got ten minutes of tape with them answering questions about the Skinhead International."

"Good. Because it's hard enough to distinguish between these Nazi pricks when they're not trying to kick you to death. When did the tape start rolling?"

"7:18."

"And we have no idea where they could have been from the time they got off the train till then?"

"Horváth and Dániel from Family Protection think the suspects might have visited a house facing Mátyás Square where one of them painted a large Arrow Cross on the front door. They're on Batthyány Street investigating a similar incident right now."

"What else?"

Balogh, his larynx tight, forced out an answer.

"Whoever painted the Arrow Crosses took time to spell out *Szolnok*."

The pink trapezoid Krebán had been turning end over end was suddenly in flight. It sailed through the air toward a point slightly above Balogh's line of sight. He ducked. The eraser hit the wall over his head and ricocheted from surface to surface, its momentum diminishing with every bounce, until it fell harmlessly to the floor.

"Please go on, Major." The launch must have satisfied something deep within Krebán. He wasn't shouting anymore.

Balogh's larynx released its grip on the words it had tried to choke down.

"Around a quarter-to-nine, not long after the Neumann assault, they were spotted entering the Kéknyelű by an officer working undercover at the bus station. He didn't see them leave."

"And they weren't seen again until half-past eleven when they abandoned the stolen vehicle outside Kiskunfélegyháza." Krebán continued calmly. "So we haven't the slightest idea what else they might have been up to between nine and, say, eleven, allowing for a forty-five minute drive to Kiskunfélegyháza."

"We're keeping our fingers crossed there's nothing else, sir."

"Have you scheduled a preliminary interrogation?"

"They won't submit to questioning without an attorney present. One will be here by early afternoon."

"A skinhead lawyer? This should be good. Does he shave his fucking head too?"

"Not exactly, sir. She's from a large Budapest firm. Retained by the suspects' parents. Seems that both suspects come from Rózsadomb."

"Lovely views of Pest and the Duna no doubt. Can't say it surprises me. Skinheads hail from much nicer places than Újpest and Kőbánya these days."

The phone rang. Krebán lifted the handset to his ear. He swore and hung up. He stared across the blank expanse of the desk, his face the color of raw meat.

"The missing flag has turned up, Balogh."

"May I ask where, sir?"

"By all means, Major." He gave Balogh the same look he used to give opponents before he sent them reeling to the canvas. "It's draped over Professor László Kellner's corpse."

CHAPTER TWENTY-SIX

Pál dismissed his final examinee at 10:37. Half an hour earlier he'd heard the faintest scratching on his office door.

"*Tessék*," Pál bellowed.

In floated a cadaverous student from Békéscsaba. The emaciated boy wore an ill-fitting, reddish-brown suit, a garish lavender-and-pink floral tie that he'd knotted and drawn noose-tight against his windpipe, and a pair of mud-caked shoes several sizes too large. Pál imagined a wasted sibling waiting for his wandering scholar of a brother to come home so he could reclaim his shoes and return to planting onions before the moon set.

During the examination, "Bony" tacitly revealed his preference for all topics dull or abstruse. He couldn't contain his excitement while answering a question about colonial laws regulating cod fishing off the New England coast. Yet, when asked to talk about the demise of General Wolfe on the Plains of Abraham, he could barely construct the merest litter of words to convey the hero of Québec to his resting place in North American history.

This victim of the recent famine impressed Pál—why hadn't he heard about the starving peasants of Békéscsaba?—and he doubted whether pin manufacture in Massachusetts, or Cotton Mather's neglected treatise on the American stink-beetle, or early Virginian efforts to distill spirits from tobacco or Smithfield ham or freshwater oysters had ever before offered the occasion for such fevered eloquence. Thus, Pál surprised himself when he grew weary of listening to the skeleton. He interrupted the gaunt examinee in mid-sentence to announce that the examination was over. The pallid corpse offered to extend his remarks on the fascinating regulations governing the North Atlantic cod fisheries.

Pál was ready for him. Feigning enough enthusiasm to make his utterance credible, he cautioned that should they recklessly undertake so adventurous a course, they might still be there come nightfall. With a touch of regret in his voice, he added that it might be best for the rattling bones to shamble or clatter or shuffle off to Békéscsaba. Undeterred, the articulate remains hopefully declared his hearse was not leaving until 2:10. Pál congratulated him on a strong performance, scratched a "5" in his index, signed it, and wished him a pleasant journey back to the land of the dead.

CHAPTER TWENTY-SEVEN

Balogh's heart sank when he saw the Arrow Cross with its dedication SZOLNOK sprayed in blood-red paint on Kellner's door. It was a taunt, a vicious mockery of the police for having lost track of the suspects for what now turned out to have been a fatal hour. He examined the lock for signs of forced entry, but found none.

The young police officer who'd been first on the scene assured Balogh that everything in the flat was exactly as it had been when he'd arrived. Nothing had been moved, no lights switched on or off, no windows opened or closed. Rózsás, the building manager, had insisted that he and a Professor Sándor Petri had been careful not to touch anything after they discovered Kellner's corpse.

"In other words," Balogh said, "their prints are going be everywhere."

"The men are in there, sir," the officer said, nodding toward the bedroom.

"Didn't your instructors at the Police Academy teach you to separate witnesses?" Balogh said, trying to hide his irritation with the apple-cheeked youth, who flushed and stammered an apology.

"Don't worry about it," Balogh said. "Just go tell the building manager to wait in the kitchen. I'll be in to talk to the professor in a moment."

Was the Sándor Petri in the bedroom the same one who discovered the first Arrow Cross last night?

Or was Petri the name of the man who lived in the Batthyány Street flat where the second Arrow Cross appeared? In either case, a third cross had bloomed on the deceased's front door sometime during the night. The residents at the first two addresses had been out when the skinheads had come round. Had Kellner died simply because he'd been the only one home?

Balogh started to work his way toward the body, looking for footprints or drag marks on the rug. He looked for stains and scuffs, anything the techs might have missed during their approach. Except for the wilted lilacs that he'd nearly trampled on entering, the crime scene appeared exceptionally clean. Death had come so swiftly that the room barely registered its arrival.

The techs were on their haunches completing a masking-tape outline of Kellner's body. A straight-backed chair lay on its side behind him to the right. Atop the great desk that loomed beyond the corpse, neat stacks of books, folders, and papers grew under the gooseneck lamp whose artificial light could not compete with the late-morning sun pouring in from a window.

Kellner lay face-up on the parquet floor; one arm stretched straight out, palm up, away from the desk, the other at his side, bent at the elbow, fist clenched. The flag with a hole through its center hid his face and most of his torso and upper legs. Tiny shards of earthenware encircled his head and shoulders, green-glazed splinters that glittered in the sunlight. Missing from the dead man's clothes were any giveaway folds or rolls that might suggest the body had been dragged into place. The patch of polished floor at the victim's heels revealed no scuffing.

The techs now went to work with cameras and gauges and stainless-steel rulers. Ignác Korbács, the medical examiner, looked on, pulling on a pair of latex gloves. Under a greasy cap of black hair, Korbács was a washed-out, lab-coated cipher with a nicotine addiction and an adder's tongue.

"Time of death?" Balogh said.

"Can't say for sure. His arms and legs are stiffer than your last good erection—my sympathies to your wife, Balogh. I'd say he's been dead for eight or nine hours at least."

"And at most?"

"Can't say until I get him to the morgue. I took his temperature before they swooped in like a pair of kites," Korbács nodded toward the techs. "But he's been in the sun all morning and I don't trust the reading."

"Just a rough estimate, Korbács." Anything less than eleven hours would make it hard to finger the skinheads who were arrested at midnight.

"Eleven hours. Possibly twelve."

Balogh looked at his watch and relaxed. They could have killed Kellner as late as eleven, stolen the car, and made it to Kiskunfélegyháza in time. Twelve hours would put the murder at half-past ten. He had his window.

"Cause of death?" Balogh asked.

"Can't say for sure. At first glance he seems to have died from a blow, perhaps two blows, to the head," Korbács said. "I'm guessing someone whacked him with whatever that was." He pointed to the splinters and shards. "He must've gotten the other when he fell."

The techs moved away from the body and Korbács moved in. The dead man's face was ashen except for a deep plum bruise that started at the middle of his forehead and spread toward his left temple where it disappeared beneath the hairline.

"He did some real damage there," Korbács said.

Balogh surveyed the shattered pieces of what had been the murder weapon. He couldn't spot a single fragment the width of a finger. The lab might be able to lift a partial print or two, but it wouldn't be easy.

"Then, he's got this really nice fracture under here." Korbács said, looking straight ahead as he cradled Kellner's head. "Not that you have to crack someone's skull to deal a fatal injury to the brain."

"Not much bleeding though?" Balogh said. He picked up a splinter by its ends and held it to the sun.

"Just enough to mat the hair some," Korbács said.

The splinter pierced Balogh's glove. A tiny red drop formed on his index finger.

"Don't cut yourself." Korbács said. He stood up and pulled off his gloves. "I'm afraid I won't be able to tell which blow killed him until I've had a look around inside his skull."

"Can we call it a homicide at least?" Balogh said. "Don't say you can't say."

Korbács said nothing and covered the dead man's face.

"All right, Korbács, what *can* you say?"

"Take a look at the breakage pattern," Korbács said. "If the killer threw down the murder weapon after he thumped the professor—"

"—would he have fallen so that the pattern was centered beneath his head and shoulders?" Balogh said. "Did someone move him?"

"If someone had rolled him onto his back, which is how we found him, say, eight hours after he died, most of his blood would have already settled in the front of the torso, the abdomen, and the front of the legs," Korbács said. "His blood has sunk to the back, the buttocks, and the backs of the legs, so all I can say is that if someone did move him, it wasn't until he'd been lying here for some time..."

This eliminated the possibility, one Balogh hadn't considered till now, that Rózsás or Petri had moved the body when they'd discovered it this morning.

"...but that doesn't mean someone couldn't have moved Kellner shortly after he was killed, since the blood can still shift from one part of the body to another for two or three hours." Korbács lit a cigarette. "Just can't—"

"—say for sure?" Balogh said.

"—hang around here all day doing your job for you, Balogh," Korbács said between drags and waved over the two bored men with the gurney.

CHAPTER TWENTY-EIGHT

Before Pál on his desk lay all the tokens of the excursion scheduled to begin from Szeged's central bus terminal at half-past seven this evening: two passports, two bus tickets, an itinerary, a document confirming their hotel reservation, their breakfast and lunch vouchers—they would take their evening meals beneath dark palms on the terrace of a seaside restaurant mercifully upwind from the fishing boats with colored sails: their day's catch that night's menu.

Next to these lay a wad of forint notes held together with a rubber band, a jar of instant espresso powder, half-a-dozen packs of Benson & Hedges 100's, two disposable butane lighters—Pál would surely lose one of them even before he and Kati boarded the bus; he lose the other on the way and his life would become a search for matches—his sunglasses, his old Olympus, five rolls of film, a tin of peppermints from Hoffnagel's of Vienna—a gift from Kálmán, who'd recently returned from a conference in the old imperial city—and a pair of vintage paperbacks whose well-worn spines bore the name of Mickey Spillane. The choice had not been easy. At length, he'd settled on two favorite Mike Hammer novels from Spillane's early period.

Pál closed his eyes: Kati's at the water's edge, tanned, happy, frolicking—was there a better word for her carefree, knee-lifting, arm-raising, hip-twisting, laughing progress through the waves?—smiling at him and beckoning every few moments, teasing him, summoning him from his place in the Croatian sun where a salt breeze ruffles the opening pages of *The Big Kill.* He closes the book, sets it down on the blanket. He leaves Hammer with a tomato who has just sashayed into the Blue Ribbon wearing a cocktail dress snug in all the right places.

Pál rises and feels the hot sand between his toes. He waves at Kati, begins making his way down the beach toward the water. An electronic bleating stops him in his tracks. He scans the beach, trying to catch a glimpse of the herd of battery-powered sheep. He hears the sound again but before he can locate its source, Kati, the waves, the sunny beach all disappear into the shattered air.

He opened his eyes and reached for the phone. Tamás Garay, his oldest friend at the University and director of the Institute, was speaking in his soft-voiced way. "I know you're there, Pál. Don't hang up."

Pál said nothing and hoped that Tamás, hearing no voice at the other end, would do what he'd just told Pál not to do.

"I've some bad news, Pál," Tamás said, "László Kellner is dead."

Kellner had been Pál's mentor once. A long time ago. He felt nothing. Or little.

"The Dean wants both of us at the funeral Tuesday morning."

"Oh no."

"I know you're trying to get away with Kati, but…"

"I'm leaving tonight."

"I told him you'd already left, but he saw you talking with Csaba this morning."

Pál and the porter had swapped *futball* rumors about *FC Szeged*'s acquisition of a brilliant young striker called Bandi Kis. Pál was resolute: "I'm still going."

"Pál, please."

Pál switched from speaking vigorous Hungarian to gruff and pulpy American: "Get that nance of a dean on the horn and tell him I'm blowing town. You'll have to shift for yourself."

"You can't Hammer your way out of this one, Pál." Tamás had heard the tough-guy routine before.

"What about Kálmán, Ilona, or Béla? Béla loves funerals. He pores over the obits every day searching for familiar names just so he can don his black suit and beam exultantly at the graveside. Let him go in my place. This is crazy!"

"They're all going. But the Dean insists you and I attend."

"I haven't talked to Kellner in twenty-five years. I hadn't seen him in ten. He kicked me out of Slavic Studies, remember?"

"We left the department together."

"You left voluntarily. I was thrown out."

"I just followed you out the nearest door. I didn't know I wasn't going back. Still, things haven't turned out so badly for us," Tamás said. "Listen, Pál, I'm not broken up over Kellner's death either. But there's no getting out of this."

"Where are you?" Resignation crept into Pál's voice. He knew that Tamás had done all he could to release him from this obligation. "Or tell me where I can reach you. If the travel agency won't refund my money I'll need to scream at someone."

"I'm in my office. Come up when you've finished sorting things out. And please extend my apologies to Kati when you speak to her."

"Why?! What have you done to her?"

"I'm apologizing, on behalf of the administration of course, for spoiling her holiday."

"I'm going to tell her it's your fault. Why let the Dean take the rap when I can turn Kati against you once and for all. She respects you far too much. And you should apologize, on behalf on the administration of course, to me too."

"Really, Pál." Tamás laughed. "You'd have spoiled your own holiday. Do you think you would've allowed yourself even a day's contentment?"

"That's exactly the question I was trying hard not to answer when you called."

"Cheer up. I'll buy you lunch."

"Not at the *menza* you won't. Under the circumstances, I have to insist we dine at a place that serves food."

CHAPTER TWENTY-NINE

Balogh instructed the officer who had met him at the door to find out whether the neighbors had heard anything unusual. The young man seemed pleased to inform his superior that he'd already made inquiries to that effect and learned from Rózsás that the widow next door was away visiting her daughter in Győr, and that the retired engineer in the flat below took out his hearing aids at night.

Balogh knocked on the bedroom door.

"I'm sorry to have kept you waiting, Professor. My name is Balogh."

Petri was sitting on the bed in the sparsely furnished room where Kellner had slept. A magazine lay open beside him on a sea-green bedspread. Petri looked straight ahead.

"I know it's been a trying twelve hours for you," Balogh said. "I'll try to keep this brief."

Petri turned to Balogh. He stood and extended his hand. "Thank you, Major. I don't mind talking now." His handshake was firm, his palm dry. "Shouldn't Rózsás be here?"

"Should he be here?" Balogh said. He pulled up a chair and motioned Petri to sit back down. So Petri saw himself as a partner in the investigation. That was fine. The more active Petri thought his role, the more information he would offer. "Is there a problem, Professor?"

"Not at all, Major," Petri said. "I'm just surprised you don't want to question us at the same time. We found Professor Kellner together."

"You have a point." Balogh said, pretending to mull things over. "Rózsás is just outside. We can send for him should we need him. Tell me, how long did you know Professor Kellner?"

"More than thirty years." Petri picked up the magazine and rolled it into a loose cylinder. His face revealed nothing. "He was my mentor."

"Did you see each other often?"

"We'd meet for lunch every few weeks and I'd visit him here two or three times a month."

"So today's visit was nothing unusual?"

"When I discovered my home had been vandalized, I called Professor Kellner and told him I wanted to come over right away."

"How did he respond?"

"He didn't like the idea." Petri rolled the magazine more tightly. "He was still shouting when I rang off."

"So you waited until morning, but why the rush to see him last night?"

"After Officer Horváth told me that skinheads were preying upon former Party members, I was worried that whoever painted an Arrow Cross on my front door might go after Professor Kellner as well."

"What time did you call him?"

"Around ten. Do you think I was the last person to speak to him?"

Balogh ignored the question. "Do you know if anyone else called or visited him last night?"

"I know Professor Borsódy had been here."

"May I ask you some more questions about this morning, Professor?"

"I don't know whether I should be flattered or worried."

Balogh looked up from his notepad and eyed Petri coldly. He decided to have a go right at the smug bastard.

"That all depends."

"On what?"

"On whether you killed László Kellner or not." Balogh waited a few seconds then smiled.

"You had me for a moment, Major" Petri said. He didn't smile back.

"Why did you ring for Rózsás when you arrived this morning?"

"László didn't answer the buzzer and I don't have the entry code." Balogh noticed the shift from Professor Kellner to László. "Rózsás let me in. We came upstairs together."

"Was the door to the flat closed?"

"I'm sure it was. The first thing we saw was the Arrow Cross. I was afraid of what we might discover inside. I knocked a few times. When no one answered I asked Rózsás to use his key."

"Didn't you check to see whether the door was unlocked first?"

"I can't recall."

"Was the door locked?"

"You'll have to ask Rózsás."

"I don't mean to press you, Professor."

"At least you're no longer accusing me of murder." Petri tried to smile.

"What did you see when you came inside?"

"I couldn't see his face for the flag, but I knew it was László."

"What did Rózsás do?"

"I heard him call the police."

"And what did you do?"

"I went to László and drew back the flag. I listened for a heartbeat."

"What else do you remember?"

"Rózsás said not to touch anything," Petri frowned. "He was too late."

"If you've no objections, we'll print you before you go."

"So I am a suspect."

"I didn't say that, Professor." Balogh tried to sound equivocal. "A few fingerprints won't be a problem as long as we know what to expect."

"That's reassuring," Petri said in a tone that Balogh couldn't tell was sincere or not.

"Just one more question: past political affiliations aside, had Professor Kellner published anything recently that might have provoked the neo-Nazis?"

"He's been a favorite target of the nationalists for a decade. Professor Borsódy had been after him of late to revise his memoirs so he wouldn't antagonize his enemies further. No one except for Professor Borsódy and Professor Kellner's typist, Éva Hegedűs has seen them."

"Where's the manuscript now?"

"Unless Éva took it home with her for retyping or the killers made off with it, it's probably still among Professor Kellner's papers on his desk. I did mention that she'd been by last night while Professor Borsódy was here?"

"You didn't." Balogh wondered if anyone else had been here last night that Petri hadn't told him about. "Thank you, Professor. I'll be in touch if I have any more questions."

"Am I free to go then?"

"Just give the officer outside a phone number where I can reach you."

Balogh went to talk with Rózsás in the kitchen. The building manager sat at the small table, his torso, sheathed in a sweat-drenched sleeveless undershirt, forming an acute angle with the tabletop. Rózsás had propped the refrigerator door open with a family-size jar of pickled red peppers, and he was leaning to one side as far as the chair and his own bulk would allow in an effort to cool himself in the chilled air from the icebox. Ample drops were forming on its racks, which held a half-carton of eggs, a block of rindy cheese, half a bottle of cherry juice, a container of *kefir*, and a small glass pitcher of milk.

"It was getting warm in here," Rózsás said, mopping his brow with a greasy rag. His eyes were bloodshot.

"Just few questions, Rózsás," Balogh said. "When the two of you came up here this morning, did Professor Petri ask you to use your key to unlock the door to the flat?"

"Didn't have to. When he knocked and got no answer, I tried the door. It was unlocked. I opened it. Hasn't been shut since, near as I know."

"Good. Now, did you see anyone in the building last night who doesn't live here? Anyone you didn't recognize?"

"Some tall bald thug tried to rough me up in the entrance," Rózsás said. "I gave him what for."

"Think you could you identify him in a line-up?"

"Well, *Biztos úr*, here's the thing," Rózsás said. "I wasn't at my best last night if you know what I mean."

Balogh dismissed the building manager and retraced his steps to the masking-tape outline. The corpse and the flag were gone. Where the back of Kellner's head had rested, blood stained the wooden floor. Most of the breakage formed a halo beyond the masking tape circuit. The Angelus bells began to ring. Noon.

CHAPTER THIRTY

Éva arrived early at police headquarters, but even before she walked through its glass doors she regretted not having accepted the detective's offer to send a car for her. The sidewalk outside was jammed with camera crews, reporters, and technicians. Fat bundles of multi-colored cables flowed out of news vans and snaked across the concrete blocking her approach. Members of the media jostled Éva as they swarmed any uniform that passed out of the building into the midday sum.

By the time she made it inside, Éva was not only late for the line-up, she was barely standing. A sallow-faced police sergeant on front-desk duty sensed her distress and eased her onto a folding chair.

"Do you feel faint, *asszonyom?*"

"Thank you, *Biztos úr.* It's passing," Éva said. "I'll sit here for moment if that's all right."

"I'm not surprised you're feeling wobbly after walking through that crush. We issued a statement about the murder at half-past ten. It wasn't fifteen minutes before the vans started showing up."

"A murder…"

"On Hajnóczy. A retired professor—"

Éva felt herself sliding off the chair just before she passed out.

When she opened her eyes, she was propped up against the cool stone wall of the lobby. The sergeant held a glass of water in one hand and his radio in the other.

"She's coming to. Send Csilla down. The lady may need someone to lean on. Right. I'll be here." He held the glass toward Éva. "Welcome back. Do you feel strong enough to stand?"

"I think so." She took another sip of water.

"So you were the one who saved an old fellow from a bad beating last night. Damn skinheads. Guess you're here to pick them out of a line-up. They may be the ones who killed Professor Kellner. But you're not supposed to know that. So *csitt!*" He put a finger to his lips. "They've not been charged yet, but there's going to be a press briefing at two. The press, *hála Istennek*, isn't allowed in here till then. I'll be off duty."

A young policewoman approached.

"Look, *asszonyom*, your escort's here. *Jó napot*, Csilla."

CHAPTER THIRTY-ONE

The Colonel's session with the reporters might have gone badly. They'd been arriving from Budapest all day by train or car and the long wait in the warm June sun made them more hostile than usual.

But Krebán had been trading blows with members of the press since his days in the ring. The media types who filed into the makeshift briefing room couldn't compare for cheek to the jaded Budapest sportswriters who used to crowd the weary bantamweight after fifteen rounds to let him know how he'd gone with the wrong combination in the third or how he might have put his opponent away in the tenth had he been a smart fighter.

The new-style journalist was no match for Krebán, veteran of so many scuffles with the old typewriter crowd, and his verbal dodge and dance hadn't let him down. He'd showered his guests with all the usual blather about "senseless violence" by "filthy cowards" and how they represented "a real evil in our midst," sounding as if he'd meant it all. Balogh glimpsed a wildness in Krebán's eyes, one the young boxer must have taught himself to contain and direct against his opponents.

The light Krebán shed on László Kellner's murder seemed bright enough to most. To Balogh, who'd watched the proceeding from the back of the room, Krebán's lamp, unlike that of truth-seeking Diogenes, had shone with all the brilliance of a birthday candle.

Asked if he was confident that the prime suspects were in custody, the Colonel responded: "I'm confident that we have two fewer skinheads on the streets and that public safety has been advanced by the action of the police."

"Do you have evidence to link them to the murder?"

"We have forensics and descriptions from several incidents and some of them fit the boys we arrested."

"Could you be more specific, Colonel?"

"No."

"What about the Arrow Crosses? Two of them appeared on the doors of ex-communists, the former and the present chairman of the University's Slavic Studies Department. Surely there's a pattern."

"Yes, yes. You're very astute. Please tell your editor I said so. But I'm afraid your pattern falls apart once we add the third victim. He's a former dean of the law faculty who advises conservative members of parliament on legal affairs. I've heard he may stand for office himself. I don't have to tell you it won't be under the banner of the socialists."

"But you have reason to believe that the two assaults and the murder were committed by the same individuals."

"Is that a question?"

"Do you have reason to believe that all three crimes were committed by the same individuals?"

"Now that's a question."

"Care to answer it?

"I'm not sure I can. You see, we have these suspects in custody on the one hand and we have all this evidence that seems to link the suspects to one or more of the incidents on the other. But until we piece it all together, it would be foolish of me to speculate, which is what you're asking me to do. So no, I won't answer your question, which, in its new form, if you don't mind my saying so, represents a major improvement over whatever it was you said the first time. I mean it was an actual question this time, wasn't it? That'll be all."

When the members of the press filed out at half-past two, the Colonel had all but convinced them they'd seen the last of skinhead violence in Szeged. Should headlines appear to the contrary tomorrow morning, he had managed to suggest, these would only attest to the media's fascination with savagery and its unflagging instinct for glamorizing evildoers.

Before he left the room, Krebán had whispered to Balogh: "I've bought us another day or two. But I want these pricks charged with Kellner's murder by Monday."

CHAPTER THIRTY-TWO

Éva snuffed out her third cigarette in a row and dropped it into the saucer. She'd lit up the third time after the first two cigarettes had failed to calm her. She couldn't remember the last time she'd fished the crinkly pack, almost empty, out of the shallow kitchen drawer where she kept things she rarely needed. When she came home from police headquarters she'd needed to smoke.

The detective had called early this morning to tell her about the line-up. They'd captured Mr. Neumann's assailants, and if she could come down and identify them a conviction was sure to follow. It had been surprisingly easy to identify the two of them, even though they looked much younger and less menacing under the lights than they had in near darkness. She'd studied the taller boy's face. Something about the set of his blue eyes, something around the corners of his smallish mouth reminded her of someone, but she hadn't been able to conjure a face or a name.

After the line-up a detective—Balogh was it?—confirmed that the boys had also been linked to Kellner's murder. Everything about the detective's face was ordinary except his penetrating ice-blue eyes.

"And since we have you here," he continued, "would you mind if I asked you a few questions about your visit to his flat last evening?

"Not at all," she said. She minded very much.

"If you have to return to work, we can do this another time."

"I've taken the day off."

"In that case," the detective smiled and began, "Professor Borsódy said you stopped by to pick up a manuscript for typing."

"Yes, Professor Kellner was writing his memoirs. I was his typist."

Where had she left the binder? She'd had it when she rushed out of the flat and down the stairs. An image of white pages scattered across the floor of the entrance hall convinced her of that. Should the detective ask her to turn the manuscript over to the police she would give him the penultimate version, the one without László's most recent corrections, without the most recent pages.

"When did you get to the flat?"

"I'd hoped to be at the Professor's by half-past eight."

"And Mr. Neumann was very fortunate that you happened to be passing through the neighborhood, but when did you actually arrive at your destination?"

"Shortly before nine."

"Professor Borsódy assumed you let yourself into the building using the entrance code. Does anyone besides the two of you have the building's entrance code?"

"The cleaning woman perhaps."

"Do you have a key to the flat itself?"

"Professor Kellner would leave the door unlocked when he was expecting me. That way I could come in without disturbing him if he was working. I'd knock first, of course."

"Was he working when you arrived last night?"

"He and Professor Borsódy were talking. I interrupted them. I didn't stay long."

Perhaps István hadn't said anything to the detective about her exchange with László. Perhaps he hadn't mentioned the pages she'd dropped off.

Why would he if the police hadn't asked about them? There were plenty of things The detective Balogh hadn't asked *her* about. He hadn't asked her about her state of mind last night. If she'd shown signs of stress during the interview, he'd probably chalked them up to her shock upon learning of László's death.

And so, she hadn't told him how upset she'd been both before the visit and after László's cruel rebuke. Or how she hadn't gone straight home. How she'd walked for hours, favoring less-traveled streets. How she'd circled back to László's neighborhood more than once so she might return to the flat and beg him not to publish those pages. How each time she'd lost her nerve and continued wandering.

She hadn't told Detective Balogh how she'd found the courage to climb the stairs to László's flat again. How she'd barely taken notice of the Arrow Cross on the front door because she was too preoccupied with what she might say to make him understand how his words had grieved her and how they would grieve István if he should, upon reading them, understand what she had understood at once. Of course, it was possible István wouldn't grasp their meaning. Yet even if István never read the pages, even if he wouldn't figure out their secret should he read them, László had been heartless not to consider their effect on her. Hadn't he imagined she might see in print his real reasons for offering the counsel he knew she could not help but follow? Was it possible he didn't care if she did?

The pages lay before her on the table. She couldn't help but read them again. She felt like one unable to avoid looking at a train wreck, except that Éva herself was among the dead and maimed.

...And I recall with sadness and remorse all those times when it fell to me to forfeit the happiness of a few for the well-being of the community I served. On one occasion, I protected a much younger, newly married colleague from exposure after his reckless personal behavior had resulted in impregnating a brilliant female student of mine.

This man, I should add, had done nothing to deserve either my empathy or assistance. Yet, at the time, it seemed likely that the ensuing scandal would compromise his effectiveness as an informer in the eyes of the Interior Ministry. My subsequent actions were thus aimed not at sparing him disgrace but at preserving his reputation with the secret police as a reliable informer. I had always been successful at containing his activities owing to the considerable influence I wielded over him as his teacher and mentor.

I acted the way I did because I knew far greater harm might come to the faculty and students in my charge than any he had caused or would cause should another be recruited to take his place. Yet I also knew my actions would cost a good man, a man who was my friend, his contentment.

She would never forget how exposed and betrayed and sick she'd felt reading these sentences the first time.

Until then, she'd never considered that there might have been another reason for her having to give up all she'd given up. How could László have told her that she must leave István because of her infidelity? Especially after she'd told him she'd been forced into the arrangement, one that, in any event, had ended after one horrible meeting.

Istenem! To see him lying there. And all the life gone out of him.

She meant to call the police for the second time that evening, but dialed Sándor instead. She told him that László was dead. He told her to wait for him, to stay calm. She waited. She tried to stay calm. She stashed the pages in her purse. Neither Sándor nor István, she'd reasoned at the time, must ever see them. She'd already deleted them from the pc at the office. Now, she needed to make sure they never saw either the printed pages or the originals. But where was the binder? Had she set it down when she took the pages and left it at the flat?

She returned from the bedroom moments later with the original draft of the pages she'd just read. Even now, she admired László's fluid hand, his elegant, errorless script. She opened the window over the sink, lay the written pages atop the typescript, and set them on fire.

CHAPTER THIRTY-THREE

Balogh sent a car to the railroad station for Dr. Gizella Kurtág. He told the driver to keep the radio off during the ride over, hoping the attorney hadn't yet heard that her clients were now the prime suspects in a murder investigation. Though the odds were against it, they weren't particularly long. The trip from Budapest on the InterCity took nearly three hours, while the statement linking the skinheads to the homicide had been released an hour earlier than Kurtág's train was scheduled to arrive. Balogh was ready to begin questioning the moment she got there and one of the skinheads was already waiting for them in the interview room.

As soon as Kurtág, a distinguished woman with quick brown eyes and graying blonde hair pulled back to accentuate her sharp features, stepped off the elevator, Balogh knew he'd made the right play. The attorney was all smiles and condescension, all politeness and clipped Budapest inflection, sure as she was that she could plead her way down to probation and community service for assorted misdemeanors and felonies. After all, her clients had only one previous arrest between them, and that for public drunkenness.

Balogh liked to begin interrogations with a few non-hostile questions to get a sense of the suspect's facial expressions, gestures, and speech patterns at a point when answering questions truthfully carried no risk. As the interrogation proceeded and the questions grew more threatening, these reactions would help Balogh establish that the suspect was turning liar. If the suspect's body language and manner of talking changed in easily discernible ways, he became a human polygraph.

"Have you been to our city before, Zoltán?"

The skinhead leaned forward, seemingly willing to answer. Kurtág blocked him with an outstretched arm. "I don't see the relevance of that question."

Of course, any attorney worth her salt would try to prevent Balogh from eliciting these baseline responses. Each time she did, Balogh would lower his head and raise his hands—palms open, fingers spread—as if acknowledging defeat.

After a few minutes, he moved on to the tougher questions, fully expecting more objections from Kurtág. He didn't have to wait long.

"Don't answer that, Zoltán," she said, and turning to Balogh: "Whether my client was in such or such a neighborhood last night is hardly the business of the police."

Balogh had had enough.

"Permit me to suggest that your clients' whereabouts last evening are precisely what you just characterized as 'the business of the police,' especially since there's ample evidence that places them at a murder scene."

Kurtág withdrew into stunned silence as Zoltán's blue eyes widened with incomprehension. Had he been caught unawares by the swiftness with which Balogh linked him to the murder? Or was it possible Zsolt had killed Kellner without Zoltán's knowledge? Balogh, after all, had already been able to determine, on the basis of paint specks discovered on only

Zsolt's hands and clothing, that of the two skinheads he'd been the graffiti artist. Perhaps he'd been the killer as well. And hadn't Rózsás, though he'd acknowledged being drunk at the time, said that he'd tangled with a tall skinhead at the entrance to Kellner's building last night? Perhaps Zoltán had stood watch downstairs as Zsolt bludgeoned Kellner to death upstairs.

"I hope, Dr. Kurtág," Balogh continued, "that I haven't offended either you or your client by suggesting his involvement in the murder of a prominent citizen and scholar of this city. Attributing guilt is the task of the courts. As a police detective, I can do little more than assemble statements, gather evidence, advance a witness or two, to assist the prosecution."

Zoltán stared at Kurtág, silently urging her to say something on his behalf. She said nothing. "We were at Bartók Square last night," Zoltán said.

Perhaps Zoltán imagined that by answering an earlier question, he might erase all the Major had said since. Perhaps he believed he could rewind the video recorder that had been running since the start of the interrogation to a point when no mention of murder had yet been made, that by answering every question he could prevent it from being mentioned again.

"I've gone over the incident reports and the evidence and I've talked to several witnesses. I've no doubt that you and Zsolt had a hand in Professor Kellner's death."

Balogh was fudging. He had witnesses for some of the other crimes, but the inebriated Rózsás was the only one who could place even one of the skinheads at the Hajnóczy Street address last night and his testimony surely would be thrown out of court.

"I don't know what you're talking about," Zoltán said, his features twisted in frustration.

"Here's what I said: there's not a doubt in my mind that you are involved in Professor Kellner's murder."

"But I don't even know who that is!" Zoltán grabbed both sides of his shaved head and began to rock back and forth in his chair.

"Are you going ask my client a question?" Kurtág said, emerging from her stupor.

"Are you going to let him answer one?"

"We'd appreciate a few minutes alone, Major."

CHAPTER THIRTY-FOUR

Appalling variations on a theme by J. S. Bach for un-accompanied cell phone shattered the bedroom's calm.

"*Istenem*! Please, not now." Dezső Markovits stretched out naked in the late afternoon light that peeked through half-drawn blinds. By his side, Csilla, similarly attired, kneeled. Within an instant, she'd taken the foil packet from her teeth and extended her lithe body—her nipples matter-of-factly grazing his hairless chest—to answer the cell phone playing on the night table. She smiled wistfully at Dezső and pressed the phone to her ear.

"Officer Horváth speaking. May I ask who's calling please?"

Csilla blushed and instinctively covered her white breasts with a tanned forearm—its down golden in the sun—before she turned away, and, swinging her legs over the side of the bed, sat with her back to Dezső.

"No, Professor Petri," she said. "You haven't caught me in the middle of anything."

Dezső admired her graceful swimmer's frame, tan but for the pale ghost of a bikini she wore all summer long under her navy two-piece.

"*Délmagyarország* ran a photograph of you with Professors Kellner and Borsódy a month ago. Let me get this down."

Csilla walked over to the chair on which her clothes lay, drew a pen and notepad from her blouse pocket, and, raising a bronze shoulder to her cheek to keep the phone from falling, wrote something down. Dezső loved watching the businesslike manner in which she made her way around the room, the routine nature of her motions. In them, he read the promise of an ordinary life together, in or out of clothes.

Drawn to life's prose, he considered himself an aficionado of the everyday. Moments like these had their magic. Csilla scribbled away, her ash-blond hair falling forward to veil half her face. He longed for a camera that might preserve more than a second's image or a certain quality of light.

"No, sir. I'll find it." Csilla continued listening. "It *is* an interesting idea, sir. I'll share it with Major Balogh when I see him."

Shortly before two, the same Major Balogh had sent her away and told her not to return to headquarters till after five. Csilla had needed a break after working late last night only to return to headquarters earlier than usual this morning and carry on straight through lunch. Too keyed-up over the Kellner case to nap, she'd resolved to burn off her nervous energy with a swim and, if that didn't work, by making afternoon love with Dezső.

Swimming had done little to take off her edge, and she'd peddled right over here from the Újszeged pool. When Dezső kissed her at the door, her hair was still wet and her lips tasted of chlorine and salt.

Csilla winked at Dezső: "Yes, sir, he *is* a good photographer."

She blushed again and covered her pubes with the notepad for good measure. "I'm not sure he does portraits, but thank you, sir. Yes, sir. Goodbye, sir."

When she came back to bed, Csilla buried her face in Dezső's chest.

"What did Petri say to make you blush?" Dezső asked, stroking her still-damp hair. She nuzzled into him some more before saying: "He asked if he'd caught me in the middle of something."

"You told him that he hadn't."

"I couldn't tell him that I was preparing to mount the police photographer."

"Maybe he could hear that you weren't wearing any clothes."

Csilla thumped him on the shoulder.

"What about the second time?"

"He asked me if you also shot portraits or nudes and told me I would make a lovely model. He added that he'd meant a portrait model, of course."

"He's not wrong, you know. The light's perfect. You wait here. I'll be right back with my camera."

"I'm going to hit you hard." Csilla cried, before she let her fist fall limply to her side. "It's my fault. I tried to be reassuring when I went over to his house with Ernő last night. I think he took it the wrong way."

"It's not your fault he's a middle-aged lecher, but I suspect he's harmless enough. He didn't talk much when I dropped by this morning to photograph his door. Though one thing he said struck me as odd."

"What did he say?" Csilla asked as she unconsciously stroked Dezső's chest, shoulders and arms, lightly brushing her fingernails backwards against his browned skin.

Dezső squirmed. "You're turning me on."

"Eeeeew! Petri said that? He's an even bigger pervert than I thought," Csilla stuck out her tongue, mock-gagging in disgust. "What were the two of you doing anyway?"

"He didn't say that. I'm saying that. Look how you're touching me."

"Oops." Csilla looked at her hand disapprovingly. "What did Petri say that seemed strange to you?"

"He wanted to know if he could go at the graffiti with some solvent he'd bought. I told him he should check with you or Ernő first."

"He didn't mention it," Csilla said. "But it wouldn't be strange if he wanted to remove that Arrow Cross before his wife and kids came home."

"Sure. But he got defensive, made a point of telling me how he'd bought the solvent weeks ago after his kids did some action painting on their bedroom wall."

Csilla squinted at her wristwatch on the night table. "I've got to be back at work in an hour."

"I guess you'll want to start getting dressed." Dezső played dumb and sat up so suddenly that Csilla rolled off his chest and almost off the bed.

"Where are you going?" she said.

"To make us some tea," Dezső said.

Csilla's voice, usually so earnest and bell clear, withdrew deep into her throat. Dezső heard only a low whisper, beseeching and full of ardor: "You're not going anywhere."

She pushed him down again and spread her body over his. She gripped his arms. She held his legs in place with hers, her thighs pressed against his thighs. She lowered her face to his and brushed his lips with hers. She held his gaze with intent eyes as she raised herself over him. Releasing her grip, she lifted her hands toward the ceiling. She tossed her head back. Bands of light and shade slanted across her breasts, shoulders, and throat. Dezső felt her body hovering inches above his own. He felt her heat penetrating him as she lowered herself onto him, but slowly, slowly, as if she too wanted to draw out as long as possible this first transporting moment of contact. Dezső closed his eyes and waited for the longest and deepest of stillnesses to envelop them.

"Csilla," Dezső said silently, "Csilla, Joy of Man's desiring."

CHAPTER THIRTY-FIVE

Zoltán and Dr. Kurtág rose from their seats when Balogh returned. He gestured for them to sit down.

"My client is prepared to accept responsibility for everything except Professor Kellner's murder," Kurtág said. "I've not spoken with Zsolt, of course, but I'm sure he will agree to this."

Kurtág was bargaining. Defense attorneys weren't in the habit of cutting deals with the police. But who wouldn't cop to a string of lesser charges if it meant getting away with murder.

"Zoltán," Balogh said, "were you and Zsolt in Professor Kellner's building last night?"

Zoltán nodded.

"I need to be absolutely clear on this point, Dr. Kurtág," Balogh said. "Your client is insisting that he and Zsolt are in no way responsible for the murder of László Kellner either directly or in accessory fashion?"

"Yes, Major."

"And, Zoltán, you do understand that you may still face murder charges if a third party killed Kellner with either your knowledge or aid."

"No one else was with us last night." Zoltán said. "I wasn't even aware there'd been a murder until now. Zsolt still doesn't know."

"So why were you in Professor Kellner's building last night?"

"We were hired to paint an Arrow Cross on his door, just as we were hired to paint the other two crosses."

"What about the assaults, the stolen flag?"

"We were paid for the Arrow Crosses. And to be seen. We needed the flag to collect payment."

"You committed two assaults just so you would be seen?"

"We weren't going to hurt the Jew. The pompous ass at the rally had it coming, but we hadn't planned on hitting him either."

"Who hired you?"

"We never met him. We got instructions through the mail or over the phone."

"This sounds like a lot of *szalámi* to me. You want me to believe that you've been framed for murder. Just remember," Balogh said to Kurtág, "young Zoltán here has placed himself and his partner at the murder scene."

"It's time you spoke to Zsolt," Kurtág said.

"Zoltán spoke suddenly: "Why would we lead the police right to us if we'd killed the professor?"

"That's a good question," Balogh said. "But people who commit crimes like this tend to believe they're smarter than everyone else. You figured you'd covered your tracks."

"And leave Arrow Crosses like bloody handprints wherever we went?"

"I didn't say you *were* smarter."

"And I didn't say we weren't stupid" Zoli buried his face in his hands.

CHAPTER THIRTY-SIX

Major Balogh could go fuck himself. If that glorified ticket-checker needed to see him again, he'd have to wait until Monday. What right had he to know that Sándor was on his way to Balaton anyway? He hadn't told the detective he'd originally planned to spend his Saturday with Monika in Mohács, so what was the point in telling him he'd changed his mind.

Sándor had called Anna from Déli Station before boarding the train for Balatonfüred. She'd been as pleased upon learning that he was already in Budapest and would be at her parents' in a few hours as Monika had been displeased when he'd called her with the news that he couldn't get away with her tomorrow after all. All right. So *pleased* wasn't the best word to describe Anna's reaction to the news of his coming anymore than *displeased* was the best word to describe Monika's reaction to the news of his going. *Indifferent* and *enraged* might be better choices. Still, things might have gone worse. Anna might have been enraged, Monika indifferent.

He'd already begged off from the Mohács trip twice before and the third time, as he might have expected of a woman as sure of her beauty and appeal as Monika was, had been the charm.

The first time she'd gone easy on him, making no fuss when she'd caught him passing off some borrowed wisdom as his own.

"Just think of it this way, *drága* Monika, *desire is kindled by everything but fulfillment.*"

"I'd never have guessed you read Osvát, Sándor?"

"Where we would be, Moni, if we'd ended up in bed together tomorrow afternoon, having made good on every pledge our hearts had sworn?"

"Why, Sándor. We'd be fucking."

The second time, she'd brushed his broken promise aside with the now-requisite literary allusion.

"I forgive you Sándor. What else can I do? Déry wrote that *even though all of us are built for love, not all of us are equally skillful at it.*"

"I'm not sure how I should take that, Moni."

"O, Sándor, I shouldn't worry if I were you. Besides he goes on to write that *whatever our natural endowments, loving demands we all be theoreticians as well.*"

"I like the old poets better. This Déry leaves me feeling, well...inadequate."

Monika laughed wickedly and hung up without a goodbye.

This time, she'd taken the news badly. Even so, her parting words had their own poetry: "*Kicsi lófasz a seggedbe!*" A remarkably expressive phrase that Sándor took as: *I wish you anal penetration by the sex organ of a modestly favored horsey.*

A shame things with Monika had ended this way, Sándor reflected, but all was changed now. A week ago he'd been rehearsing ways to say goodbye to Anna. Today, he was bent on staying with her. Monday's call from the Minister had made matrimony a desirable state again. Wednesday's revelations, courtesy of Éva's pc, had made it positively necessary for future happiness. Now, László's death had sent him running

142

back to his wife for good, even though Éva had since deleted the distressing files.

Anna knew him and must have known all along that he would never leave her. He acknowledged her power over him. He'd been gazing the length of the sunny carriage when a few rows up the aisle he spotted a dark-eyed woman in a lime-green blouse and fawn skirt that rode up her thigh each time its hem threatened to slip over her polished knees. She was smiling in a way that both frightened and charmed him. He imagined her dragging him to the car's lavatory, a dingy cubicle so small, grimy, and rank that it was barely suitable for two with more on their minds than washing hands. Would women always exert such power over him?

Sándor smiled back and stuffed the black binder that lay beside him into his satchel. There'd be time to extract and destroy the incriminating pages. The rest of the memoir posed a more serious problem—far too many knew of its existence, two persons had read everything but the appendix, at least one had read the entire manuscript. He couldn't return the binder to Éva, but he couldn't keep it either. He'd think of something.

CHAPTER THIRTY-SEVEN

The little red light on Balogh's phone was blinking. He despised the call indicator and, during slow periods, he would cover it up with a snippet of electrician's tape. At times like this, he grudgingly put up with its madding intrusions.

Good, he thought, only one message to delete. But that turned out to be from Viktor Uborka demanding immediate compensation for the stolen flag currently locked up in the evidence room. Balogh dropped the handset into the desk's cavernous bottom drawer and kicked it shut. He'd hoped for a satisfyingly loud bang but a soft spiral of phone cord had caught itself on a sharp corner and prevented good metal-on-metal contact. Annoyed, Balogh opened the drawer again and dropped the rest of the phone into it, making sure this time to pull taut the wall cable as he kicked the drawer shut again. A prodigious boom echoed through the office. Method was all.

Zsolt's shock upon learning he faced a murder charge hadn't stopped him from offering an account of last night's events that differed just enough from Zoltán's to lend credence to both accounts. Had the versions been any closer to each other, Balogh might be more inclined to reject their stories. Years in interrogation rooms—so many that he could no longer smell the acrid pong of cigarette smoke, rancid sweat, and antiseptic hanging in every corner like a filthy ghost—had taught Balogh that truth preferred minor discrepancies over agreement in each particular. He wasn't ready to believe that the skins were telling the truth. He'd simply begun to question their dishonesty.

And he didn't expect his doubts to outlast a careful review of the facts. In their statements, Zoltán and Zsolt had placed themselves in Kellner's building around the time of the murder. Even without confessions, the circumstantial evidence was unusually strong, certainly strong enough to support a murder charge if not a conviction.

Tomorrow morning, Korbács would produce the incriminating forensics. Balogh would file charges and turn the case over to the county prosecutor. He would spend the rest of his Saturday nodding off in his arbor while Ildikó and the children, armed with a weather-beaten ladder and cane baskets, harvested ripe cherries, hard and sweet and shaped like hearts, from fruit-heavy branches.

He wondered if he would feel cheated by so tidy a conclusion to the case. He valued good policing and though he occasionally experienced mild disappointment when his skills as a detective proved unnecessary for breaking a case open, this didn't feel like one of those times. After a bad start, the police had wrapped thing ups quickly: the suspects had been in cuffs by midnight. The evidence had come together nicely, the witnesses had been cooperative. Even the interrogations had gone well in the end: the "Z's," as he had taken to calling Zoltán and Zsolt, had confessed to every crime with the exception of what the autopsy would surely prove was a homicide.

Thus, he felt neither discontent nor accomplishment at the prospect of closing the case quickly. It would be a relief to have the case over. But why? The case file had been open for all of eight hours. He couldn't have grown bored with it so soon.

The case was anything but dull and its political dimensions made it unlike any case he'd even worked on before. Perhaps the ideological nature of the case had frightened him. After all, he'd grown up in a nation where crime and politics had been anything but strange bedfellows. They'd been more like an old married couple.

He was too young to remember the show trials of the Stalinist 40's or the reprisal hangings of the 50's, but he was not too young to remember how the merest mention of the $\acute{A}VO$, the State Security Department, could awaken such fear in his elders. As one commentator on the period wrote: when Magyars used to say they were afraid of each rap on the door, they really meant they were afraid of *each rap on the door*, especially those heard in the middle of the night. He couldn't recall ever having heard a single joke about the secret police, even in a country where the best punch lines had always been directed against arrogant and arbitrary authority.

The hard criminality of a regime maintained through terror and starvation in time gave way to the soft corruption of one maintained by its refusal to impose more Soviet-style restrictions on an already impoverished populace. This shift spelled a relatively secure and peaceful if humble and stagnant life for most Magyars and until recently, even a decade after the changes of '89, Hungary could boast one of the lowest violent-crime rates in Central Europe. Even now, murders occurred infrequently enough that most homicides made the national news.

But the murder of László Kellner was another matter. Depending on whom you listened to, the victim was either a hero of the Hungarian Revolution of 1956 or a collaborator with the late dictatorship. The killing of so controversial a figure could not help but evoke memories of past crimes: other murders, treasons, betrayals, and frauds, all carried out in the name of the Hungarian people by the old Stalinist regime.

As word spread that László Kellner had been bludgeoned to death, many sober-minded people said they could hear the phantoms of Hungary's tragic past shaking ages of grit from their chains and warming up their dusty pipes with easy scales of moans before attempting the blood-curdling, full-throated wails for which they were celebrated. And who's to say these ghost-boosters were wrong, since the killers, just as they had at Szolnok one year ago, had draped the famous corpse in a Hungarian flag with a hole through the center. It was perfectly reasonable for people to believe that the Szeged police had a political murder on their hands.

Still, it was Balogh's duty to ask himself what other motives might lurk behind Kellner's murder. He recalled his morning conference with Krebán and remembered thinking that the skinheads might have acted on instructions. Their testimony, if true, had just confirmed this, but their odd behavior last night had given Balogh pause even before he learned of the slaying.

Now, Zoltán's rhetorical question began to bother him: *why would we lead the police right to us if we'd killed the professor?* They'd gone out of their way to be seen at Bartók Square and near Kellner's building. Doubtless, skinheads adored publicity, but why would these two want to draw attention to themselves if they were about to commit murder? Especially when capture would spell long sentences in the old Szeged jail? Most dungeons were more inviting. It just didn't make sense.

Had the suspects been set up as both claimed they'd been? Had the setup been botched? What if the murder hadn't been planned at all, either by the skinheads or by the party or parties they claimed had hired them? If they'd been hired only for those actions to which they'd confessed, was it possible their mysterious employer hadn't intended them to be nailed for murder, but only for the crimes they'd just admitted to? Balogh wondered what result a third party might hope to achieve by last night's hate spree.

The only thing of which Balogh could be sure was that László Kellner was either the victim of a political murder or that someone had gone to unusual lengths to make him seem like the victim of one. If there'd been a cover-up, he'd need to uncover the pedestrian motives hidden beneath the mutilated flag, the sorts of routine motives—money, sex, revenge—that served as springs for most of the murders Balogh had solved.

He'd already established, based on interviews with several of the last persons to have seen the professor alive, that László Kellner could be difficult, perhaps even cruel at times. His oldest friend and colleague, István Borsódy, had admitted to quarreling with him, while his typist, Éva Hegedűs, had been guardedly cooperative the way someone is when they don't want to recall the nastiness of their last encounter with the deceased. Even that peacock Sándor Petri had been rebuked by his mentor last night.

Balogh remembered that Pál Berkesi, his former brother-in-law, had once been a prize student of the murdered scholar. Hadn't Pál, enraged by something the professor had said, left his mentor's charge? Balogh could barely recall the story of their falling out, the incident having taken place so long ago that even when Pál told Balogh about it years later, it had seemed like ancient history. Yet Pál had still sounded hurt as he related the episode. And though Pál had a forgiving nature, he seemed not to have forgiven his mentor. Maybe Kellner had driven others to act rashly, even violently. A call to Pál was in order. Balogh lifted the phone out of the bottom drawer.

CHAPTER THIRTY-EIGHT

At sunset, a draught of easy wind sped a great green moth over the flowering sedge and ruffled the glowing reeds along the Tisza's shore. The fishermen's flatboats waited for dawn in yellow mud, their slimy bottoms afire in the summer dusk. Waiters lighted the terrace lamps.

"...Besides," Kati reassured herself, "we're only postponing our trip."

Rising above her disappointment, she descended upon her catfish *pörkölt* like the intrepid marsh bird that swooped down now and then to carry off a shiny fish head from a fellow diner's plate. After each successful foray, Pál cheered the winged raider with a *huzzah*!

Pál looked up from his Serbian-style carp and dabbed a daub of sour cream with a red napkin. "The waiter told me that your dinner, in its wild state, pulled linens from the hands of unsuspecting laundresses up river."

Kati refused to take the bait.

Pál cast again: "He told me your fish took hold of a billy goat's leg once and dragged the stupid beast to the river bottom."

"I think someone's taken hold of *my* leg," Kati said.

Pál lifted the checkered blue cloth and peered under the table.

"You're mistaken. Or perhaps you mean to call our waiter a liar?"

"I just didn't hear him say anything about my catfish, Pál."

"Of course not. You were busy translating the menu."

"But the menu's in Hungarian!"

"So you work quickly. There's no need to boast, Kati."

She resolved to change the subject, though she expected their conversation would continue in the same vein. She didn't mind. He'd been very sweet to take her to her favorite restaurant as part of his plan to make up for their aborted vacation plans. The teasing was another part of that. Bicycling to Lake Ludas tomorrow yet another.

"I met Gabi at the Bécsi Kávézó today."

"And how is your friend the nymphomaniac? Ships that pass in the night have nothing on her."

"She's not a nymphomaniac."

"Of course not. What was I thinking? Your chaste friend is the epitome of feminine virtue."

Kati laughed. "I wouldn't go that far."

"Neither would that nice American youth here from Salt Lake City last summer."

"He was leaving the Mormons anyway, Pál."

"She led him down iniquity's path to the vale of defilement. He'd not even completed the first month of his ministry when she placed his soul at hazard."

"Gabi hasn't placed any souls at hazard."

"No? How many Magyar gentlemen did she corrupt in two weeks at Lake Balaton last August? Can you tell me that, madam?"

"Oh, Pál, I doubt she corrupted any of them."

"You're absolutely correct. Your Magyar gentleman is incorruptible. The lads ensnared in Gabi's web of lust must have been foreigners."

"Enough, Pál."

"I'm sorry, madam. I did not mean to impugn our foreign guests. As for your friend…"

"Gabi's a little promiscuous."

"And the Alföld is a little flat."

"She's pretty. Most men are attracted to her."

"She's attracted to most men. To most men *and* women probably. I'm surprised she hasn't tried to bed you. No matter. At least I know why you don't let her visit the flat more often."

"I've never told Gabi not to visit. I trust her."

"Yes, yes. But do you trust me?"

"You can meet her alone anytime you wish."

"Good, because I've invited her over tomorrow for a cozy little chat."

"We're biking to Serbia in the morning."

Pál opened his pocket calendar. "Here it is," he said and pretended to read: "17 *June. 11:30 PM. Cozy little chat with Gabi.* You'll have to find something to do with yourself for a few hours. Come to think of it, you may want to arrange to stay overnight with a friend. These cozy little chats can last a while."

"Pál, don't you want to know what Gabi told me?"

"Not really."

"She spent most of yesterday afternoon with a skinhead boy."

"A skinhead boy! How nice for her. Our little Gabi is doing well for herself. And what did he say when she told him she once made love to a dark Roma boy she met while waitressing at..."

Pál broke off. The day's events had conspired with his memory to put him in mind of last night's murder. When he spoke again, his tone was softer, sober, apologetic.

"I'm sorry, Kati. I'm not thinking clearly," he said. "Where did Gabi say she met this skinhead?"

"On the train ride from Kecskemét."

"Did she say what his name was?"

"I think she said his name was Zoli. Why?"

"Kati, the police may be looking for Gabi. She was seen leaving the train with two skinheads being held in the Kellner case."

"The police think Gabi has something to do with the murder?"

"They just want to talk to her. Besides, her Zoli may not be the one in the lockup. If he is, maybe she's his alibi."

Kati's eyes misted over. Pál took her hand and stroked it.

"Kati, listen to me, the police wouldn't care if she'd entertained an entire company of well-favored Hitler youth..."

Kati glared at him, drew her hand away.

"I'm just saying that she probably doesn't figure in the investigation," Pál said. "Unless you're not telling me something she told you about this Zoli, she has nothing to worry about."

"She didn't say much about him," Kati said. "Only that he'd saved her from being molested by a drunk on the train. And that she was surprised by how sweet he'd turned out to be, how safe she'd felt with him."

"You see. She has no reason to be afraid."

"Call Balogh," Kati said, "I'll go with her to police headquarters tonight."

"I've heard of people like you," Pál said, taking out his phone. "Friendship. Loyalty. Compassion. Make sure you don't go all soft-eyed should Gabi kiss you. You don't want to send her the wrong signal."

CHAPTER THIRTY-NINE

Ernő knew the Kéknyelű by reputation only as the saddest wine joint in town. The acrid scent of failure hung about the place like a gold chain on a gypsy king. Chewed-over husks of pumpkin seeds carpeted the floor.

"*Jó estét kívánok!*" Ernő checked his notepad, "Géza Eperjesi?"

"*Jó estét, Biztos úr! Tessék parancsolni!*" The tall, gaunt Eperjesi had the grim face and the washed-out blue eyes of an undertaker. His smile was vaguely menacing. "But I take it you are not interested in my wine."

"Have a few question for you, Mr. Eperjesi. Can we talk here or would you like more privacy?" Ernő gestured toward the dead-enders at the bar. Through the bluish nicotine haze, their bloodshot eyes looked like they had stopped seeing anything beyond the rim of a wine glass years ago.

"The living dead will not disturb us." Eperjesi passed a grayish hand back and forth before the face of one permanently drunk. "And we will not disturb them."

Ernő began: "Two skinheads came in here last Thursday evening. Would you like to see their mug shots?"

"I remember them." Eperjesi said.

"How long did they stay?"

"They were in the front door and out the back in five minutes," Eperjesi said, his face blank.

Ernő jotted down Eperjesi's words. "You've already answered my next question. Tell me, had they been here before?"

"I'd never seen them before Thursday evening, but I have seen them in the paper since. They are in trouble?" Ernő wondered if Eperjesi was curious about the case or merely feigning interest to create an impression of ignorance.

"They claim to have conducted some business with you."

Eperjesi remained stone-faced. "They came here for an envelope."

"One with a hundred thousand forints in it," Ernő said.

"Really. A hundred thousand? I guess I will be more careful in the future about giving away stationary."

"Save your wit for your customers," Ernő said, not trying to hide his irritation. "Anything written on that envelope?"

"Just some numbers."

"Do you recall which ones?"

"No, only that there were six of them."

Ernő jotted down "local number."

"Did they take the envelope with them?" he asked.

Eperjesi shook his head no and flicked his lighter.

"Any idea who may have sent the money?"

"I received an anonymous phone call. Payment arrived by truck the next morning and left by skinhead that evening."

"And that was the first time you heard the caller's voice?"

"And probably the last if word gets out that we have spoken," Eperjesi said. "I do not know if it matters but I think he was calling from a pay phone. I heard coins dropping." Eperjesi was growing positively expansive.

"But how did he get your number?"

"I have done favors for many people over the years."

"What kinds of favors, Mr. Eperjesi?"

"Nothing illegal. I have my tavern license to protect. They generally involve the discreet transfer of funds from one party to another."

"And do these favors come cheaply?"

"I am afraid, *Biztos úr*, that is none of your business. I am cooperating and I cannot see what possible..." Ernő had misjudged Eperjesi. He hadn't expected to meet the same indignation a respectable citizen might show in the face of unwarranted allegations.

"Calm down, Mr. Eperjesi. I didn't mean to wind you up. But how do you know you're not passing drug money? You'd be over at Csillag jail in no time if you were tied to a syndicate in any way."

"Which is why I am particular about those for whom I do favors."

"A moment ago you said you didn't know the person who called you."

"I have other ways to determine risk."

"So who delivers the money?"

"With all due respect, *Biztos úr*, may I observe that while you get paid to ask questions, I get paid *not* to answer them."

"Perhaps you'd rather go over our job descriptions in detail at headquarters."

"A driver from a Budapest wine distributor. I know him a long time."

"Can I get a name?"

"If you come to the office, I can even give you his cell phone number, but he does not know the person you're trying to find either. His dealings with the man you seek have been strictly through courier."

Eperjesi led Ernő to his office and opened the door. A red, white, and green flag lay heaped on the desk.

"I see you are admiring my flag. I have been meaning to hang it since the other day. To brighten up the place. What do you think, *Biztos úr*?"

Saturday, 17 June

CHAPTER FORTY

In the dream, Jancsi is seven years old. He and his little sister Elena and the other children from the orphanage are loaded into hay carts at sunrise and driven out to the cornfields. Crows already blacken the sky. The keepers hand out rattles: some are seed-filled dried gourds, others are wooden blocks with cranks. The tiniest children wear bell collars. All of them begin to run, little, darting scarecrows, up and down the rows of corn as long as crows fill the sky. Above them always that swath of summer blue. To either side, always those high green walls of spindly stalks.

With too few rattles to go around today, Jancsi and Elena have to wave their arms in the air as they run and sing old Roma songs to scare the crows away. By late morning, they are so tired they fall down and sleep in warm earth. One of the minders has Jancsi by the shoulder and is shaking him awake. He opens his eyes.

A police officer stared down at him.

"Wake up, Jancsi. Time to leave the park."

The bright morning sun made it difficult for Jancsi to see the officer's face, but he recognized his voice. This *zsaru* was kinder than most, a little bossy but friendly. No name calling. No stick. He hated the stick. He wanted to ask the police officer where he was, but thought better of it.

"Forgive me, *Biztos úr*, I'll leave at once." Jancsi tried to stand up, but faltered. He sat back down on the grass.

"Go easy, Jancsi. Get your bearings. Say, you've a nice raincoat there."

Jancsi made it up without staggering this time and stood at attention as if waiting for inspection. The officer adjusted the coat around the homeless man's frail shoulders, smoothed his lapels, and took a step back to admire his handiwork.

"There's a proper gentleman," he said.

Jancsi recalled the slip-slap of footsteps in haste and the muffled thud of a soft bundle landing on wet grass. Someone had dropped the coat within arm's length of where he lay the previous night. Jancsi had somehow found it in his sleep and pulled it on in the chilly dawn.

"Looks like someone caught it in a bicycle chain." The officer stared at the hem. He leaned over to take a closer look. "You know what, Jancsi? That's not rust or grease. Would you mind coming down to the station with me? I promise it won't take long."

Jancsi shied.

"Don't worry. It's just that I may be able to find you a better coat."

"This one's fine, *Biztos úr*." He shuffled his feet in the dust.

"I'm afraid I have to insist you come with me, Jancsi."

They left Dugonics Park just as the music started and the fountain jets began to gush and spray.

The officer made good on his word. Jancsi, arrayed in a new used coat from the police station lost-and-found, was back on the streets by lunchtime, begging half-eaten cutlets and unfinished bowls of bean or cabbage soup from patrons leaving the Dóm Square canteen.

CHAPTER FORTY-ONE

Balogh swung around in his swivel chair, planted both elbows on the blotter, and opened his hands to support his sagging countenance and spirits. The murder case against the skinheads was growing weaker by the hour. It had begun to break down late yesterday when Ernő came back from the Kéknyelű with the flag left there by the suspects.

That turned out to be only the first of three bad omens. An hour ago, Balogh received news that a police officer, while making his rounds downtown, had found a homeless man wearing a bloodstained raincoat. The man had come into possession of the coat while he slept under a bush the night before last. A search of its pockets yielded short strands of red, white, and green threads. Balogh ordered the coat sent to Korbács so the ME could check the blood type of the stains against Kellner's.

And just twenty minutes ago, Mr. Szalonna, supplier of the flags for Thursday evening's Bartók Square rally, confirmed the flag retrieved from the Kéknyelű was one of his. He didn't recognize the flag with the hole found at the crime scene, but suggested that might it have been stolen from a public institution—a firehouse, a school, one of the university faculties—given its weathered appearance.

"These colors are all washed out," Szalonna said, brandishing a hand like a matured ham over the faded cloth. "The wind and rain have done their job."

"Or just old?" Balogh ventured. Perhaps the flag had a past.

"Not old," Szalonna said. "Just badly worn."

"Any idea how the hole was made?"

"He may have rushed a bit, but the cutting's too clean for a knife," Szalonna said. "Scissors most likely."

Balogh watched the fat man lumber toward the door.

"I'll send you an invoice for the flag," Szalonna said over his shoulder, the tang of bacon grease and onions in his wake. "When I get payment, I'll reimburse Uborka."

The telephone's shrill warning jarred Balogh back to the present.

"In on a Saturday morning, Balogh?" Korbács was at the other end of the line. "Things at home must be worse than I thought."

"Do they match?"

"You know, Balogh, marital aids have come a long way since the days when one would have to poke around the kitchen garden in the dark for the right cuke or tuber," Korbács said. "I can send over some catalogs if you like."

"Was the blood on the raincoat Kellner's?"

"Yes," Korbács said. "But you're disheartened, Balogh. And just because you couldn't hook an eel for Mrs. Balogh's kettle last night?"

"What about the fibers found in the coat pocket?"

"They match one from the crime scene," Korbács said. "By the way, we found similar fibers in Kellner's mouth and nose."

Doubts as to the cause of László Kellner's death began, like waves, to test the lines securing Balogh's basic assumptions about the case to the dock of certainty.

"Are you there, Balogh?" Korbács reassured him: "I'm still leaning toward a blow to the head as the cause of death. The front and back lobes are badly bruised and we've found major bleeding in and around the brain. But I still can't say which killed him. Or whether both did. Or, for that matter, whether neither did."

"Neither?"

"It's possible that Kellner suffered a stroke after the first or second blow."

"What about these fibers in his mouth and nose?"

"Seems the old professor might have been alive when they covered him with the flag. I should know everything by late tomorrow afternoon, but to be safe, I'm going to have a brain specialist in Budapest look over my report before I send it to you."

Balogh suppressed a groan.

"In the mean time, I'd keep an eye on that wife of yours."

Balogh was up against it. Yesterday, when the case against the skinheads seemed strong, Krebán had given him until Monday to charge them with murder. As things stood, he wouldn't even know the cause of death by then. His only hope was that the crime lab report, due tomorrow morning, could place one or both of them inside Kellner's flat the night he died.

He left headquarters at once and hastened to the open-air market at Mars, formerly Marx, formerly

Mars Square, where he sought out the only person who could help him. Balogh made his way through stalls redolent of frying meats, hot paprika pods, boiled cabbage, spirits, fish—he'd come back tomorrow morning to purchase a carp for tomorrow's dinner with Pál—pickling brine, Makó onions, garlic sausage, freshly baked bread, and *kávé*, past all this to the little caravan where a round woman with full rosy cheeks and forgiving eyes waited for him behind a sliding window of smudged plastic.

"One with peppers and tomatoes, Marika."

While he waited, Balogh watched country folk milling about in the sun, eating their *lángos* cakes, dripping sour cream and garlic juice onto their dusty shoes. *Lángos* was something eaten away from home at markets and fairs and these poor folk had likely wandered here straight from the bus station nearby, having risen before dawn to flag down one of the Szeged-bound coaches that crossed the Alföld day and night. Perhaps this was their way of easing into new and strange surroundings just as it was Balogh's way of orienting himself toward a case grown new and strange again.

Marika sliced a tomato and arranged it with green pepper rings atop the golden fried round. Balogh passed a two hundred forint note to Marika. With his other hand, he received the still hot cake on a leaf of wax paper. The first bite brought tears to his eyes, and as soon as he wiped them away, he began to see things clearly again. No denying it. The case seemed much weaker now. But what had changed to make it seem so? Balogh took another bite. The cool pepper's crunch blunted the acid tang of the tomato. Balance was all.

In one respect, the case against the skinheads had grown stronger. Hadn't they admitted to breaking into Kellner's building around the time of the murder? In most other respects, the case looked shaky. Given their consistencies, the skinheads' stories of having been hired to paint Arrow Crosses at several address-es seemed at least plausible. Ernő's discovery of Szalonna's flag at the Kéknyelű corroborated an im-portant detail in both accounts, while Szalonna's con-firmation that the flag found draped over the corpse was not the one stolen from Bartók Square deprived the police of a major piece of evidence that would have placed one or both skinheads not merely within Kellner's building, but inside his flat. Still, the skin-heads could have stolen more than one flag that night.

More damaging was Szalonna's revelation that someone had gone at the flag used to cover Kellner with scissors rather than with a knife like the one Zoltán had been carrying at his arrest. And, of course, if someone else had cut the hole out of the flag, it made the skinheads' claim that they'd been set up that much more convincing.

The bloodstained raincoat was a complicating ra-ther than a damaging piece of evidence, but it left Balogh with the task of learning whose coat it was, why it had Kellner's blood on it, how fibers from the flag had gotten into its pocket, and who had made off with the coat only to discard it within easy reach of a sleeping homeless man.

It wouldn't make much of a difference should it turn out that Kellner had still been breathing when his killer drew the flag over him. He died shortly thereafter and whoever brained him could be charged, at the least, with manslaughter. Yet should it turn out that Kellner had been suffocated—well, how might that change things?

If nothing else, the simple account in which skinheads murder a controversial leftist scholar in a way that recalls last year's slaying at Szolnok would have to be modified or abandoned. Bludgeoning someone to death was consistent with the skinhead m.o.. Smothering someone was not. It seemed unlikely that one of the skinheads—Zsolt, say—upon seeing that Kellner wasn't dead would shove the circle of cloth, which he'd cut from the flag's center—with scissors!—into someone's raincoat; wrap the flag around the balled-up garment; and suffocate his victim, before draping the flag over the corpse and fleeing with the blood-stained raincoat in tow.

Soon, Balogh would return to headquarters and begin sifting through all the evidence as if he were examining it for the first time. He knew that, without completed reports from Korbács and the crime lab, all efforts to arrive at a convincing interpretation must fall short. But the point wasn't to choose among plausible versions. The point was to generate as many versions of the murder as possible. The wealth of circumstantial evidence against the skinheads had led Balogh to favor one interpretation over others. The unsettling discoveries of last night and this morning had freed the detective in him to poke his nose into the fabric of things. His eyes found Marika's.

"Another," said Balogh.

CHAPTER FORTY-TWO

Pál and Kati set out for the Serbian frontier from the little market across from the lower town cemetery. The coffee machine was out of order, but the cane-wielding owner informed them that the fountain service was open. She offered them a choice, one familiar from Pál's youth, of "blond" or "brown" cola, a choice no more exotic than that between orange soda and Coke. Kati chose the former: its hue went better with her lipstick and eye shadow, to say nothing of her strawberry blonde hair. She sipped the sherbet-colored beverage through a paper straw as they strolled beneath a late-flowering stand of cherry. A light wind weaved the falling blossoms into her hair.

By midday, they had pedaled the dozen or so kilometers of level road to the border and followed the Körös stream all the way to Lake Ludas's reedy northern shore. By one o'clock, they'd taken a table under the lindens in the garden of the lakeside Mosquito Inn. Baskets full of red poppies hung from the eaves of the thatched roof. A green lizard sunbathed on a weathered fencepost and a fat stag-beetle lighted on Kati's hand. From the shallows, mating crested grebes swam ashore, furiously shaking their heads and offering each other soaking wet bundles of new grass. Only the shriek of a water rail pierced the afternoon calm.

By three, on Hinga hill above Nosza village, Pál furiously shook his head and offered Kati a mouthful of new grass. She laughed and threw her hands around his neck and kissed him through the tender blades.

Searching among periwinkles for her other sock, Kati asked Pál if he wanted to talk about László Kellner.

"You're after me about him too?" Pál said, pulling on Kati's other sock. "Balogh's invited me over for *halászlé* tomorrow evening—'just the boys'—to pump me about Kellner for his investigation."

"I just don't think it's healthy for you not to talk about the death of someone who was important to you once."

"Thank you, Kati," Pál said and laced up a muddy shoe. "If I find myself in desperate need of therapeutic chestnuts from a women's magazine, I'll know who to ask."

Kati threw his other shoe into a thorn bush.

"What?!" Pál said.

An hour later they crossed the border again and loaded their bicycles and themselves onto the Szeged-bound train. Pál drifted off as soon as they pulled out of Röszke station. He might rouse himself once or twice along the way to survey the Alföld unfolding in cereal bands of gold, endless under a cloudless sunset sky, or to glare at a fellow passenger for introducing the heady scent of *szalámi* and garlic-stuffed pickled plums into the close compartment. Otherwise, he'd be out cold until he and Kati reached Szeged. Then, he'd jump up, yank down his bag from the overhead rack, and be off the train even before it came to a stop. Occasionally, he'd remember that he wasn't traveling alone and wait for Kati to join him on the platform before heading for the station exit.

Kati had grown used to being alone while riding trains with Pál. Soon after they started seeing each other, Kati suspected that her companion's rapid descents into oblivion at the outset of any longish rail journey were contrived to avoid chatting. But whenever she would confront him about his locomotive slumbers, he'd protest that he'd always fallen asleep on trains and that the sound of an express in the distance could make him yawn. He'd even been known to nod off at toy-store windows while watching model railroads.

Kati recalled how brave Gabi had been last night at police headquarters, how much she had wanted to help clear Zoli of suspicion to no avail. All day long, Pál had brushed off her questions about the Kellner murder. But she was soon brought up to speed by the headlines of newspapers scattered around their compartment. They ran from the respectful *LÁSZLÓ KELLNER, MTA SCHOLAR AND HERO OF '56, SLAIN* to the revelatory *SZEGED PROF'S MURDER RECALLS SZOLNOK SLAYING* to the tabloid *SKINS TOP SUSPECTS IN OFFING OF RED LACI*. Kati picked up the broadsheet nearest to her, turned to the obituaries, and began to read.

CHAPTER FORTY-THREE

László Kellner, Historian, Nagy Circle Member

Born at Székesfehérvár 9 October 1924;
died at Szeged, 16 June 2000.

Historian László Kellner, who worked to transform Hungary from an authoritarian regime into a multi-party democratic state during the 1956 Revolution, was found dead in his flat yesterday. The cause of death has not yet been determined. A spokesman for the University of Szeged, the institution at which Kellner taught for three decades, said that Kellner is survived by a sister, Mrs. Edit Toth of Székesfehérvár. His wife of 35 years, Zsuzsa, died in 1980.

Kellner is best remembered for composing a defiant statement on behalf of Imre Nagy's government in which he condemned the Kremlin-sponsored overthrow of Hungary's legitimate authority as he urged passive resistance against "the forces of occupation" and "the imminent puppet regime." Asserting that "the Hungarian people with their blood have proved their devotion to the ideas of liberty and social justice," he ended his communiqué with a plea for the free nations of the world to come to Hungary's aid in her struggle for freedom.

During the October Revolution, Kellner served as advisor to Prime Minister Imre Nagy on political affairs. He belonged to a cohort of younger, reform-minded Marxist intellectuals who hoped to create a more humane socialist republic dedicated to improving the lives of ordinary Magyars. It was they who persuaded a reluctant Nagy to embrace democratization. Within days, Nagy formed a multi-party government, ended censorship, declared Hungary's neutrality, and withdrew from the Warsaw Pact.

After the Soviet army crushed Hungary's fledgling democracy on November 4, Kellner was among the last of the reformers to accept the Yugoslav embassy's offer of asylum. Three weeks later, with the others Kellner agreed to leave the embassy after the newly installed government of János Kádár guaranteed their safety. They were apprehended by Soviet troops and flown to Romania, where they were interned while awaiting trial.

Kellner was among the defendants at the secret trials held in Budapest in June 1958. While Nagy and several of his associates were found guilty of treason and put to death, Kellner chose not to protest his innocence and, in turn, received a sentence of life imprisonment, a sentence later reduced to five years. His detractors often cite his decision to plead guilty to lesser crimes against the state, as well as his later reinstatement to an academic post upon his release from prison in 1963, as evidence of special collaboration with the regime. The second point remains a source of as much controversy as Kellner himself. While the scholar's critics insist that he was the only Nagy circle member who, after incarceration, was returned to a university position during the Kádár period, evidence for this claim varies.

"I see you're reading your horoscope again." Pál awoke and shifted in his seat. "Has it changed since this morning?"

"No, but yours will if you don't go back to sleep," Kati said. Pál shut his eyes.

Rehabilitated and granted a professorship at the University of Szeged's Slavic Studies Department, Kellner became department chairman in 1968, serving until 1990, when he retired. He was elected to the Magyar Academy of Sciences in 1970.

Kellner was educated at Eötvös Loránd University where he took degrees in Slavic Languages and Modern History. In 1943, he joined the Hungarian Communist Party and served in the anti-Nazi resistance during the last year of the war. After liberation, Kellner rose quickly in the Party hierarchy, though he later said he'd feared being arrested throughout the Stalinist period.

As a scholar, Kellner published extensively on "the Muscovites," a group of Hungarian Marxists, including Nagy and theorist Georg Lukács, who fled to the Soviet Union after the collapse of the revolutionary government of Béla Kun in 1919. Many of its members returned with the Soviet Army in late 1944 to orchestrate both the Hungarian Communist Party's rise to power and the surrender of Hungarian autonomy to the Kremlin.

In recent years, Kellner divided his time between archival research at the Historical Office of the Ministry of the Interior and writing a memoir. It is unknown whether he had completed the memoir at the time of his death. After the changes of 1989, Kellner emerged as a favorite target of anti-communist polemics and editorials denouncing his socialist past and his compliance with the Kádár government.

Despite such efforts at censure, Kellner is assured a lasting place in the pantheon of Magyars who fought to bring democratic reform to Hungary in the second half of the 20th century.

Kati lay down the paper and wondered how a man such as the Kellner described in the obituary could have lost Pál's loyalty. Pál's devotion to his teachers sometimes verged on blind hero worship, even when the object of that devotion seemed less than deserving of such admiration.

Last fall, Kati had gone with Pál to the seventy-fifth birthday party of a beloved *gimnázium* teacher. On the bus ride to Baja that morning, Pál had spoken of nothing other than his old teacher's charisma and his selfless dedication to all of his young charges. By party's end, the man, who had seemed to Kati more boorish than charming, more self-important than self-denying, had barely acknowledged Pál. Instead, he'd doted upon a handful of former students who had grown wealthy through shady dealings. On the bus ride back to Szeged, Pál had asked Kati if his teacher hadn't lived up to, even exceeded the praises he had heaped upon the old man on the way to Baja. Kati merely smiled.

Whatever Kellner's character flaws might have been, she doubted Pál would have been able to see them, at least in a way that might lead to an irreparable split between mentor and student. And, since she never sensed a hint of shame in Pál's voice on occasions when he'd darkly allude to the episode that caused it, what could Kellner have done or said to foster so permanent an estrangement?

CHAPTER FORTY-FOUR

"What do we know for sure?" Balogh said.

He was sitting with Horváth and Dániel at a table on which lay, in hefty file upon file, in report upon thick report, every piece of information generated by the investigation so far. With neither the crime lab's nor the autopsy results in hand, the three of them were, as the Magyars say, under the frog's ass.

"What do we know," Balogh started to repeat the question before changing his mind, "about Professor László Kellner?"

"That he was a favorite target of the nationalists, who held him up as a living symbol of the old regime," Csilla said. "That he was working on a memoir."

"But even if the nationalists knew that, they hardly could have been threatened by it," Ernő said.

Balogh covered his mouth with a hand, and rocked back and forth. His palm slipped down to cover his chin as he tapped a cheekbone with an index finger. "In that case, who might have been threatened by the memoir?"

"Someone who didn't want details about their past showing up in print," Csilla said.

"But we don't even know what's in the memoir," Ernő said. He scanned the folders and papers on the table. "I don't even see it here. Is it in evidence?"

"According to Professor Borsódy, Éva Hegedűs, Kellner's typist, came by for it on the night of the

slaying. Presumably, she still has it. When I interviewed her, I was so preoccupied with charging the
skinheads with Kellner's murder that it didn't occur to
me to ask her for the manuscript."

Both Csilla and Ernő lowered their gazes.

"Don't be embarrassed for me," Balogh said.

When they looked up again, he was smiling.

"And don't look so surprised." Balogh repeated
the wise words of Colonel Hegyes, his mentor at the
Police Academy: "Remember: the competent investigator must never be ashamed of owning up to mistakes or oversights, especially in cases where their
negative effects can be remedied. Should these same
errors prove irremediable, the competent investigator
must by all means remain silent."

Balogh was pleased to see the young officers
smiling with him now. Somewhere, he hoped, old
Hegyes was smiling too. That mountain of a man,
who'd been a Police Colonel in Miskolc before he was
called to teach at the National Police Academy, had
retired six years ago to a little house in sleepy Sa-
jószentpéter.

A year later, while attending a regional police
conference, Balogh had learned from a classmate that
Hegyes slumped over in his chair while doing the
crossword, dead of heart failure at sixty-three. He
wondered if Pál, upon learning of László Kellner's
death, felt the smallest part of what he'd felt when he
heard the news about Hegyes.

"We'll need to go through that manuscript before
we can determine who might have been threatened by
its publication." Balogh made a mental note to call
Éva Hegedűs later. "Now, merely on the basis of
what we've said so far, what motives for murder rec-

ommend themselves?"

"Hatred and a desire for revenge on one side," Csilla said.

"The fear of exposure and a desire to stop the publication of an incriminating document on the other," Ernő said.

"So it's possible that Kellner had aroused violent feelings at both ends of the political spectrum?" Balogh said. "Now, we don't have a cause of death yet, but it's safe to say that someone acted in a way that caused his death."

"Can we say that this person acted in a way *to* cause his death?" Ernő said.

"You tell me," Balogh said.

"We'd need to establish premeditation, or at least intent, to call Kellner's death a murder," Ernő said.

"And until Ernő discovered the flag taken from Bartók Square at the Kéknyelű, we thought we had the evidence to prove it," Csilla said. "Now it's not so clear."

"I'll tell you one thing," Ernő spoke up. "You don't whack someone on the back of the head with an earthenware jug by accident. Someone tried to kill László Kellner."

"And," Balogh wanted to be careful about what he said next, "thereby initiated the series of events by which the professor died. He may not have died from the first blow, but from the blow he sustained when he fell as a result of the first, or even from a stroke. That's as much as we can say without the ME's report. What else do we know about the slaying?"

"We know where it happened." Csilla said. "Even without the autopsy report, we know approximately when it happened."

"On this point we have the testimony of both Borsódy, who left him after nine o'clock on the evening of the fifteenth, and Petri, who called on him a little before ten o'clock the next morning." Balogh consulted his notes. "The telephone records confirm this. So what's our time frame?"

"If we set aside the arrest of the skinheads at midnight for the moment," Ernő said, "we can place the murder between ten o'clock and early morning the next day."

"The autopsy report will show that Kellner died sometime between ten in the evening and one in the morning," Balogh said. "Korbács tells me there's evidence that he didn't die right away, but even then we're looking at a time frame of three hours. And I don't think the autopsy report's going to narrow things down much more."

"Anything after eleven would put the skinheads out of the running," Csilla said.

"I tend to agree with you," Balogh said. "Now, what about witnesses?"

Ernő said: "We know Eperjesi, owner of the Kéknyelű, showed the skinheads out of his place a little before nine. And that Rózsás talked to one of them in the entrance of Kellner's building around ten."

"We know who was in the flat earlier that evening," Csilla said. "Borsódy visited for several hours, leaving sometime after nine. The telephone record tells us that he was home by 9:50 because Petri rang him about that time and he answered. Of course, he could have gone out again."

"We know that Éva Hegedűs dropped by around nine to pick up the manuscript and left shortly thereafter. Is there anything to prove that she went straight home afterward?" Balogh said.

"Ernő and I thought you might want the call records," Csilla said, brushing her bare arm against Ernő's as she passed a little chart across the table to Balogh. "So we prepared this timetable. We've some gaps, but it's a start."

"And a good one." Balogh did his best to ignore the domino effect Ernő's recoiling elbow had set off among the half-filled cups and empty cola cans that had been accumulating on the other side of the table.

Call	Time	Caller	Called	Line out	Line in	From	To
1	8:28	Hegedűs	Police	cell 1	landline	Jósika	HQ
2	8:31	Petri	?	landline	cell 2	Egyetem	?
3	8:47	?	Petri	cell 3	landline		Egyetem
4	9:13	Petri	Police	landline	landline	Mátyás	HQ
5	9:51	Petri	Borsódy	landline	landline	Mátyás	Batthyány
6	9:53	Petri	Kellner	landline	landline	Mátyás	Hajnóczy
7	10:38	Hegedűs	Petri	cell 1	landline	?	Mátyás
8	10:43	Hegedűs	Porter	cell 1	landline	?	Egyetem
9	10:47	Horváth	Petri	landline	landline	HQ	Mátyás

"Petri was on the phone quite a bit last Thursday," Balogh said. "So was Éva Hegedűs. Why do we know the names of some cell phone users and not others?"

"We don't have the mobile phone records yet, sir," Ernő said, having regained control of his flailing elbow. "We only know Éva Hegedűs's cell number because she called in the assault on Mr. Neumann. We don't know who owns cells one or three yet."

"Let's try to translate what we do have into a narrative," Balogh said. "Csilla, why don't you start us off."

"Éva Hegedűs is walking along Jósika Street on her way to Kellner's flat when she witnesses the assault on Oszkár Neumann. She calls the police and waits with Neumann for officers to arrive before continuing to the Hajnóczy Street flat.

"Around the same time, Petri places a call to an unknown party from his office in the Ady Square building. Fifteen minutes later, the skinheads arrive at the Kéknyelű. They exchange a stolen flag for an envelope containing a hundred thousand forints and one of them uses his mobile phone to call the local number written on the outside of the envelope."

Insight flashed in Ernő's eyes. "Didn't Petri get a call at his office about then?"

"You're right," Balogh said. "How long did that call last, Csilla?"

Csilla looks at her notes: "Just eleven seconds, sir. Wouldn't it be a remarkable coincidence if the skinhead punched in the number for Petri's office by mistake?"

"Beyond remarkable," Balogh said. "Take over, Ernő."

"Petri arrives home from his office a little after nine to discover an Arrow Cross on his front door. He calls the police and Csilla and I get there inside ten minutes."

"Excuse me, Ernő," Csilla interrupts, "but if we're doing this strictly chronologically, Éva Hegedűs has already arrived at Kellner's to find him with Borsódy. She doesn't stay long: she takes the manuscript and leaves. Borsódy leaves no later than half-past nine."

"How do we know that, Csilla?" Balogh said.

"He has a twenty-minute walk ahead of him, if, as he says, he went on foot, and he's home to take Petri's call by 9:51. We couldn't have left the Petri residence more than five minutes before that. At 9:53, Petri calls Kellner."

"And we're absolutely sure that it was Kellner who answered the telephone?" Balogh asked.

"We only have Petri's word for it," Ernő said.

Balogh bit his lower lip. Csilla and Ernő waited for him to speak: "It wouldn't be in Petri's interest to say Kellner answered the phone if he hadn't, especially since he has an alibi for the whole time you're with him. On the other hand, it's convenient that Kellner gave him an alibi for the rest of the night by insisting he not come round. Let's take him at his word for now: Kellner was still alive as ten o'clock approaches."

"Things get sketchy now," Csilla said. "Sometime after ten o'clock, Rózsás comes home from his local and has words with one of our suspects, probably Zoltán in the vestibule. Though Rózsás was heavily intoxicated at the time, I'd guess his version of the events is accurate given that the Audi the skinheads stole was parked one street away and that its owner has confirmed he'd just returned from the filling station at a quarter past ten."

"What do either of you make of these two calls by Éva Hegedűs after 10:30?"

"She might have just called Petri to say she wouldn't be at work the next day," Ernő said. "Maybe Petri told her to call to the porter."

"Be sure to ask the porter on duty that night what she said. You can ask him if he's missing a flag while you're at it," Balogh said, recalling his earlier conversation with Szalonna. "Now, Csilla, I see you called Petri at 10:47."

"Just to tell him that the photographer would be around in the morning. I got the answering machine."

"Find out if Petri was asleep," Balogh said. "If he went out for some air."

"We'll drop by and ask him first thing Monday," Csilla said, looking at Ernő. He didn't return her gaze. "I can use the pretext of thanking him for drawing our attention to the news photo. After all, he used it as a pretext for calling me up to flirt some more."

"You think that's the main reason he called?" Balogh chuckled and took the grainy picture from Csilla. The caption contained the names of the three professors and their common affiliation with the University's Slavic Studies Department.

"He's a flirt, but he also might have been trying to help us, suggesting the means by which the skinheads linked him to Kellner," Csilla said.

"But not to Borsódy." Balogh frowned. "What was the address where the second Arrow Cross was discovered?"

Ernő checked. "Thirty-two Batthyány Street. Borsódy lives a few doors up."

"What's his street number?" Balogh said.

"Twenty-three."

"Csilla, there's a Szeged directory on the shelf behind you. Look up the listing for Borsódy."

Csilla opened the phone book near the middle and rifled through several pages until she found the listing: "Thirty-two Batthyány."

"Borsódy was supposed to get the second Arrow Cross. He was spared by a misprint," Ernő said. "Someone sent the skinheads the photo in the paper. They got hold of a phone book when they got to town."

"So," Balogh said, "there was a plan."

"A plan that doesn't contradict the skinheads' accounts of having been hired for a particular job," Ernő said.

"And Petri has gone some way toward lifting any clouds of suspicion that may have been hovering over him."

"Why do you say that Csilla?" Balogh said.

"Why would he give us help corroborating the skinheads' story unless he believed himself beyond suspicion?"

"There's another way to look at it, sir," Ernő said. "Maybe he doesn't believe himself beyond suspicion so much as he believes that, if he supplied us with an important clue, we'd come to the conclusion at which Csilla just arrived."

"And since three's the Magyar way," Balogh said, "here's one more interpretation: he wants us to believe that he believes he's beyond suspicion."

Sunday, 18 June

CHAPTER FORTY-FIVE

"How was I to know you were afraid of live fish, Pál?" Balogh said as he hosed down the board on which he'd scaled and gutted and cut into pieces two kilos of wild Tisza carp. Alaszka, the cat, brushed against his calves, meowing impatiently. "I mean really. I just asked if you wanted to watch me clean the thing."

Pál had stopped hyperventilating—Balogh could no longer hear his high-pitched panting behind the door of the garden shed—but he still refused to join Balogh in the yard.

"I'm all finished Pál." Balogh wiped his hands on the grass. "*Istenem.* Come out of there and help me with the soup."

Pál emerged from his shelter, looking as clammy and white as the belly of the finny creature Balogh had just eviscerated. Over a lifetime, he'd accumulated a repertoire of fears, not one of which could be traced to a trauma suffered in infancy. Besides live carp—he cherished its boiled, baked, and fried cousins—he was terrified of heights, chalk, cats *sans* tails, ping pong balls, canned stewed tomatoes, months whose names ended in "P," Yorkshire pudding, men called Ferkó, short-sleeve shirts, paper plates, parasols, and the by-all-other-accounts benign woman who sold bus and tram vouchers at the corner of Somogyi and Tisza Lajos.

"You'll ruin it if I don't watch you." The phobic Pál eyed his former brother-in-law with suspicion and gingerly made his way to the large kettle suspended over an open fire from a tripod by a rusty chain.

The steaming carp had already begun to whiten on the onions as Balogh, wielding his wide-bladed *bicska*, sliced tomatoes and green peppers into the kettle.

Pál looked into the pot and said: "I see I'm too late." He sat down on a rock and lit a cigarette. "Where's the *paprika*? How do you intend to make *halászlé* without *paprika*?"

Balogh held up a small cloth bag tied with a red, white and green ribbon. The sweet hot aroma hit Pál even before he untied the tri-color band. He pressed the little sack to his nose. The heat generated while grinding the dried red pods had coaxed the oils from their skins and seeds, imparting to the crushed spice an earthy fragrance that haunted every Magyar's dreams of home.

"Did you grind this yourself?" Pál said.

"Of course." Balogh said. He poured a large jug of water into the kettle.

"Mortar and pestle?"

"The one you gave us as a wedding present."

"Seeds and pods together?"

"Isn't that the way you taught me?"

"Let's face it. You were never a very good student, Balogh."

"Then let me ask the questions."

"Just don't ask me about Kellner."

"Why don't you want to talk about him?"

"Why don't you and Kati mind your business?"

The water had begun to boil and Balogh gently rocked the kettle from side to side. The milky stock has turned bright red.

"We've a little while before we eat," Balogh said.

"I'm going for a nap in the arbor." Pál rose from his perch. "Wake me when it's time to eat."

"Pál, I need your help. The Kellner case is coming apart."

"I thought you nabbed the suspects the same evening he died."

"So did I."

"I'm going for a nap in the arbor."

Pál turned away and began walking to the shadiest corner of the yard. There, beneath leafy vines and waxy clusters of new grapes Balogh's hammock awaited.

"Pál." Balogh said, his voice on the edge of pleading.

Pál turned and stared back at him through the kettle steam. He shook his head.

"All right," he said. "After dinner."

Pál drained off the last of the fishy broth, sopping the residue with a hunk of white bread. He popped the red-white sponge into his mouth and closed his eyes. At his feet, Alaszka, her coat less polar white than charcoal gray with dust and ash, rolled atop the carp bones she'd just licked clean.

"The summer of '89 was different," Pál resumed. "By then, we'd sensed that the dictatorship had begun to wither away. Remember how Kádár died on the day the courts rehabilitated Nagy. Even so, the changes here seemed less dramatic than what was happening in Poland or Czechoslovakia.

"The spring of '68 in Prague was more like '56 in Budapest when everyone—even Party members—started to question and reject freely all that Moscow said was true."

"Why where you in Prague?" Balogh said, uncorking another bottle of *bikavér* and refilling Pál's glass.

"Kellner arranged a three-month study visa for me. I was still in his good graces."

"What did you study there?"

Pál laughed.

"I didn't see the inside of a lecture hall more than once my entire stay. When I arrived in March, I knew nothing of Dubček's 'socialism with a human face,' but signs of the thaw were everywhere: Forman's *Loves of a Blonde*, Kundera's *The Joke*, The Rolling Stones' "Satisfaction," and an endless parade of long-legged Czech girls in miniskirts. I was nineteen."

"*We* weren't lacking for miniskirts, as I recall," Balogh said, "though I was just a child."

"No, the Magyar girls had long legs too. It's just that here we rarely discovered the remarkable goings on beneath those little skirts."

"I understand."

"Soon after arriving I made friends, for life, I thought, with Jan Hodek. Then, I fell in love with his sister Zdena." Pál paused. "This was long before I ever laid eyes on your sister."

"Of course," Balogh said, touched by Pál's delicacy.

"Jan and Zdena, along with every other young Czech that spring, talked, sang, chanted, dreamed—I'm sure—of nothing but freedom. Once, after a long night of drinking beer, the three of us danced together by the banks of the Vltava. By sunrise, our little troupe had grown to several dozen strong. Every young passerby, it seemed, had joined our ranks. And everyone was singing."

"And not a policeman in sight," Balogh said. "What did you sing?"

"Songs by the Beatles. 'Hello, Goodbye' was the only one to which we knew all the words in English." Pál's eyes welled up.

"Were you still there in August?"

"My visa ended in June. In July, Jan and Zdena visited me at my aunt's house near Balaton."

"Too bad they couldn't have stayed."

"In early August, Zdena wrote to say she'd applied for a visa to study here. The Russian tanks rumbled into the Old Town Square two weeks later. No mail service. No telephone. They closed the border. I couldn't reach her."

"Was that the last you heard from her?"

"A notecard arrived in October. The little folded kind you send with wedding gifts. Pink roses against a white background. The address on the envelope read: Pál Berkesi, Szeged University, Hungary. No stamp. It hadn't come by post."

"How then?"

"By hand. Many hands."

Balogh wanted to ask how the Czech girl's note could have found its way across a sealed border through barbed wire and mine fields all the way to her boyfriend in Szeged. He only said: "What did it say?"

"She was with relatives in Moravia. She had no news of Jan."

"And that was how you learned that Jan was missing?"

"Jan wasn't missing. He was dead. On the night before the invasion, a friend visiting Jan from Budapest went home with a young woman who'd invited him to see the lights of Prague from the window of her Vinohrady flat. The next morning, he awoke to see that tanks had clogged all the boulevards. When he reached Jan and Zdena's building in Malá Strana, a neighbor said that Jan had been shot at a demonstration in Václavské Square and that Zdena had disappeared. He wrote me with the news when he returned to Hungary. Zdena's card came a month later."

"And that's about the time you fell out with Kellner."

"I was still mourning for Jan and trying to accept that I would never see Zdena again when I ran into him at the entrance to the Ady Square building. He was annoyed I hadn't come to see him since my return to Szeged. He insisted I meet with him that afternoon."

"Didn't he know what happened?"

"I'd written him for permission to take a leave of absence. I'd explained as much as I could in the letter," Pál watched the dying fire. "He never wrote back, so I stayed in Szeged, attending his lectures and seminars."

"And he never said anything to you about Prague?"

"That wasn't his way. He was aloof with students. But he could be generous. I'd never have gotten to Prague without his help and he secured Tamás a fellowship at the University of Leningrad the previous autumn."

"Why was he intent upon seeing you that day?"

"Before I left for Prague, he'd invited me to join the Party adding that it would make things easier for me. I'm not sure why he wanted an answer *that* day? I guess I'd kept him waiting long enough" Pál's speech grew thick, his tone mixed petulance and guilt. "I hadn't meant to. I'd thought about his invitation the whole time in Prague, despite all the changes taking place there. I'd thought about it the whole summer."

"Even after the Russians invaded in August?"

"Even then," Pál said. He remembered he was ten years Balogh's senior and added: "You need to understand the mindset. We'd witnessed Moscow's brutal responses to reform efforts in '56 and yet we'd failed to connect the bloodshed here with the Party. Nagy was a communist after all. So when Brezhnev ordered the Warsaw Pact into Czechoslovakia in '68, we regarded it as just another crude show of force by a ham-fisted Soviet leadership."

"So what stopped you from joining the Party?"

"Something my father said to me when I came back from Prague: 'You really want to think about this, Pál. Becoming a member of the Party isn't like getting married. It's much easier to get out of a marriage.'"

"Wasn't he a Party member?"

"That's why his advice puzzled me. He didn't leave the Party until he left the Health Service in 1977. On the day, he walked straight to the worker's hall and turned in his card. A brave thing to do in those days."

"But your father's remark must not have settled the issue. You were still at odds after you received Zdena's note. So what made you tell Kellner no?"

"I went to his office certain that I wouldn't. To me, László Kellner *was* the Party. To reject the Party was to reject him."

"But you did."

"Not...not really." The thickness in Pál's voice gave way to a stammer. He struggled to speak clearly, to compensate for the tiny, invisible lead weights depressing his tongue. "I just...I just stood there stalling, trying to get over my squeamishness, reproaching myself, asking why shouldn't I feather my nest and accept Kellner's invitation. He grew weary of my shilly-shallying and dismissed me."

"Just like that?" Balogh turned the last glowing coals over in the ash with a spade. "He said nothing else?"

"He said: 'I never would've guessed that you would have such difficulty choosing between the Party and a Czech whore, but it seems filth's more your element than ideals. Now you can go live among pigs.'"

Monday, 19 June

CHAPTER FORTY-SIX

Balogh knocked and entered Krebán's office swiftly, depriving the Colonel of the element of surprise he treasured when launching his makeshift projectiles doorwards.

"Please tell me you've charged the skinheads in the Kellner case," the Colonel said, returning a leather pencil holder full of soft felt tips and stubby highlighters to its place on his desk, which, for barrenness, increasingly had begun to resemble the Alföld. Surely, Terézia would soon find a way to blunt the edges of a sheet of paper.

"There've been some interesting developments, sir." Balogh braced himself, expecting to be scolded like a pig bought for a pengő.

"You've bad news, haven't you? Why not just give it to me: 'Say, old fuck, I've some tidings for you that'll make passing a kidney stone seem like a birthday present.'"

Balogh was about to speak when Krebán preempted him with this warning: "Just remember, Balogh. Anything short of charging these skinned pricks with murder will be as an ill wind to me. Budapest's already called twice today. They don't usually call a third time, preferring instead to send a '52 Pobeda to take the uncooperative parties for a ride in the country."

"Sir, I…."

"O yes, Balogh! They've hidden away a fleet of those black beauties in perfect running order, part of an effort to remind provincial dogberries like us that the bad old days could come roaring back at any time. But don't take my word for it."

For all his waxing nostalgic, Krebán's confidence was waning. His voice barely rose above a half-roar while his color hovered between bubblegum and not-so-hot pink. Balogh wondered if his sneak-arrival had robbed the Colonel of the seconds required to hoist the mainsail of his self-possession. Be that sail set or shortened, Balogh chose his words with care.

"We may want to widen the scope of the investigation, sir."

Krebán tugged on a halyard: "Which is a pleasant way of saying what?"

"That the cold body of evidence against the skinheads, while compelling, awaits a toe-tag bearing the designation 'irrefutable,'" Balogh said, continuing to weigh words.

"Which is an unpleasant way of saying what?"

Though he heard the rustle of sailcloth taking wind, he could equivocate no longer: "Our case could be stronger, sir."

"*Baszd meg*!" Krebán slammed his palms down on the desk.

Well, if the prick was out, as the Colonel had just proclaimed in hoariest Hungarian, then it was out. Balogh spoke freely. "I'd like to add a few names to the suspect list."

"*Az Isten faszát!*" Krebán bellowed.

Then again, if it was the Lord's prick that was out, as the empurpled Colonel now indicated, Balogh could only bow before the power and the glory of the divine member and be silent.

Krebán lunged for the pencil holder, but merely succeeded in knocking this quiver and all of its blunted arrows to the floor. Frantic, he scanned the desk for alternatives. Terézia had done a thorough sweep this morning and few choices remained: a featherlight box of rubber bands, a macaroni-and-glue sculpture, lovingly if hastily assembled by his granddaughter (he'd never been sure whether Panni had meant the grotesquely curled figure to stand for a policeman or an alien pasta-based life form), and a cellophane bag of stale sunflower seeds.

Clean out of weapons of least destruction, Krebán grunted. All color drained from his face. He whimpered: "Balogh, you've thrown us to the wolves!"

"While shepherds weep, wolves work." Oddly enough, it was Balogh on whom assurance now sat like a cocked fedora on a Józsefváros pimp. "All I'm saying is that the murder case against the skinheads looks weaker than it did twenty-four hours ago. They're still our prime suspects. You may want to remind the press of this. You can also remind them that in the course of any ongoing investigation, we follow all sorts of leads, even a few that might seem to argue against the guilt of the suspects. They needn't find anything unusual in this."

Krebán, consoled: "And we've already charged them with two counts of assault and a long list of hate crimes. That should keep Budapest at bay for a little while longer."

Balogh told Krebán about the flags (the Colonel raised an eyebrow), the blood-stained raincoat (the Colonel raised the other eyebrow, pursed his lips, and nodded gravely), the curious cell-phone calls on the night of the murder (Balogh: "Csilla is still waiting to hear back from Westel about the anonymous recipient and caller of the second and third calls on this chart."), Korbács's thoughts on the cause of death (Krebán: "There's something very strange about that man."), Korbács's delayed release of the autopsy findings (Krebán: "Please remind my to rip his balls off the next time I see him."), the intended address for second of three Arrow Crosses painted that night (Krebán: "So that part at least *was* planned."), the skinheads' tales of having been hired to make mischief only to end up implicating themselves in Kellner's murder (Krebán: "Fuck them with a whore's prick!").

The Colonel then sat quietly as Balogh concluded the briefing with results from the crime lab.

"None of the fingerprints found in Kellner's flat belong to the skinheads. No boot prints on the carpet inside the flat either. But the crime techs did find Zsolt's fingerprints on the hallway walls and on the doorjamb and boot prints matching Zsolt's Doc Martens on the runner leading to Kellner's flat."

"You're saying he was never *inside*?"

"*I'm* not. Though Kurtág will use the absence of his prints there to support Zsolt's claim that he wasn't."

Krebán leaned back in his chair. "Whose prints *were* found in the flat?"

"Excluding Kellner, we end up with a short list: Borsódy, Hegedűs, Petri, Rózsás, and the woman who cleans most Wednesdays."

"Did she clean last week?"

"She dusted and wiped everything down with lemon oil on Wednesday afternoon, and since we're reasonably sure that Kellner received no more visitors until Thursday evening when Borsódy and Hegedűs came by, we're reasonably sure that none of the fingerprints were more than a day old when the body was discovered."

"Have you been able to eliminate anyone from your list of possible suspects at this point?"

"The cleaning woman and her husband threw a little party for some other couples at their place Thursday night starting around eight. It lasted until at least 2:17 because that's when one of their neighbors called us to complain about the noise."

"2:17. That's out of the probable range for Kellner's murder."

"We can probably rule out Rózsás as well. His alibi only lasts until ten when he staggered home from his local, but by then he would have been too drunk to make it upstairs."

"So if Petri wasn't among Kellner's visitors on Thursday night, that leaves only Borsódy and Hegedűs," Krebán said, much calmer now. "How sure are you that Petri wasn't there that evening?"

"Not at all. His story doesn't square with the one the fingerprints tell. Everyone I've mentioned left their prints on the inside of the front door, but I can only imagine two ways that Petri's prints could have gotten there."

"And one's that Petri closed the door when he and Rózsás entered the flat," Krebán said.

"But Rózsás insists the door stayed open once he opened it. That doesn't mean Petri couldn't have touched the door when he entered the flat Friday morning, of course."

"And the other way?"

"That Petri *had been* to the flat the previous night. We can only place him at home from nine until around 10:30 when he received a call from Éva Hegedűs. When Officer Horváth rang him fifteen minutes later, he didn't pick up. He doesn't have an alibi for the rest of the evening."

"Neither do Borsódy or Hegedűs. What else can you tell me about those two?"

"They were both in Kellner's flat at least once that night."

"Why do you say 'at least once,' Balogh? Start with Borsódy."

"He called this morning to ask if he could retrieve his raincoat from Kellner's flat. Thing is, we hadn't found any coat matching his description in the flat."

"What did you tell him?"

"That everything was being held as possible evidence and that it might take us a few days to return the coat to him."

"But on Saturday morning, a bloodstained raincoat turned up in Dugonics Square, right on Borsódy's way home from Kellner's flat."

"Either he doesn't know the coat went missing from the flat or he's just pretending not to know because he went back for it. I don't want to bring him in for an ID right away, because if he's telling the truth, he'll think that someone's trying to frame him. He's shaken up by Kellner's murder as it is. There's also a chance that he's in touch with the murderer, though he probably doesn't know it. I'd like to keep the killer in the dark as long as I can."

"What about Hegedűs?"

"I don't know what to make of her. She was co-operative enough during the interview, even if she was confused about certain details."

"Is that so unusual?"

"Only when you contrast her statement about her visit to the flat Thursday night with the one she provided the officers who answered her call when she happened upon the skinheads attacking Mr. Neumann. She had all of thirty seconds in bad light to get a good look at the two of them, and she remembered everything about them. She knew which skin passed off the flag to the other before they disappeared around the corner. Compare this to her statement concerning the Kellner case: the second is almost devoid of details."

"For instance."

"Borsódy said she'd dropped by the flat around nine on Thursday to pick up a manuscript for typing and left shortly thereafter. She didn't challenge this. Yet when I asked her if she took the manuscript with her, she waffled before saying that she must have."

"What's your point, Balogh?"

"That people tend to be good at remembering details or not. Éva Hegedűs possesses remarkable powers of observation and memory. So what happens to these powers once she arrives at Kellner's flat?"

"Nothing, Balogh. You confused the poor woman with your idiotic questions." Krebán ruffled.

"What sort of bonehead asks a woman if she left with the manuscript she came for?"

"The sort of bonehead who wants to know if anything happened during her visit to make her forget why she came."

"You *have* asked her to turn in the manuscript as possible evidence?"

"Yes, sir. I'm sending someone to pick it up this morning."

"Say more about this signal instance of catastrophic memory loss."

"That's just it, sir. I don't think she lost her memory. But if she visited the flat twice that night, isn't it conceivable, given the sheer number of details which her very good memory would have retained during two such visits, that she'd be afraid of confusing them? Doesn't it make sense that she'd pretend to be absentminded rather than take the chance of getting some details wrong because she can't block others out?"

"Is there any evidence that she returned to the flat later?"

"We haven't found any, sir. But that's not surprising. It would be difficult to separate evidence from two visits so close together."

The Colonel nodded. "Fair enough, but where is this going, Balogh?"

"Ostensibly she went there to pick up the manuscript, and we've no reason to doubt that. I'm just wondering if there wasn't another reason for her visit."

"Such as?" Krebán said.

"Borsódy told me he hadn't expected to see Éva Hegedűs that evening though Kellner did. So perhaps she hadn't expected to find Borsódy in the flat when she arrived. Perhaps she wanted to talk to Kellner privately. I'm wondering if she returned later that night to have the conversation she may not have been able to have earlier."

"And you regard this as a possible motive, Balogh? Unfinished business?"

"We'd need to establish that something was bothering her, to know *what* was bothering her, before we even begin talking about motives. But both Borsódy and Hegedűs admitted to having some conflicts with Kellner lately."

"Over what?"

"Neither offered specifics and I didn't see the point in asking for them. The case against the skinheads seemed so strong."

"Any motives for Petri?"

"None that I can see. The background checks turned up nothing unusual." Balogh referred to his notes. "Married for twenty-odd years to the same woman, Anna (née Klapka), who runs a clinic here in Szeged. Two daughters: ages eight and eleven. Did both his undergraduate and graduate work here under Kellner, taking his doctorate in Slavic Studies in '74. Joined Party in '68. Resigned in late '89. Professor and Chair of Slavic Studies since '90. He's up for a post at one of the ministries. Education, I think."

"What was his relationship with Kellner like?"

"Kellner mentored Petri to the top of their profession. He selected Petri to succeed him as Chairman of the academic program that Kellner built."

"You've neglected fear and resentment as possible motives, Balogh. One who owes his success to another never forgets that the one who made him can unmake him."

"It's possible, but Petri strikes me as the sort who wouldn't have any problem believing that he alone was responsible for his success."

"What else do we know about him."

"A relation of mine who knows him since they attended university together tells me that Petri, while likeable enough, was something of an ass-licker as a student and that he's been plagued most of his adult life by the chronic vascular condition our American friends call 'zipper trouble.' But, as a gloomy Dane once said, 'Accuse every man that's chased a skirt, who should 'scape whipping?'"

CHAPTER FORTY-SEVEN

They'd always gotten on well as partners. So well, in fact, that others on and off the force just assumed that Csilla and Ernő were grabbing more than a bite at lunchtime.

Over drinks with friends at The Laughing Policeman, they'd separately endured repeated and not always so oblique gibes ranging from the glib and open-minded *Of course, the traditional notion of mounted police involves horses, saddles, bridles, and such, but you mustn't let that deter you* to the deeply silly and euphemistic *Don't make mudpies in your own summer kitchen* to the scriptural and vituperative *Woe to the flock whose shepherds lie down in filth!* And separately they'd insist that they were happily involved with other people: Csilla, after all, had her Dezső, Ernő his Zsazsa. "No," they'd object, "we're good friends," refusing to add the qualifying "just" or "that's all" and risk cheapening something they both valued.

Their comportment toward each other had always been open, easy, and free of the envy that often evolved between less equally matched partners. So it troubled her that he seemed even more tight-lipped and tense this morning than on Saturday when, during the briefing with Major Balogh, she'd first sensed an unfamiliar coolness in her partner's manner.

She'd told herself that she was making things up, that she merely felt self-conscious having returned to headquarters, for the second time in as many days, after a daytime frolic with Dezső. What came across as Ernő's emotional distance was nothing more than a projection of her own schoolgirlish embarrassment at the thought of being found out. She'd wrapped her ruffled equanimity in this wisdom as a woman preparing for the movers swaddles a mirror in an old quilt. Calm descended on her mind's meadow as she turned her attention back to the investigation.

Moments later, her composure decomposed again when she accidentally brushed Ernő's forearm with hers and he started like a spring hare frightened by a breeze. She'd smiled at him, but he'd only looked away as if to hide disdain. After the meeting, when she'd asked him about his plans for the evening, he'd mumbled some words she couldn't make out and darted from the room.

Now she pulled up in front of the hardware store nearest the Petri residence and let the Astra idle. Ernő folded his newspaper and unbuckled his seatbelt.

"Petri's house in twenty minutes?" He pushed the passenger door open.

"Ernő, wait. I've been meaning to ask you something."

He dropped his chin and gazed straight ahead.

"Why did you run off after the meeting on Saturday?"

"I was trying to make it to the washroom before my bladder gave out."

"But you're all right?"

"Too many Cokes, that's all." A frozen smile cracked his lips.

"I meant is everything all right otherwise? With you? With us?"

"No problems," he said, trying to mean it, and fled the car.

The store owner must not have heard Ernő come in for all the paint-mixing machine's racket. Having placed both hands atop the lid of a vibrating canister, the stocky man, who combed his hair back like Stalin and sported his hog-bristle mustache, hunched over the violently shaking contraption. After a moment, he looked up to see the young police office waiting for him by the seed display. He lifted a shaking index finger and shouted a phrase, which, for all the owner's sympathetic vibrations, had come out sounding like *éjjeli pillangó* or "streetwalker" rather than the *egy pillanat* or "one moment" Ernő was intended to hear. Ernő waved back at the quivering man to indicate he wasn't in a rush.

He was grateful for a few minutes to compose himself after the scene with Csilla in the car. For the second time in forty-eight hours, he'd obeyed the impulse to flee from her. At least this time he'd been able to utter an intelligible string of words before running away.

What must Csilla be thinking? That her partner and friend of two years could no longer stand to be in the same room or car with her? And how had she taken it when he'd reacted to her innocent touch the other day by withdrawing his arm with such force that he'd sent every cup and bottle within elbow's reach flying?

He couldn't tell her how he'd felt when he saw her sitting alone in the conference room before Saturday's meeting. How he'd stopped and looked through the little window in the door before entering so he'd seen her, her face bathed in late afternoon sun. How he hadn't been able to bring himself to go inside because he hadn't been able to take his eyes off her as she sat there letting the dying light wash over her. She'd worn an expression that he could only call angelic, a complexion equally so, because her face and eyes at that moment seemed illuminated from within, the outer light serving only to show off her inner light more brilliantly.

What was he saying?! He couldn't tell her how he'd fallen deeply in love with a vision of her. He couldn't tell Zsazsa that. But he couldn't continue avoiding Csilla's gaze either, recoiling from her touch, running from her whenever she asked him any question requiring a coherent answer.

And he had to stop making up these little poems. They weren't poems. They were merely random words gathering themselves in his head. All right. They weren't random words. They were *all* about Csilla. It's just that they seemed to come from nowhere. Already, he regarded them with as much affectation as he bore hives and sinus trouble and plantar warts.

Even worse, he could never tell when the fit was upon him until it was too late. Like now. *When I see her I don't know what, having so much, to say. In her I see all that is beyond praising.* Enough! *May she know this, since she will never hear it from me, unless my heart should learn to speak.* Fuck! No more! *Not even the Tisza, from the icy waters that roll and swell her at the thaw, has such torrents as these that rise and rush with love within my heart when I see her.*

Ernő might have continued in this manner for some time had the owner not interrupted his reverie: "…help you, *Biztos úr?*"

"Yes. My name is Officer Ernő Dániel and I'd like to ask you a question about a sale. Do you recall ringing up any paint solvent last week?"

Ernő followed the owner to the counter where the latter opened a loose-leaf notebook filled with sales records and inventories. "Here it is. Last Wednesday. One can solvent, two cans of spray paint. Poor guy doesn't trust himself, does he?"

"You're sure he bought the spray paint with the solvent?"

"That's what it says here. Last Wednesday. I think I remember him. In here first thing that morning wearing a suit. On his way to work. Said he needed to paint some children's furniture. Bright red."

Petri came to the gate wearing a gray polo, jeans, and sandals.

"You just missed Anna and the girls, Officer Horváth. We all got back from Balaton late last night."

"I'm sorry for not calling first, but I was in the neighborhood and I wanted to thank you for the tip about the newspaper photo."

"Not at all. And you should feel free to drop by whenever I'm here." He smiled.

Whenever you're here alone? It had taken him all of a minute to make his first play. *Jaj!* The man worked fast.

"Perhaps you'd like to come inside, Officer Horváth?"

"We can talk out here. Officer Dániel will be by any minute," Csilla said to let him know reinforcements were on the way. "I meant to ask you when you called me on Friday if you'd gotten my message from the night before."

"Didn't I mention it? I listened to it when I woke up the next morning."

"You must have gone to sleep right after Ernő and I left?"

"It had been a long evening. You can imagine how exhausted I was," Petri said.

"Éva Hegedűs mentioned that she phoned you that night. She couldn't have called you long before I did. Can you remember what you talked about?"

Petri looked at Csilla as if she had broken some rule of conversational etiquette before responding as if their exchange was still friendly.

"It wouldn't surprise me if Éva told you I nodded off during the call. I only half-remember her saying that she wouldn't be in for work."

Ernő showed up just as Csilla thanked Petri again for the tip on the news photo. "The skinheads used it as a visual hit list to come after the three of you," she added.

"Professor Borsódy's flat wasn't vandalized."

"No, but he was the intended target of the attack on Batthyány Street."

"How do you…What makes you say that?"

"I've told you too much already, Professor." Csilla smiled. Ernő glared. Petri smiled back nervously.

The amiable man inside the porter's station introduced himself as Csaba Szalay and said he'd been on duty the evening Kellner died. Csilla asked him about the phone call from Éva Hegedűs that night. He continued to wave and greet people entering or leaving the building as he answered.

"She didn't sound too good. *Jó reggelt kívánok, uram!*" As he spoke he winked a little, either from tic or habit. Since his black eyes twinkled anyway, he gave off the impression of taking nothing seriously. "She said she wouldn't be in the next day— *Viszontlátásra!*—and could I get some letters— *Szervusz! Sziasztok!*—from off her desk and post them for her first thing in the morning. I took care of it right away. *Szia*, Gyuri!"

"How long were you gone from your desk."

"Five, ten minutes at the most. *Kezét csókolom*, Antalné! I didn't even bother to lock the office. *Viszontlátásra!* No one comes at that time of night— *Igen, igen. Jó, jó.*"

"You wouldn't be missing a flag would you?"

"How did you know?" Impressed, Csaba ignored all passersby. "I'd taken the old one down Thursday evening and put it away. When I showed up Friday morning, the man coming off shift told me it was missing. Lucky we keep an extra one handy."

Csaba gestured toward a shelf on which lay a folded flag still encased in its plastic sheath. "That's the replacement's replacement."

Csilla finished writing and closed her notepad. She was about to slip it back into her pocket when she thought to corroborate Sándor Petri's account of his whereabouts Thursday evening. Ernő had just told her on the ride over that Petri had purchased paint and solvent on Wednesday. He was beginning to think that Petri painted the Arrow Cross on his own front door. That would explain the absence of any evidence of intruders on his property. Ernő's theory had a major flaw. The skinheads had confessed to all three jobs. But could Petri have been in cahoots with them?

She asked the porter: "Did you happen to see Professor Petri that night."

"He went out for dinner and came back. I remember he said something about catching up on work while his family was away for the weekend." Csaba paused. "That's funny. I don't think I saw him again that evening. I know he was gone by the time I went to the Slavic Studies office for those letters, though."

"When was that again?"

"A quarter to eleven? I had to run out two other times. Once at around half-past eight when a janitor's key snapped off in an office door. The second was right before Éva Hegedűs rang. I went downstairs for a pee."

The kindly porter took Csilla's expression of mild frustration for disapproval. Petri probably arrived home after nine as he said, she thought. It seemed unlikely he would have been able to paint the Arrow Cross himself. But why had he purchased the spray paint then? And if not the skinheads, then for whom?

Tuesday, 20 June

CHAPTER FORTY-EIGHT

Pál slipped into the institute director's office so quietly that Tamás Garay, immersed in the morning edition, wasn't even aware of the intruder until Pál lit up.

"Smoking is strictly forbidden in university offices, Professor Berkesi." Tamás said, setting the newspaper down and lighting up. Though he was the same age as Pál, his sandy hair had only begun to streak with gray. His bony, beautifully shaved face, was still smooth. Expelling a column of smoke from his small mouth, he spoke in his usual soft-voiced manner: "You leave me no choice but to report you to the authorities."

"Quickly!" Pál said. "Name the three pagan concubines of Ladislas IV."

"Édua, Mandula, and…" Tamás cried out in frustration. "*Istenem!*"

"No. The third's name definitely wasn't God."

"*Bassza meg!* What was she called?! Didn't the good king once enjoy her before the whole royal council?"

"They excommunicated him on the spot," Pál said. "Those thirteenth-century bishops were far too easily scandalized. Ladislas was merely showing them the best way to disseminate Christianity among the heathen."

"Kúpcsecs! She was called Kúpcsecs," Tamás said and grinned, "which translates loosely as she of the pointed breasts."

"Thank you for the etymology lesson, Professor Garay," Pál said. "You should have specialized in historical linguistics."

"Our colleague Kálmán has arranged for our transportation to and from the cemetery," Tamás, a specialist in historical linguistics, said. "He'll be here any moment."

"I suppose Béla insisted on hitching a ride in the hearse so he could make his entrance astride the casket?"

"He's picking up Ilona in Újszeged. They'll meet us there."

Kálmán knocked three times and waited for Tamás's *"Tessék,"* before entering. He'd managed to tame his impossibly wavy black hair—Pál often amused himself by referring to Kálmán's tsunami look—with lavender-scented hair tonic for the occasion. His ensemble was black, his manner subdued, his countenance somber.

"Well," Kálmán said soberly.

"We're not graveside yet, Kálmán," Pál said. "You may smile if you like."

"Well." Kálmán's solemn expression at once relaxed into the customary wide grin.

"That's much better," Pál said. "You walked in here a minute ago looking like someone died."

The baffled but smiling Kálmán said: "Csaba is downstairs with the car."

"But then," Pál intoned, "who's with Csaba?"

Pleadingly, Kálmán looked to Tamás.

"We mustn't keep Csaba waiting," Tamás said. "Thank you again, Kálmán, for arranging things."

"Yes. Thank you, Kálmán," Pál said, holding the door for the others. "But how will you get to the funeral?"

"But, Pál, I am going with you...." Kálmán waved a finger at his mischievous colleague.

Only when they reached the car did Kálmán understand that Pál had spoken in earnest. Tamás and Kálmán offered Pál the more comfortable front seat, but Pál claimed the back seat for himself. He was terrified of oncoming traffic, he protested, and couldn't bare to watch vehicles hurtling toward him at astonishing speeds. Tamás then suggested Kálmán take the front seat and that he himself join Pál in back, but Pál nixed the plan, insisting he could only travel by car stretched out face-down in the rear.

The reason wasn't hard to understand: Pál Berkesi lived in a world without faith. But faith, for him, was a physical condition, a bodily sense of security arising from the conviction that others could generally be counted upon not to steer their vehicles into the opposing lane. Most persons who lived and operated motor vehicles in reasonably well-ordered societies shared this assumption, among others that enabled them to go about their daily business without fear or misgiving. Pál did not.

Further negotiation yielded a compromise: Pál would sit upright in back. Tamás, seated to his left, would block Pál's prospect of rapidly approaching and certain death by suspending his jacket inches before Pál's eyes. (The dangerous impracticality of Pál's simply keeping his eyes shut for the length of the journey was established when Pál himself argued that one might as just as easily blink without warning when one's eyes were closed as when one's eyes were open and that he hated to think about the irreparable harm that might be done him even by the briefest involuntary glimpse of vehicles bearing down on them.)

Whenever Csaba needed to make a left turn, Kálmán would kneel facing backwards in the front seat and lean over to drape the rear right window, blocking Pál's view of the now perpendicularly flowing automobiles and buses and trucks. For his part, Pál would sing Bulgarian workers' songs in his rich *basso* accompanied by Tamás and Kálmán to drown out the sound of passing cars and to divert the other passengers from their labors on his behalf.

The late morning traffic across the Old Bridge had not been heavy enough to prevent Csaba from delivering his fascinating cargo to the Újszeged cemetery in time for László Kellner's funeral. Pál sent his companions ahead and lingered by the lime green Škoda. From a distance of several car lengths, he watched Ilona embrace Tamás and Kálmán and allow herself to be escorted by them toward the crowd, four or five deep, assembled at the burial site.

On the far side of the grave, Béla had taken his place in the first row between the Dean and the President of the University. Next to them, Pál thought he recognized a dozen gray eminences from the Magyar Academy as well as the Ministers of Culture, Interior, and Education, the last of whom was talking with Sándor Petri. To his right, István Borsódy comforted an elderly woman who, to judge by her penetrating gaze, could only be László Kellner's sister. The mayor of Szeged towered over the gathering. His assistant looked at her watch and rose up on her toes to whisper something in the leaning mayor's ear. An official called the mourners to attention.

"Don't you want to join the others, Professor?" Csaba said.

"I'm going to have one more cigarette first," Pál said and offered Csaba his pack.

"My wife won't let me smoke anymore," Csaba said, lit up, and took a long drag, slowly exhaling with obvious pleasure.

"Who's manning the porter's station anyway?"

"It's Tuesday, so it's Ábel. He's Thursdays eight to four as well. I'm Mondays and Wednesdays eight to four and Tuesdays and Thursdays four to midnight."

"But didn't we chat last Friday morning?"

"Tibor's wife had a thyroid operation."

"That's right," Pál recalled. "You were tired. You'd worked the evening before."

"I was befuddled as well. I thought I'd mislaid a flag."

"Perhaps someone stole it."

"That's what I've come to believe."

"Did you tell the police?" Even as he spoke, Pál remembered Balogh talking about a missing or stolen flag over dinner Sunday night.

"No. But I suspect they knew it was gone."

"What makes you say that, Csaba?"

"Yesterday morning, a pretty young thing in a uniform comes round to ask if we were missing one. She must have heard that we might be. Why else would she ask?"

"How do you think word found its way to the police?"

"That's anyone's guess. But it must have spread quickly because as soon as Officer Lovely left, Professor Petri asked me if the flag had turned up. I hadn't even told him it was gone."

"Maybe another porter mentioned it."

"I was the only porter to see him Friday. He came in for an early meeting and left for Professor Kellner's flat around half-past nine." Csaba took one last drag from his cigarette and crushed the butt under his heel.

Someone must have requisitioned the only operational tape deck from the University's warehouse of defective audio-visual equipment, for as Pál approached the mourners, he made out the severe, even penal opening chords of Beethoven's *Egmont Overture*. The choice of music for the interment might have struck some as too surgingly exuberant for a funeral, once the early measures' brooding pre-dawn darkness lifted, but even Pál had to agree that whoever was responsible for selecting the *Egmont* had done well by László Kellner.

Beethoven penned the overture for Goethe's play about the execution of the eponymous Count by the occupying Spanish army. The nobleman's crime: leading the Netherlanders in an uprising against their foreign masters. Through an accident that must stand as just one more of History's cruel jokes at the Magyar nation's expense, the overture reemerged a century and a half later in 1956 as the theme of another failed revolution. In Kossuth Radio's cramped, makeshift studios, the *Egmont* was the only classical disk among a catalogue of urbane and effervescently light operas including such favorites as *Merry Widow*, *Land of Smiles*, and *Csárdás Princess*.

At the time, it must have seemed fitting that an overture bearing the noble Count Egmont's name should kill airtime between news bulletins tracing the euphoric discharge of revolutionary energies rather than the enchanting and heart-fluttering melodies of *Countess Maritza*. At least until the Russians arrived with their soporific and toothless recordings of *Swan Lake* and *The Sleeping Beauty* on the Kremlin label. It wasn't long before these had cast their melodic spell over the Magyar people, easing it into a national stupor that would last a generation.

In the last row, at the edge of the thick ring of mourners, Pál spotted Éva Hegedűs standing alone. He hadn't seen her since they'd passed each other on the Ady Square building's great staircase a week ago and had wondered aloud together, as they always did, why two old friends couldn't find time to meet for coffee. Had it really been twenty five years since Éva, a soft-eyed teenager from Karcag, listened appreciatively, hands folded in her wool-skirted lap, as Pál, a new assistant professor, urged her, citing a remarkable performance in his seminar, to continue reading in American history?

The young Éva had impressed him with her grown-up response to his praises—no blushing, gushing or false humility—and with her resolute declaration that she had already made up her mind to pursue Slavic Studies. He could still hear the endearingly earnest tone with which she announced that she'd be grateful if she could come to Pál with questions about historical method occasionally. How could he have said no to this dazzlingly bright, utterly winning second-year phenom? Their academic consults evolved into friendly chats and had Pál not been so in love with Ágnes, whom he'd met the previous summer at a wedding reception in Baja, he was sure he would have fallen for the adorable and spirited Éva.

Now, she stood beside him like one starved from grief. He took her hand. She regarded Pál through tears, said his name in a voice that sounded as if it had traveled a long way through steel wire. She threaded a slender arm through his and leaned into him.

By the time Pál turned his attention back to the funeral rites, the music had ended and István Borsódy was well into his eulogy. He was speaking without notes and though he appeared frail, his voice carried in the bright summer air. Pál thought he heard, just beneath the measured cadences of Borsódy's words, the burden of honest rage.

CHAPTER FORTY-NINE

"...Could he yet speak, László would urge we not trouble ourselves with such fools. He would gently remind us that some will heed any slander. Yet these fools and scandalmongers, never lovers of the truth themselves, continue to proclaim that while László Kellner lived, while he pursued the historian's craft, he did not merely abide but deliberately and maliciously advanced the late dictatorship's campaign against the truth.

"And since their hatred—one out of all proportion to the sin of which they wrongly and rancorously accuse him, a hatred powerful and violent enough to bring about his death—I say again: since their hatred knows no bounds, I can only imagine that they came, in their malice-twisted minds and spite-filled assemblies, to view László Kellner as a emblem of the inhumanity and dishonesty of Stalinism. To these detractors, I say that they offend not only the memory of a decent and honest man, but History herself. And so, standing here beside the grave of my oldest friend, I would exorcise such vengeful ghosts as still haunt László Kellner's good name.

"On that November morning when Russian tanks aimed their turrets at our Parliament, when few officials of the revolutionary government remained, László Kellner repeatedly rejected the Russian commander's offer of safe passage out of the building. On the floor of a rubble- and glass-strewn office—its walls and windows shattered by mortar and tank fire—he banged out one more declaration of principles on an ancient Underwood from whose keys and type bars dust and debris flew each time he struck a character. This plea to the free world turned out to be the last official act of the Nagy government, one that would not only nurture the dream of Hungarian independence for thirty years, but give the lie, as it does now, to the slander of László's treason.

"Only after copies had been cabled to the leaders or the representatives of the major Western democracies did he yield to the enemy's demand to leave Parliament. He took refuge, with Nagy and the others, in the Yugoslav embassy as the treads of Russian tanks tore up the streets of our capital and buried its youth. He was shipped off to Romania, again with Nagy and the others. In a sealed railroad car, he was returned to Budapest and, *unlike* Nagy and several others, rewarded by his captors with life imprisonment for his actions on behalf of a free and sovereign Hungarian nation.

"After the last round of secret trials, of reprisals, of executions, and renunciations, another thaw began and his life sentence was commuted. László was released from prison five years later.

"I often wonder if those six or seven years, when our lives as men and our roles as actors in history entwined so, were not less trying for him than the times that followed. I don't know what László would say, but I can tell you that during the revolution and the subsequent reprisals the important choices seemed far less difficult to make. It happens only rarely in our lives, perhaps only when we are young and find ourselves in dangerous circumstances, that we attain a degree of moral clarity.

"It was only after prison that choices became harder. László chose to transform himself not into a model of party discipline but into its image. He chose to pretend to give over his rage at all those who'd invited Russian tanks into Budapest, who'd ordered the execution of Nagy and the others, who'd originally sentenced us to life. Some lines of a great poet that László would recite now and then explain his choice better than I can:

Who can neither revenge
nor everything forgive,
inextinguishable
burns his black lamp of gall.

"He chose to pretend to do all this because the alternative was either not to pretend and poison his life with bitterness or not to pretend and actually forget the total injustice of totalitarian rule, the absolute injustice of a world in which no wrong whose source lay in the state itself can ever be redressed. He knew that he could never give over his memories of that horror, that to do so would mean nothing less than to give over hope itself, hope that one day the power that sought to deny all hope might itself falter and fall. Thus, long before Kundera wrote that 'the struggle of man against power is the struggle of memory against forgetting,' László Kellner knew instinctively that to give over memories of past horrors was to condemn oneself to a slavish life and a living death.

"And just as he had to struggle not to forget, he also had to struggle to forgive. But to forgive or even to pretend to forgive one's enemies, and worse, to dwell among them, he had to learn to think of himself as someone else. László knew this. We who are old enough to remember how things were forty years ago knew this. We know that everyone who must learn to think of himself as someone else comes to think of himself as someone else in a different way.

"László could have chosen, with many, perhaps most of us, to live a double life. To split his life down the middle. To strive for the appearance of transparency while secretly preserving the distinction between public and private life. Perhaps, as the years went by and the regime relaxed its grip, this is all the regime expected of us. Just the *appearance* of transparency: the illusion that we live in a glass house, that the desire for privacy is dangerous and deluded, and that we are ever revealing our lives, our loves, even our deaths to public view.

"Such an unsustainable illusion required constant attention from the regime. This arrived in the form of a national system of spying, of betraying one's family, of denouncing one's friends. The regime, it turns out, never learned much of importance about us for all that, but this was never the point of the internal spy system. The point was to keep us living in fear, to force on us the illusion of living an entirely public life.

"László Kellner was never one for illusions, for appearances. And so he chose, perhaps fatally, another sort of life for himself, one that challenged the spy system and the reasons for its existence. He chose transparency itself. His colleagues and students recall him as a man of integrity. A man of honor, surely. A man who was honest, yes. But when I speak of László's integrity now, I speak of László as one who refused to be divided against himself, who would not allow his life to be split in two, to rat itself out, to turn against itself..."

Pál caught sight of Sándor nodding in agreement across the pit. It troubled him that Sándor knew the flag had disappeared before Csaba, or anyone else, could tell him it was gone. Why would Sándor advertise such knowledge and thereby risk implicating himself in the larger investigation? Did Balogh know about this exchange?

Pál wasn't sure he would call Balogh, since, to him, tipping off the police still smacked of informing. Besides, Balogh would learn of the exchange even without Pál's intervention. The only way he might drop a dime was to convince himself that Sándor's admission pointed toward his innocence rather than the recklessness of a guilty man. He'd need to think about it some more.

"...Rather than live a double life, to admit a division between public and private, László chose to keep himself whole by burying his private life. Unlike those who chose to live a double life, to maintain two faces—one for the Party, one for ourselves and a trusted few—condemning privately what we publicly endorsed, László's choice of transparency freed him to maintain just one face, so that the face he showed the Party was the face he showed the world. Whatever you may think of his choice, László Kellner was not a hypocrite.

"You may ask whether one can really bury one's private life and live publicly at all times. Perhaps one cannot keep one's old life buried forever. As it happens, László's buried life was exhumed when the remains of Nagy and his associates were exhumed eleven years ago this week. The man László Kellner became again on the sixteenth of June 1989, the man he himself buried upon his release from prison, that is the man we rebury today.

"Again, I do not know whether one can bury one's authentic life and live as another. I do know that to the extent that one can, László succeeded. He achieved transparency or something very near it. He complied fully and publicly with the regime's diktats. But we also have to remember that the events of 1956 changed the regime also, that after the uprising, it required only the rituals of compliance and László observed these. Most of us did, even if we did so only tacitly, passively, whereas László observed them expressly and got the reputation among the malicious and ignorant as a hard-liner if such a thing ever again existed after the national tragedy of revolt and reprisal.

"I suppose it is possible for one who didn't know him, for one who hadn't known him before his release from prison, for one who didn't work beside him after his release, for one who hasn't studied his work, to reject the proposition that the László Kellner who, like the rest of us, had to endure another quarter century under the dictatorship before the changes, could not have compromised himself or the truth any more than the László Kellner he buried could have. But this is the truth.

"I did not always understand László's conduct toward others myself. But it would be unfair to László if I didn't mention a time when I'd argued with László over how he'd dealt with a certain student only to realize many years later—for I am as stubborn as László Kellner was—that he'd been right all along. I pause to ask myself how many other times he was right and I wrong on matters as important as the education of the youth, the future of our profession, of the nation itself.

"László Kellner served his community and country as few have served either. This is a common graveside sentiment. Let me express it in a way less common and sentimental: László Kellner's choices and actions rendered the choices of others easier, their actions less dangerous, their freedom possible, even when this meant being accused of motives and emotions and deeds that he never entertained or felt or performed.

"Earlier we listened to the overture Beethoven composed for the execution of another patriot. My words of tribute have been but a paltry tune compared to that grand music. Perhaps you will allow me to offer the briefest coda, one that might redeem what has gone before it.

"László Kellner was executed the night before the anniversary of the execution of Imre Nagy and his associates, and, as importantly, that of their reburial as heroes and martyrs more than thirty years later. A sixth coffin lay alongside the coffins of Nagy and the others on that June day eleven years ago. The sixth coffin commemorated those unknown Magyars who gave their lives so that their nation might know liberty once again. No one could have known at the time that more blood would be shed for freedom, that the sixth coffin would come to symbolize not only those who had already lost their lives in the name of a free Hungary but *all* the lives that would yet be lost. Before us, we see the sixth coffin once again. Within it lies one who sacrificed his life not merely for others but for the truth that keeps us free."

Pál's eyes met Sándor's as two cemetery workers in grimy jumpers lifted the ropes on which the coffin had rested beside the grave and started lowering it into the earth. In an imaginary reversal of roles with the workers, Pál envisioned himself and Sándor in those grimy jumpers holding the ropes and balancing Kellner's coffin between them. But cooperation gave way to mortal competition and Pál had the sense that this contest would end only when the loser was lying at the bottom of the pit with the coffin, covering his face with hands tangled up in the ropes as mourners shovelled dirt upon him.

CHAPTER FIFTY

István Borsódy's graveside account of László Kellner's life after prison haunted Pál as he waited at the schoolyard gates for Erzsi. As a teacher, Borsódy had loved Zen-like paradoxes as means of illumination. Pál couldn't begin to imagine what living transparently would be like unless it merely meant being the person you presented yourself as publicly. But Borsódy had hinted at something more.

A transparent life would be a life without masks, without hiding or any of the guilt that goes with that. A life with none of the intellectual's sense of drift, of feeling as though you were floating in the air, until, as some found during the worst of the old days, you found oneself not so much floating in the air as falling through it, someone having tripped the lever, the trap having swung open, the darkness rushing up to meet you.

Maybe *that* was it. Maybe László Kellner, who'd passed through the shade of the prison-yard gallows each day for five years, had simply traded the principles for which he'd nearly been hanged for those that might place him beyond the shadow of the noose. Had Borsódy meant nothing more by transparency than willed self-destruction prompted by one's desire to escape hanging?

Then again, hadn't Borsódy's final point been that his friend had chosen the life he chose not to save his own life but the lives of others? If he'd rejected the compromise offered by a double life, he'd also rejected his own past to protect the future of others. Kellner understood that all those he loved were in danger because the Party knew that it could hurt him most by hurting them. Had Kellner repudiated his own life not to win the Party's forgiveness, but, as Borsódy suggested, to save the lives as well as the souls of others? Didn't Kellner know better than anyone that it wasn't the Party's way to forgive and that its willingness to readmit him into it ranks could only be taken as a guarantee of further soul-killing compromises?

Kellner also knew that he could never return to his old life among those he loved if he wanted to keep them from harm. As Pál figured it, Kellner had three options as the time of his release. He could cease to live among them or he could cease to love them or he could cease to be himself. Since he could not cease to live among them, since he could not cease to love them, he chose to cease being himself. Pál had found Borsódy unnecessarily cryptic on this point, but, as the eulogy went on, he'd also found himself warming to the portrait of Kellner being unveiled. One didn't have to like Kellner to respect him, to mourn, from a safe emotional distance, for a man who'd made hard choice upon hard choice.

Yet Pál's revived if chilly respect for Kellner only served to swell the smart, that sting he'd felt this morning when Borsódy told him privately, as he had told everyone publicly if obliquely, that he had come to agree with Kellner about "a certain student" who it turned out was Pál himself.

Borsódy had sought Pál out after the funeral. At first, his former student had been tempted to ask him to say more about Kellner's transparency. But the aged professor who'd spoken so movingly of his dead friend afterward appeared so old and near the end of a long journey that Pál could only bring himself to offer meager yet honest words of comfort.

"Thank you, Pál. I looked for you during my remarks."

"I was in the last row as usual, Professor. Tamás was up front."

"I wanted to make sure you heard the bit about how László and I argued about you. How, in the end, László had been right."

"Thank you, Professor." Pál tried to hide his bewilderment and hurt. He chalked up the remark up to confusion occasioned by the old man's grief.

Borsódy had searched Pál's eyes for a sign of understanding. "I'm not sure you do," he said. "Come by the flat tomorrow so we can talk some more."

Pál wondered how a teacher who had always been so kind to him could declare that Kellner had been right. After everything that happened in Prague? After Kellner had all but thrown him out of the department? Though his sympathy for the bereft Borsódy far outweighed any anger Pál might have felt on hearing the poor man's admission, he couldn't help but feel as if he'd been dismissed from his old department again.

An obnoxious electric bell went off and the doors of the school flew open. The first children to emerge were a jovial crew of tow-headed boys swinging their satchels and twirling neckties like steamrolled snakes in the air. Immersed in tribal business, they didn't even notice Pál as they thundered past him at the gate. Two more waves of yapping boys full of beans spilled out into the schoolyard before the first of the girls appeared in the doorway in small groups of three and four.

Unlike the boys, who at this point in their social development could only be seen as parts of a composite personality, as products of their tribal identity, the girls had already begun to perfect their personal styles. From their choice of scrunchies and colored shoe laces, from the way they decorated their book covers or adopted what they thought were adult gestures and intonations for expressing opinions about people they did or didn't like, it was clear to Pál that they were well on their way to becoming the persons they would become. As they passed, they smiled or nodded their little heads in acknowledgment of the rumple-suited professor waiting for his dawdling daughter. Some he recognized as Erzsi's playmates from movie matinees and dance recitals, in turn recognized Erzsi's father and reassured him that Erzsi herself would be along any moment.

Five minutes later, she was skipping toward him across the asphalt. Like the tail of a kite, her long beribboned braid steadied the bouncing Erzsi as she pranced his way. From the amused expression on the grizzled janitor who'd accompanied her as far as the door, Pál surmised that she had just finished offering him pointers on the correct use of a mop. He was at a loss to understand how should it have happened that advising all sorts of people on how best to perform their given tasks was his daughter's chiefest pleasure and preoccupation in her bright young life. Yet she must have had a gift for telling others what to do. Even though Pál feared she would make a pest of herself, she seemed never to invite anything worse than tickled thanks and gently teasing laughter from the recipients of her wisdom.

Pál loved to tell Tamás and Kálmán of how she'd honed her skills on family pets. Her earliest efforts had been directed toward coaching their sheepdog on his barking technique. No use telling her that Kongó's deep and cavernous woof was one of his fine points, that he'd been named for its rich, hollow tone. The three-year-old Erzsi followed her preliminary instructions by getting down on all fours to demonstrate the proper pitch and volume. The lesson failed. Erzsi merely succeeded in getting her little face, its eyes and nose and mouth all scrunched up in anticipation of the deluge, licked clean with three swipes of the slobbery pup's considerable tongue.

Now, having released Pál from her adoring embrace, Erzsi looked her father over and said: "It's a Tuesday, so somebody must have died."

"Why would you say such a thing?" Pál said.

"Because you're wearing your dark suit and you only do that when somebody marries or somebody dies?"

"How do you know I didn't get dressed up just for you."

Erzsi tilted her head, raised her eyebrows, and regarded him with upcast cornflower-blue eyes. She wasn't buying it. Instead, she took his hand and led him onto the sidewalk. "Who was it anyway?"

"Who was who?"

"Who died?"

"A man I knew."

"Are you sad?"

"I knew him a long time ago."

Erzsi waited for what to her must have seemed an unusually long moment before changing the subject.

"I'm going to Miki's birthday party tomorrow afternoon. *Anyu* took me to the store to pick out a present yesterday."

"What's this?" Pál said.

"When someone invites you to their birthday party, you have to bring a present."

"Sounds like a scam to me. When I was a boy, it was all I could do to keep other children from throwing me down the well on my birthday. I don't know anything about this 'present' business."

"You do too."

"Well, since you've already bought the present I suppose you'll have to pass it along to the little grifter. But this is the last time. Next year, he'll have to shift for himself or look for a new set of patsies."

"*A-pu.*" She said the Magyar word for Daddy as she would scold a doll.

"What did you get him anyway? Goose liver? Blood pudding? Escargots?"

Erzsi had long ago learned to press on in the face of her father's incessant silliness: "And then on Saturday…"

"Yes?" Pál said.

"On Saturday afternoon…" Erzsi elongated each syllable, especially the last. She spoke this way whenever she would draw her *faux* gruff father out.

"I have plans." Pál was onto her.

"You're coming to my party!" Her playfully haughty tone let him know she was enjoying this tussle.

"What party? What's with all these parties?" Pál blustered. "How do you expect anyone to get anything done in this dingy little country of ours if everyone's off attending parties all the time?"

"You know my birthday's Saturday," Erzsi said in a voice that had begun to display the slightest impatience. "And *you're* going to be there. And *nagymama*. And *nagypapa*...." She could only mean his parents. Ágnes's parents lived in America now with her younger sister and they wouldn't make their yearly visit until August.

"Is there something special you'd like for your birthday this year, Erzsi?"

"I want you to surprise me." She was clearly not her father's daughter in all respects, but she was still young enough that a surprise would do her little nerve-endings no lasting damage.

"And your mother knows that you've been planning this...well...gala? How is your mother anyway?" Pál stopped short a few meters shy of the entrance to the pleasant block of newish flats. In its shady courtyard, dark green bushes sported button-like pink flowers.

"You're not coming inside?" she said a little glumly. "*Anyu*'s fine, but, why don't you ever want to talk to her except on the phone or unless Bertalan is around?"

"Is that what you think?"

"It's what *Anyu* and I both think, *Apu*."

"That's silly." They were right, but he hoped he hadn't been so obvious. "I'll see your mother at the party. We'll talk then."

"With Bertalan and everyone else there."

"Try not to let it bother you, Erzsi? We both love you very much."

"Didn't you once love each other very much?"

"What's that got to... Erzsi, that's between your mother and me."

"I just liked it better when we all lived together."

"How can you even remember? You were so little then."

"I think I do. Maybe I don't. I don't know."

She sounded wistful, a rare humor in a child, even one as precocious as Erzsi. Could one so young sense time sealing away past joys, feel a longing for happier days? He bent over to kiss her on each cheek and once atop her head. He pulled her close and stroked her hair. She buried her face in his shirt. "You go inside now, Erzsi. I'll see you Saturday."

He waited for her as she took out her key and opened the door. He turned to go. Upon reaching the curb, he looked back and saw that she was standing in the doorway watching him as he walked away. She waved goodbye, wearing a sad little smile, and disappeared into the sunlit lobby.

CHAPTER FIFTY-ONE

"I thought you left for Budapest after the funeral," István said, leading Sándor to the small sitting room. Early-evening sun polished the dusty leaves and dusky petals of the African violets on the window sill.

Sándor looked through a bright pane at the traffic thinning along Szentháromság Street. Turning to lay eyes on his host, he said: "You look tired, István."

"The doctor prescribed something." From off the sofa, István lifted an open book he'd laid down spine up when Sándor rang and closed it. "It's good for knocking me out, but I wake up feeling exhausted anyway. Please Sándor," he smoothed and patted the cushion where the book had been, "won't you sit?"

"I should have called first." Sándor lowered himself into a club chair instead and dropped his satchel on the rug. "I wanted to see how you're faring."

"No better that I should be. How is it with you?"

"I'm bearing up. I wish I could say the same about Éva."

"The poor girl. László was hard on her the last time she saw him."

"Some think that wasn't the last time she saw him." Sándor said, flipping mechanically through the latest issue of a journal with a pale blue cover.

István might have expressed alarm had he not felt oddly hampered by Sándor's nonchalant manner of relating this news. He said: "I thought the case was all but closed with the skinheads' arrest."

"The police must have turned up conflicting evidence or discovered a motive because, apparently, they're interested in Éva now."

"That you don't sound worried comforts me a little." István said, silently weighing the possibility that Sándor had things wrong. His fears for Éva now got the better of him: "They can't think that she has anything to do with László's murder." After another pause, he shook he head and continued. "No, forgive me, Sándor. I don't think the police consider Éva a suspect in the case at all."

"What *do* you think?" Sándor asked, bemused.

"I think you might be projecting your own misgivings about Éva onto the police because you refuse to admit having doubts about her, doubts that have nothing at all to do with László's murder. I think you should tell me what these are and not worry about upsetting me."

"I grant that much of what she's done and said during the last week gives me pause, but I'm not projecting. The police *are* interested in Éva. I didn't say they necessarily regarded her as a suspect at this point. They probably just—"

Someone began to vacuum in the flat above. István and Sándor looked up at the ceiling and then at each other. The appliance's wheels rolled heavily back and forth. "My neighbor cleans all hours of the day and night." István said, grateful for the distraction. "I think she spends most of her waking hours cleaning. She must get something out of it besides a spotless flat."

"Cleaning's always been one of the more therapeutic metaphors. The urge to tidy up must be universal given life's messiness," Sándor paused, self-pleased. "As I was going to say, the police probably just want to…well, tidy up, to rid themselves of any remaining doubts about the suspects' guilt by sweeping away rival motives for László's murder."

"What rival motive could they imagine involving Éva?"

"Perhaps one to do with the argument she had with László."

"They didn't argue. I made that clear to the police."

"Maybe they just want to know what moved László to rebuke her. When two people argue…" Sándor stopped and started again: "When one person takes another to task only to be found murdered the next day, the police are going to be interested in the survivor. But you still haven't told me what happened that night. You were there. You must have heard and seen everything."

"I was trying to mind my own business. Éva dropped by. Then she left."

"But only after László rebuked her. She must have done or said something to provoke him."

"I can assure you, Sándor, she did nothing to provoke that response. It wasn't the first time there'd been a misunderstanding between those two. And it wasn't the first time that László had reprimanded her. You can deny it all you want, Sándor, but I still say you're projecting whatever doubts you have about Éva onto the police."

"You won't believe me, István, until I tell you all I know. I'd hoped I wouldn't have to do that, especially on the day we buried László." Sándor leaned forward and rested his hands on his knees. He took a deep breath and exhaled. "The night he was murdered, Éva called me a little after 10:30. She was sobbing, but she managed to stop long enough to explain that she was calling from László's flat and that someone had painted an Arrow Cross on the front door. Then she started to sob again. This time, I had no trouble making out her words. She kept repeating: 'László's dead.'"

István nodded. The news of Éva's return to the flat troubled him, though he'd expected worse. He wondered if he'd been too quick to dismiss Sándor's claim that she'd attracted the interest of the police. She hadn't reported László's murder to the authorities even though she was the first to discover his body. If the police found out, she could have some difficulty explaining herself. Even so, he felt a small wave of relief break over him. He waited until it passed and said: "Why didn't she call the police?"

"She seemed frightened. I told her *I* would call them, then come right over so I would be there with her when they arrived. She started sobbing again, harder than before. She begged me not to place the call. She'd convinced herself that they would charge her with László's death. I told her she had nothing to worry about. I tried to explain how with everything else that the skinheads had done that evening—the vandalism, the beatings—they'd all but convicted themselves of murder. She didn't believe me. She wanted me to promise that I wouldn't contact the police. What else could I do, István? She sounded desperate. I was afraid she would hurt herself."

"But if she couldn't bring herself to call the police, and she didn't want you to do it for her, what did she want from you?"

"An alibi." Sándor sounded as if he himself din't believe what he'd just said. "She wanted an alibi, István. She thought that if she could prove she'd called me to say that she was ill and that she wouldn't come to work the next day, then the police would be more willing to believe that she'd gone straight home after leaving László's flat earlier that evening. Then, the next morning, the building manager and I could find László and inform the police of his death. She said that László was already dead and it wouldn't make any difference to him whether I called that night or the next morning."

István removed his eyeglasses and balanced them on a knee. He leaned back on the sofa, and placed the heels of both palms over his eyes. When he uncovered them, he gazed at Sándor: "So you've both figured out a way to implicate yourselves in László's murder by conspiring to withhold your knowledge of his death from the police."

Sándor looked away.

"I'm not judging you, Sándor. You wanted to keep Éva from going to pieces. But you knew that László was dead when we had our meeting and you didn't tell me. No wonder you seemed so distracted."

"I wanted to tell you, but I couldn't risk implicating you as well."

"Sándor, I'm not upset with you. I just cannot imagine anything more terrible than having to carry that knowledge around with you."

"I can imagine something more terrible." Sándor let his head drop, catching his forehead in his hands.

István experienced the mind-flash that precedes the most painful recognitions. "You haven't told me everything."

"I didn't know everything until a few hours ago." Sándor didn't lift his head from his hands. "Today, when I saw Éva at the funeral, she seemed overcome with remorse. She said that she needed to talk to me, that she'd done a terrible thing. I kept telling myself that it was only her guilt over unresolved bad feelings between László and her. All through your eulogy, I weighed what I felt—that she couldn't have killed László—against something I'd learned yesterday— that she'd called Csaba the night of the murder with an errand that took him away from the porter's station long enough for someone to steal the spare flag they kept behind the desk." He dropped his hands and turned to face István. "Even after she told me, I didn't believe her. I couldn't believe that she could kill László and then have the presence of mind to make it look like another Szolnok."

"She told you that she killed László?"

Sándor nodded. Dazed, István couldn't speak.

"I shouldn't have told you this today. It's too much. I'm going to get you some water and one of those pills so you can get some rest. Where are they?"

"No pills," István said. "I don't want to sleep."

"Just some water then. I'll be right back."

István watched him leave the room. He heard water running in the kitchen. A cupboard, possibly a drawer, opened and closed. The faucet squeaked shut. Sándor returned with a glass of water and waited for him to drink.

In the interval of stunned silence, the meaning of Sándor's words bubbled up little by little in István's mind like slow-to-rise marsh gas blistering the surface of a murky pond. Finally, the older man spoke in a voice that sounded like wind lost in the dry reeds:

"But the skinheads killed him. They covered László with the flag. What about the Arrow Cross?"

"It was already there when she arrived. By the time she got back to the flat, she was so distraught over her exchange with László earlier that evening that the sight of it may not have registered at first. She said she only remembered seeing it later after László was dead and she was trying to figure out a way not to get caught."

"But how could it even have come to that, Sándor?"

"László must have thought she might come back because he'd left the door unlocked. She finds him at his desk. They argue but after a little while he turns his back on her and orders her to leave. She's not too clear on what happens next but she thinks she must been on her way out when she sees the large green jug full of withered lilacs by the door. She drops the dead flowers onto the floor. She runs back to where László is bent over his books and strikes him on the head."

"She must be delusional, Sándor. No matter how distraught she may have been, she wouldn't have done that."

"She killed him, István."

"And you're convinced she took the flag from the porter's station after making sure that Csaba would be off running an errand for her? Sándor, do you really believe she would have risked leaving the flat to return a second time?"

"I have to believe that, István, since I can't bring myself to believe that her act was premeditated. And I'm sure she stole the flag. Why else would she draw Csaba away from his station?"

"I'm sorry, Sándor." István laughed bitterly. "It's so absurd."

"What's absurd?"

"For months, you and I did our best to discourage László from publishing his memoirs as they are. So much there that might have provoked his enemies to come after him. If you're right about Éva, then our worst fears were realized anyway. László's book had nothing to do with his murder."

"But it had everything to do with László's murder."

"I'm not sure I understand, Sándor."

"Of course you do. István. All afternoon you've been trying to avoid talking about the pages Éva dropped off. You may not have read them but you must have figured out that Éva didn't want anyone else to know what was in them."

"Didn't Éva mention them to you?" István said, still trying to stall.

"If she killed László to stop others from reading them, she wasn't going to tell me about them." Sándor pivoted to face István. "Why don't you tell me what *you* think she was afraid I might find out?"

"Anything I could say would be a guess."

Sándor's smile suggested disdain. He reached into his satchel and pulled out a small device that István could not identify.

"This is the hard drive from Éva's pc."

István stared at Sándor. "So you have read them."

"I haven't. Éva's always been careful to delete sensitive documents."

"So if what you want has been deleted, why—"

"Because the hard drive contains a record of every keystroke. Any text processed can be retrieved and I've found someone in Budapest who knows how. I'm going to see him tomorrow and it shouldn't take him more than a day to retrieve what I want to read. István, I want to know what you think was in those pages. I'm going to read it for myself anyway."

István stalled some more. "Do you think it's a good idea, Sándor, removing the hard drive? I understand that you're trying to protect Éva, but what if the police discover the hard drive is missing?"

"You speak as if I'm only trying to protect Éva. I'm trying to protect myself, too. You know that I'm up for a ministry post and if my name appears in László's manuscript among those he condemns for collaborating with the regime, my nomination will be withdrawn. I've worked my entire life for this and I won't let a dead man take it away from me."

Indignation rouged István's cheeks: "You're talking about your mentor."

"And I honor his memory. I owe everything to him. But that doesn't mean I'm going to let him take it all back just because he had an hyperactive superego and couldn't forgive himself for complying with the regime in ways that didn't matter."

"You've made your point, Sándor. You have a right to know if László was going to expose you. I just don't see why you want me to speculate, when you'll be able to read the pages for yourself soon enough, as you've just said yourself."

"I want to know what kind of monster you think you've been dealing with all these years."

"I don't think you're a monster, Sándor. I know you were an informer. I had my fears about you in the past, but I kept them in check because who wants to imagine he lives and works in a world where his own students are informing against him. László confirmed my fears the night he died."

"So I've been found guilty of betrayal by a jury of my teachers."

"I stopped thinking in terms of guilt and innocence long ago. Why do you think László and I argued so over the years? He could never accept my view that it wasn't the historian's task to calculate blame and blamelessness since these weren't factors that belonged to history. It falls to the propaganda-artist, not the historian, to furnish us with the labels 'guilty' and 'innocent,' to lend them enough power to warrant acts of revenge which would otherwise be seen for what such acts are: crimes motivated by greed, lust, resentment, fear, and pride. I cannot judge you, Sándor."

"Before we're through you may hear something that will change your mind. Tell me, István, what else do you think you know about me?"

"That you used your power as a member of the Party and an informer to get what you wanted. The temptation to do so must have been great, Sándor."

Sándor looked at István in that way some beggars regard passersby before they hit them up for change. "Don't be so circumspect, István. Just tell me what you think I did."

"That you took advantage of Éva. That you threatened her. That you told her you would inform on me if she refused to go to bed with you. Afterward, I think that she was unable to live with me and with the shame of what she'd done at the same time. So she left. Besides the two of you, only László knew what happened. Éva told him. He must have promised her that I'd never learn the truth, and when she discovered he was going to break his promise all the shame and rage she'd ever felt rose up inside her."

"Is that what you think, István? That I'm the reason she left you? I won't lie to you. I tried to bed Éva for the longest time. It embarrasses me even now to admit that I never gave a thought to her feelings or yours, that I only considered my own desire. And you're right. I used what leverage I had as a Party member, but she wouldn't give in no matter how much I pressured her. She really loved you, István. You had a chaste little girlfriend there. And a pretty one too.

"So I slipped something into her glass while we were having a drink. I took her to a room in an abandoned wing of one of the old clinics by the river. A friend in the Party, a radiologist, lent me his key. I doubt she even remembers how she got there, how I undressed her and carried her to the bed. Fucking her was like fucking a rag doll, István. I doubt she even knew who she was."

"Please go, Sándor. I want you to leave."

Sándor didn't move.

"You need to hear this, István. It may make you feel better. The whole time I was on top of her, she wouldn't look at me. I tried to force her to, but she'd just wrench her face away. She kept her eyes locked on a spot on the wall. You would've been proud of her, István."

"I was wrong about you Sándor. You *are* a monster."

"We've never talked about what happened that day. I suppose we have an unspoken understanding.

She never wanted you to know we'd been together and I've never told anyone. Perhaps she thinks the price of my silence is her civility. But we've been more than civil to each other over the years. I would even say that our secret has drawn us closer together."

"Get out."

"But that's only half the story, István."

"I don't care. Get out."

"Don't you want to hear why Éva left you?"

"I've heard too much already."

"The answer may surprise you, István. Several weeks after our one and only time together, Éva learned she was pregnant."

István closed his eyes.

"I know what you're thinking, but it wasn't mine. It couldn't have been. I didn't know it at the time, but I was sterile. Years later when Anna wanted children and she couldn't conceive, we went to a specialist. Turned out I had weak swimmers. The treatment was successful and Anna got her children. So there's no doubt about it, István. It wasn't I who got Éva with child. It was you!"

"Éva was pregnant with my—"

"Yes, István, you were the father. Of course, Éva didn't know that. She was certain I was the father. Only you would know for sure if the two of you had been taking precautions at the time, but I assume you were and one got through.

"That's right, István. She thought she was pregnant with *my* child. When she turned to László for advice, he insisted that she leave Szeged rather than put you through the pain of knowing that your girlfriend was going to have a child by one of your own students. He was thinking of me, too. Remember, I'd only been married for a year."

"But what happened to the child?"

"There was no child, István. Éva had the pregnancy terminated here in Szeged. So you see, István. Éva didn't leave you because I took advantage of her."

"You raped her."

"That characterization doesn't offend me, István. But as I was saying, Éva didn't leave you because she was ashamed of having slept with me. She didn't even leave you because she thought she was pregnant with my child. No, she left because László said she must. László even made arrangements at the abortion clinic for her. Seems that as Zsuzsa got older and her illness progressed, she also grew careless with her lovers and László had to help her through the termination process more than once. He knew the drill by the time Éva got pregnant."

István sat silent for a long time. He felt as though he was on the verge of a decision, though he couldn't make out what it was. Still distracted, he said: "Did Éva say anything about the raincoat?"

"What raincoat, István?"

"My raincoat. The one I left in László's flat."

"She didn't say anything to me about it and I didn't see one when I was there. She must have taken it with her and ditched it somewhere. She didn't want the police to think you'd forgotten it because you'd been in a hurry to leave the flat. At the same time, she didn't return it to you, because she didn't want you knowing she'd gone back to the flat."

"Yes. That's what I thought." István made a decision. "Sándor, I need you to promise me something."

"Of course."

"Sándor, I'm going to confess to László's murder. Éva cannot go to jail. Promise that you won't tell anyone about what we've said here."

"I promise. But the police will never believe you."

"They'll believe me." He felt sure they would. "It's best you go now, Sándor. I have some things I need to take care of."

WEDNESDAY, 21 JUNE

CHAPTER FIFTY-TWO

The note lay on the white duvet beside the dead man. A thumb's breadth of water remained in the glass beside the empty pill bottle on the night table. István Borsódy had removed his jacket and tie and draped them over the back of an arm chair in the corner. A pair of ancient slippers—in faded gold lettering, the name *Church's* was printed inside them—lay on the floor with their toes pointing away from the bed.

The news of István Borsódy's suicide had arrived at headquarters just about the time Ernő handed the mobile phone records to Balogh. It seemed that the professor, distraught over the murder of his dear friend, had swallowed a bottle of sleeping pills the previous night. The cleaning woman had found him.

"I'll look at these when I get back from Batthyány Street," Balogh said, closing the folder in which the phone records lay. "Anything surprising?"

"Nothing to contradict what the skinheads told us, if that's what you mean," Ernő said. "Petri's role gets more interesting all the time and we haven't even asked him about the spray paint yet."

"I think we can accept Zsolt's claim that two cans of the stuff were waiting for him." Balogh came around the desk and gestured for Ernő to follow him out of the office. "Call Petri. Tell him I'd like to talk with him about Borsódy's state of mind after the funeral yesterday."

Now, as he waited for the crime tech to dust the envelope and suicide note for prints, Balogh asked Korbács: "Any word from Budapest about the Kellner case?"

"Maybe tomorrow. Friday's more likely," an unusually subdued Korbács said. "Nothing peculiar here. Twenty-odd secobarbital, judging from the prescription. Then, lights out."

The only prints were Borsódy's. His handwriting was refined, conveying both confidence and gravity:

I, István Borsódy, killed László Kellner during an altercation that began early on the evening of 15 June and escalated as the evening progressed.

The fatal episode occurred when I returned to Professor Kellner's flat to retrieve my raincoat, which I'd forgotten when I walked out in the midst of one of several angry exchanges. We'd resumed arguing even more heatedly than before. Enraged, I started to leave again but my anger turned me around and led me to cross the room again to strike László Kellner on the back of his head with a vase I found by the door. The blow killed him. I attempted to disguise my act as a political crime committed by extremists. Fearing that I might have blood on my coat, I abandoned it in Dugonics Park.

I have acted alone. The personal matter over which Professor Kellner and I fought could be of no interest *to the authorities and I will not disgrace either of our memories by describing it here. Guilt has not been the chief motive behind my confession. One may kill a friend, but even death may not cancel a friendship that stretches back to youth. I do not wish to live without that friendship. I had not counted on feeling such loneliness.*

Borsódy had signed his name without a flourish in the same elegant hand and folded the heavy bond writing paper in thirds.

The detective unfolded, reread, and refolded the note several more times as he struggled to accept its testimony. He recalled another murder case he'd worked on years ago involving two old men who'd been friends for most of their lives. The similarities even extended to the murder weapon, an empty wine bottle with which one friend had repeatedly struck the other one's head until bottle and skull both shattered.

Resemblance between the two cases ended there. Like so many other destitute pensioners, these two had subsisted on *krumplipaprikás* and cheap wine. They'd apparently just finished off their third liter of the night when one drunk decided that the other had stolen his last five hundred forint note and tried to strangle him. The other had reached instinctively for anything with which to fend him off and continued fending him off even as his assailant lay all crumpled up on the linoleum. As for the five hundred forint note, it lay all crumpled up on the linoleum under the table where its owner had dropped it an hour earlier.

Balogh was not displeased when his mental image of that squalid murder scene yielded to a real one consisting of Korbács holding a pencil from which two pairs of scissors were suspended in one hand and a see-through plastic bag containing a cloth disk in the other. On closer inspection, he noticed a sliver of green on the white round.

"Where did you find those?" Balogh asked, making a mental note to send someone over to look for scissors in the Kellner flat.

"In a kitchen drawer." Korbács jogged the pencil, causing the shears to swing back and forth. "The flag circle was at the bottom of a dustbin a few feet away."

"Does it seem strange to you that Professor Borsódy kept this evidence concealed even after he decided to confess to murdering his friend?"

"It's not as if he hid it well. Perhaps he wasn't confident that his confession would be enough to establish his guilt."

"Perhaps he wasn't the one who hid it."

Not only did the flag circle match the flag found draped over Kellner's body, but the officer sent to search Kellner's flat for a pair of scissors called to say that he'd found none. Now, Ernő stood before Balogh's desk again: "Petri wasn't at his office number. Éva Hegedűs wasn't there either."

Word of the suicide traveled fast once the Colonel alerted the University and the local news outlets. It was wise of Krebán to have done so quickly rather than to wait and risk fomenting rumors of a second politically motivated slaying in one week.

"I tried Petri at home," Ernő continued. "His wife said she'd been trying to reach him to tell him the sad news."

"He's skipped town, then?"

"He's attending a Slavic Studies conference in Budapest. His wife said she would leave another message for him to call us. She said he turns off his cell phone during sessions. I have the hotel and conference info."

"Do we know when he arrived in Budapest?"

"He checked into the Hotel Korona at Kálvin Square a little after two yesterday afternoon, having gotten a lift to Budapest with the Minister of Education straight from Kellner's funeral."

Ernő had talked to one of the conference's administrators who verified that Petri registered at the conference desk no later than half-past two and while he hadn't attended the welcoming address at five, she'd met him for a drink later that evening. Balogh asked Ernő if the conference administrator had sounded young and attractive. Ernő said it was difficult to judge such things over the phone but that he seemed to recall her saying something about how Petri had been eager to call it a night so he could wake up in time for the morning sessions.

"What are you implying, Ernő?" Balogh asked playfully, in spite of or perhaps because of this morning's grim discovery. "That Petri's a cad. That he threw the poor woman out as soon as he had his way with her? You'd never do such a thing, would you Ernő?"

But Ernő was too busy trying to hide his mortification at being held up as a target of sexual speculation, even in jest, to attempt to answer Balogh. He consoled himself with the thought that at least Csilla hadn't been there to hear this. But his mind soon began to resonate with her name like a cloud seeded for rain and in no time he found himself drenched with another word-shower: *If it please him, may Love wish that she and I lie together in some blue chamber. There, attended by all joys, we will seal a great covenant. There, robed round with laughter and my embrace, she will reveal to me that perfect body clad in the glimmer of the lamplight.* Would he ever know peace again?

Balogh looked at his watch: it was nearly noon. "We should be hearing from Petri shortly. Why don't you get Csilla and we'll go over these phone records together."

Ernő was baffled by the announcement: "But didn't Borsódy confess to killing Kellner in his note? Wasn't there evidence found in his flat linked to the murder scene?"

"Yes and yes," Balogh answered. "But I'm not sure how these facts are related. I'm not sure that taken together they reveal the truth about Kellner's murder."

"I'm confused, sir."

"Of course you're confused. You think that facts and truth are the same. But that's never the case, Ernő. We arrive at the truth by means of the facts but it's the relation *between* the facts which concerns us most. Are you still confused?"

"Yes, sir."

"Good. It's confusing," Balogh said. "Now, go get Csilla."

CHAPTER FIFTY-THREE

Csilla, looking efficient and blonde, glided into the office. Ernő, looking cowed and blond, dragged his feet a few steps behind her. Shuffling to the table, he seemed to be of two minds, one too narrowly focused on something, the other distracted, unable to concentrate on anything. He'd been poised to take the chair next to his partner as he always did, but apparently he thought better of it and, stepping sideways, perhaps a little too deliberately to escape Csilla's notice, seated himself in the next chair down. Tiny furrows appeared above Csilla's sun-bleached eyebrows. Ernő looked around in every direction but hers.

Balogh slid a blue vinyl folder across the table. "I don't know if you've both seen the preliminary report on Borsódy's suicide, but have a look."

Csilla corralled and guided the folder to a spot equidistant between Ernő and herself so they could read it together. Ernő resisted—"You go ahead, Csilla."—and at once assumed a position that could only be described as "the fetus seated." Aghast, Csilla pulled the folder back her way and buried herself in the report.

As he absorbed these workplace theatrics, Balogh wondered why he was so reluctant to accept a murder confession supported by evidence found in the self-proclaimed murderer's flat.

Balogh was running out of suspects. The skinheads, at least with respect to the murder charge, seemed to be in the clear. And if he could prove that Borsódy had made a false confession and that the physical evidence linking him to Kellner's murder was planted, Balogh would have just two candidates left. In spite of some rather unusual behavior, the accumulation of evidence around either was still so slight that neither could be considered a promising suspect in the murder investigation.

To be sure, Petri had emerged as a rather curious victim of politically motivated vandalism. How often, after all, does a homeowner supply the vandals with the tools of their trade? Yet aside from the weak evidence of a few prints discovered on the inside of Kellner's front door and the even weaker non-evidence of Petri's failure to answer a late-evening phone call from Csilla, Balogh still couldn't connect Petri to the murder.

As for Éva Hegedűs, what were the chances that she would have gone to Kellner's flat not just once, but once to kill him, and once again to make the murder look like another Szolnok? And if she had, short of a confession, how could Balogh prove it? If the dearth of physical evidence made it impossible to place Petri at the flat on the night of the murder, then it was the wealth of evidence left in the wake of Éva's visit there earlier that night that made it impossible to determine whether she'd gone back there later.

So why did he feel as if he'd come back to life as a detective at the very moment when the prospects for a successful outcome to the investigation seemed so unpromising? How was it that he felt alive again, challenged, even with the stench of death hanging in the air?

But challenged in what way? Hadn't the case become challenging when Ernő returned to headquarters with the flag stolen from the Bartók Square rally intact? The case *had* begun to feel challenging last Friday, but that was different from feeling, as he did now, as if he'd been challenged personally, as if someone had thrown down the gauntlet, though in this case the gauntlet had taken the form of an extra pair of scissors and a white flag circle with a narrow strip of green.

It was less of a duel than a race in which foiling your competition before they foiled you was more important than your individual time, one in which you found yourself striving to make out a pattern that would lend a structure of coherence and inevitability to a bunch of stupid and unruly facts even as your opponent was striving to substitute another pattern, other patterns, and false ones at that, for yours. It was as if you'd been set against one another to see who could write the story that would best explain why everything had happened last Thursday night the way it had. The difference was that your opponent was trying to write your story for you, to slip his own story between you and the events themselves, to have you take his version for yours.

When Ernő closed the folder to signify he'd finished reading the report, Balogh turned to Csilla and said: "I've already vexed your partner by rejecting a too-convenient linkage between Borsódy's confession and the evidence found in his flat. We can't just assume one exists. We have to establish it. Let's begin by assuming the opposite case: that the fact of Borsódy's confession and the fact of the evidence found in his kitchen are unrelated."

"Since there's no doubt that Borsódy ended his own life," Csilla said, "you want us to consider as separate questions whether or not his confession is true and whether or not he hid the scissors and the flag circle in his kitchen."

"So what evidence suggests the confession is true?" Balogh said.

"Only his raincoat, which turned up in the park with Kellner's blood stains on it," Ernő said. "Just because the park is on Borsódy's way home doesn't mean that *he* was the one who abandoned the raincoat there."

"That's it as far as physical evidence, leaving aside the scissors and the flag circle," Balogh said. "There's nothing in the flat that indicates a second visit that night."

"But going back to the confession itself," Csilla said, "is it so hard to believe that an argument between two people grew so passionate that it ended with one killing the other in a fit of rage?"

"It's not that I have a hard time believing that Borsódy and Kellner fought," Balogh said. "It's just that I have a hard time believing that in all the years they knew each other, they hadn't fought like that before."

"So why was it only this time that one of them reached for the nearest heavy object to smash the other's skull?" Ernő said, completing Balogh's thoughts.

"Let's assume that the confession *is* false," Csilla said. "Why would someone confess falsely to killing his best friend?"

"Make it simpler," Balogh said. "Why does anyone confess to something he knows he hasn't done?"

"Extortion, or some other form of coercion, the desire to protect another?" Csilla said.

"I'm not sure how easy it would be to wring a false confession out of someone who could see his way to killing himself," Ernő said. "If he had a death-wish, you wouldn't get much leverage with threats."

"No," Csilla said, happy for an excuse to address Ernő directly, "unless you threatened him by threat-ening someone else."

"Maybe you wouldn't have to use threats at all if that someone else were in trouble," Balogh said. "What would you do if you learned that someone you loved had committed a terrible crime?"

"I would turn her in at once," Ernő said and let out a high-pitch squeal that Balogh decided was either a laugh or the sound of pure anxiety.

"Ernő's response is probably unique," Csilla said, "Most people's first impulse would be to shield their loved one from prosecution."

Balogh said: "Who might Borsódy have wanted to protect? I've a fairly good sense of his relationship with Petri, but we'll need to know more about his his-tory with Éva Hegedűs. Let's move on."

"If we're going to consider the possibility that the raincoat was ditched in the park by someone other than Borsódy," Csilla said, "then perhaps we should also consider the possibility that the scissors and the flag circle were planted."

"In that case," Balogh said, "I'll set aside my own proposal that we take the evidence and the confession separately. Would you would try to frame someone with material evidence if you thought he might con-fess and then kill himself?"

"It could've been insurance," Ernő said. "Get Borsódy to say he'll take the fall and then plant the evidence in case he backs out."

"But think about the risk," Balogh said. "Whoever hid the flag circle in Borsódy's dustbin is either the murderer or someone implicated in the murder. He would have to make sure the flag circle couldn't be traced back to him."

"How could he make sure of that?" Ernő said.

"Well, for starters, if he knew the flag was missing from the Ady Square building porter's station, he wouldn't want us to know that," Balogh said, "He'd keep that knowledge to himself."

"Especially since most people still think that the flag found at the murder scene came from the Bartók Square rally," Csilla said.

"Here's something to think about," Balogh said. "Yesterday, my former brother-in-law told me that Petri surprised the porter when he asked about the missing flag on Monday morning."

"How could Petri be that foolish?" Csilla said. Even if we didn't already know that he knew about the Ady Square flag, wouldn't he figure we'd find out soon enough?"

"You would think so," Balogh said. "But maybe he's *trying* to point the finger at himself."

"Why would he do that?" Csilla said.

"Maybe he's counting on us to conclude that he's not foolish enough to incriminate himself," Ernő said.

"That *would* be foolish of him," Csilla said. "People make foolish mistakes all the time. There must be some other reason he would willing to take that risk."

"Because if Petri seems too fast on his feet to plant this evidence *after* he lets on he knew the flag was missing," Balogh said, "then someone who hasn't told anyone that she knows it's missing—because she was the one who stole it—might be more likely to plant it."

"You think Petri is attempting to frame Éva Hegedűs?" Csilla said.

"That's one possibility. There are others." Balogh reeled off a few: "She killed Kellner but Petri, for whatever reason, can't bring himself to turn her in so he's trying to help us out. She killed Kellner and she, not Petri, planted the evidence to implicate Petri even after she, God knows how, got Borsódy to confess to her crime. Petri and Hegedűs are both linked to Kellner's murder but in order to get Borsódy to confess, Petri or Hegedűs had to persuade him that only one of them was guilty and that would be the one, guilty or not, for whom he would most likely sacrifice himself."

"And we can't rule out the possibility that Borsódy is telling the truth," Csilla said.

"Or that Borsódy is telling the truth *and* that someone unaware of his intention to come clean planted the evidence to finger him," Ernő said.

Csilla looked like she wanted to say something. Balogh asked her what was on her mind.

"I was just thinking how difficult it's going to be coming up with a sequence of events in which any of them—Petri, Hegedűs or Borsódy—could have murdered Kellner, walked to the Ady Square building to steal the flag, and returned to Kellner's flat again without being seen."

"That's why I'm beginning to wonder if two or all three of them weren't working together," Balogh said. "Which leads us to the phone records that you've assembled."

Ernő explained again how the mobile-phone records confirmed everything the skinheads said last weekend about the unidentified calls and the news photo just as their testimony on Monday confirmed Ernő's suspicions about the spray paint purchase.

Both skinheads explained how they'd received the captioned news photo of Kellner, Borsódy and Petri one day before they boarded the train for Szeged. They'd used it to find the street addresses of each of victim's residences in the telephone directory shortly after they arrived.

With the news photo, they'd received a cheap mobile phone and a note informing them that the spray paint would be waiting for Zsolt at Petri's house and that they would get paid at the Kéknyelű, where they would also be given a number to call.

"Zsolt dialed the 'wrong number' to Petri who seems to have been waiting for the call in his office," Csilla said.

"What about the call Petri placed just before he answered the wrong number?"

"He called his wife, sir," Ernő said. "The skins were told they should wait for a signal before starting the third job, and at 10:03 Zsolt received a call placed from a pay phone at the railroad station."

"How far a walk is it from Petri's house?" Balogh said.

"Ten minutes," Ernő said.

"We need witnesses," Balogh said. "Find out if a train came in or left around ten. Check with anyone working at that hour in the shops across from the station."

Balogh clasped his hands behind his head and leaned back in his chair. "Petri called Borsódy from home to make sure he'd returned from Kellner's before calling the skins. It must have vexed him that Borsódy didn't mention coming home to an Arrow Cross, but the important thing was that the skinheads make it to Kellner's."

"But why would someone hire the skinheads just to paint some Arrow Crosses and create enough mayhem to make their presence felt in town?" Ernő said. "If Petri had wanted Kellner dead, why wouldn't he go all the way and hire skinheads to do that too."

"That's just it, Ernő," Balogh said. "I'm convinced that Petri planned everything through the last of the Arrow-Cross business, but I don't think he intended either to murder Kellner himself or have someone else do it. Borsódy had been trying to persuade Kellner not to publish his memoirs because he feared for his safety. Petri may have had another reason for wanting to stop this book from being published. And perhaps he thought an Arrow Cross on the front door would be more persuasive than any argument that Borsódy could make. László Kellner's murder wasn't premeditated."

"But you said before that you thought more than one person might be involved in the murder. Do you think that Petri and Hegedűs were both involved?"

"It's possible. It would be nice to know if Éva Hegedűs placed those calls to Petri and Csaba from Kellner's flat."

"I can try Westel again, sir," Csilla said.

"It's also possible that Borsódy was surprised by Hegedűs or vice versa after one or the other killed Kellner in a rage. Both had reasons—unresolved business, a raincoat, a potentially damaging document—for returning to the flat. It wouldn't be the first time that night they'd surprised each other at Kellner's flat."

"What's our next step, sir?" Ernő said.

"I think we want to know if either Petri or Éva visited Borsódy last night."

Balogh's phone buzzed. Csilla rose to answer it.

Balogh asked Ernő: "Do you think that Petri could've made it to Szeged and back to Budapest in time to meet that conference organizer for an evening cocktail?"

"Probably not by train, sir. I'll check the car rental agencies."

Csilla pressed the receiver tightly to her shoulder and whispered: "It's Mr. Uborka. He sounds angry. Something about a reimbursement check and a lawsuit."

Friday, 23 June

CHAPTER FIFTY-FOUR

Arriving alone at the cemetery for István's funeral, Éva had for some time been unable to find the mourning party even though the burial site abutted László's grave. For ten minutes, she strayed over pebbled paths among tombstones, though at no point during her meander was she ever more than fifty meters from the small group of mourners assembling beside István's grave. They'd been screened from view, first by a stand of dark cypress and then by a high, flowering hedge which trembled whenever a light wind passed through its branches, loosening its blooms.

When she spotted a small funeral party, she scanned faces in vain for one she knew, but these all belonged to strangers. Even the sight of László's freshly mounded earth beside a newly dug grave failed to reassure her she was in the right place. She had to ask another mourner whose funeral it was.

Now, under an overcast sky, Éva wondered whether her morning's confusion was born of her inability to absorb István's death. When the Dean had called her Wednesday morning with the news, she'd replied that he'd been buried the day before, having, in her shock, confused István and László. For the moment, she grasped the fact of István's death and the soft notes of her weeping gradually assumed the cadence of those who mourn the suicide. In the trees, a murder of crows clamored.

The hand that proffered the handkerchief belonged to Pál, though, this time, the arm which supported her belonged to Tamás. Both men had known her when she was happy, when she and István had been happy together. But all that had changed.

Where was Sándor anyway? Everything had changed from the moment more than twenty years ago when they'd scuttled up the stairs and out of the little Serbian tavern called Vrnatchka Banja, where they'd often meet for a friendly glass of wine, and onto the sidewalk. Sándor had grabbed her roughly above the elbow and shoved her toward his Trabant. She'd been so surprised by the change in him that for days afterward she would rub her still-sore arm to remind herself how he'd seized her, scared her.

She'd felt only vaguely nauseated from whatever drug he had slipped into her glass, but she could barely remember walking, not a little unsteadily, from the car to the rear entrance of the clinic where they ducked into a freight elevator that stank of fouled linen. She remembered the spare, ugly room. The bed sheets hadn't been changed.

She'd been oddly unable to object when he told her to undress. And she remembered how he'd left the lights on and how she'd stared at the bare bulb hanging from the ceiling. She remembered how he'd pulled her legs apart, rather easily since her strength was gone, and how, having entered her, he tried to kiss her and how she turned away to stare at the wall.

How after each time, he would tell her to stay on her back and to keep her legs spread and how, when she began to cramp from not moving, he'd refused to let her change her position; how after each time, he'd sat down in the chair he'd dragged to the foot of the bed and stared at her as he smoked, drank plum brandy, and said terrible things to her until he'd grow bored and climb atop her again.

The obsequy had begun—still no sight of Sándor—though she didn't hear much of what was said.

She remembered thinking about his wife. She remembered thinking how this wasn't making love. She remembered how, after he had satisfied himself for the third time, he threw her clothes at her and told her to get out. She remembered pulling on her sweater and skirt and leaving the way they entered and, as she walked home in a light autumn rain, praying that István would not be home when she arrived there.

How strange that it was Sándor, a few months later, who'd insisted that she miss her appointment at the abortion clinic when, after much questioning, she'd admitted to him that she was with child and that László had made arrangements for her to terminate the pregnancy before leaving town. And it was Sándor who'd offered to contact the "right" people to manage the adoption. Though she would never trust him again or think of him with anything other than anger coupled with disgust, she accepted his help. She'd never wanted to abort the child and she was eager to avoid doing so despite her apparent willingness, understandable given her compromised position, to follow László's instructions.

She never worried that László would find out that she'd disobeyed his instructions. Since Sándor

had counseled her against László's counsel to terminate the pregnancy, she decided it was unlikely Sándor
had ever told László that the child had been born. She
took what comfort she could take from knowing her
son was alive and in a good home. She drew what
peace of mind she could draw from the strength of
László's promise never to utter a word to István
about the saddest time of her life, and she assumed,
István's as well.

She was old at twenty-three when she came back
to Szeged, having lost her man and given away her
son and with no hope of ever being happy again.
She'd never been the type to dwell on happiness lost
and, though she was embarrassed to admit it, even to
herself, she tended to be hard on those who did. But
her loss had been real and final. Now it was real and
even more final if such a thing were possible.

It didn't have to be that way. Losing István a
second time wouldn't be any less painful for having
found her son, but at least something of the life they
might have lived together as a family might yet be
saved. It's just that she couldn't know for sure that the
boy sitting in jail right now *was* her son, even though
she *felt* he must be. She saw István's face in his, especially in his eyes and around the corners of his mouth.

She now experienced for the first time a phe-
nomenon common among the recently bereaved:
when she tried to remember the sound of István's
voice, she found she couldn't remember his face; and
when she could remember his face again, she could
no longer remember the sound of his voice.

She prayed that she might trade places with
István. She was the one who killed László, yet István,
gallant even in dying, had confessed to the murder to

draw suspicion away from her. She couldn't bring herself to accept István's parting sacrifice since it was not the mother's but the child's life that must be saved. She'd already framed her own confession which she'd make in person to Major Balogh after the funeral. The number 60 bus would take her as far as Mars Square and it was only a short walk to police headquarters from there.

As they started to lower István's coffin into the grave, she feared she might collapse or weep uncontrollably. Her grief finally betrayed her. Without calling out for help or making a noise loud enough to be heard over the squeaking of the pulleys, Éva lost her grip on Tamás's arm and sank helplessly toward the ground as though she'd forgotten how to stand.

CHAPTER FIFTY-FIVE

Krebán was ready for Balogh this time, but the detective tricked him by opening and closing the door fast enough to avoid being struck by the paperclip dispenser the Colonel had smuggled into work for the purpose. The canister came apart on meeting the door's frosted glass and showered the floor with a coppery rain of fasteners.

"Are you coming or going, Balogh?" Krebán said. "Help yourself to some paperclips. Terézia ordered too many last quarter."

"Thank you, sir." Balogh walked over to the desk carrying two documents. He handed the first to Krebán and pointed to the title. Krebán began to read:

```
CONFESSION OF ÉVA HEGEDŰS (Transcript)
Date: Friday, 23 June
Time: 2:36 PM
Officer Present: Major A. Balogh

- Please state your name.
- Éva Hegedűs.
- Do you wish to have an attorney pre-
sent?
- No.
- You have not been coerced into making a
statement?
- No.
- You may begin.
```

– I want to confess to the murder of László Kellner.

– Would you please state the time and day of the murder?

– About half-past ten on the night of 15 June.

– Would you please describe the circumstances leading up to your act?

– I'd been to Professor Kellner's flat earlier that evening to drop off work he'd ask me to type for him. I'd hoped to discuss a personal matter with him at that time, but Professor Borsódy was there and I did not want to discuss the matter with him present. When I tried to bring up the matter indirectly, Professor Kellner rebuked me. I decided to wait until I could speak with him in private. I waited an hour until I was sure that Professor Borsódy had left before returning to the flat.

– Do you think Professor Kellner was expecting you?

– I don't know. He may have been. I'd let myself into the building and went upstairs. Someone had painted a large Arrow Cross on his door along with the word *Szolnok*. I was afraid and knocked. Professor Kellner answered and said that the door was open. So he may have been expecting me. He was at his desk. I asked him if he'd seen the Arrow Cross. He said he had. I asked him if we could talk about the matter I had touched on earlier. He reluctantly agreed. Things went badly from there and we argued.

– Could you say something about the matter itself? Any details you can provide will lend your statement greater credibility.

- You don't believe I'm telling the truth?
- People have been known to make false confessions.
- He'd made me a promise years ago and now it seemed he was about to break it. I reminded him of his word and pleaded with him not to go back on it. He said that while he hadn't felt any compulsion to break it until recently, he wouldn't be bound by a promise he'd never made in good faith. He told me he never would have promised me anything if I'd been reasonable and taken his advice without assurances.
- Would you care to be more specific about the nature of the promise?
- He promised that István Borsódy would never learn of the real circumstances of my leaving him. In the typescript I returned to Professor Kellner that night were several paragraphs in which he revealed the reasons I left István Borsódy. I didn't want István to see them.
- You didn't turn over that document with the draft of the memoirs.
- I destroyed both the originals and the typescript after I talked to you last Friday.
- And the manuscript you turned in, was that the most recent draft?
- I lost it between the time I left the flat the first time Thursday evening and when I went back.
- Did you continue to argue with Professor Kellner?
- No. He ordered me to leave and returned to his desk. As I was walking toward the door, he said that as long as I was going I could throw away the wilted lilacs in the large jug by the door. His request

enraged me for some reason.

I remember dropping the lilacs on the floor and running over to where he sat with his back to me. And I remember hitting him on the head with the jug.

As soon as I hit him, time seemed to slow down and I recall everything. Instead of falling over, he tried to stand. With his back still toward me, he placed one hand on the desk and the other on his chair to steady himself. Then, one of his knees buckled, and as he struggled to stay upright the chair shot out from under his hand and fell over on its side. He lost his balance and collapsed, slamming his head on the side of the desk as he fell to the floor. He didn't seem to be breathing and when I checked for a pulse I din't find one.

– Do you recall whether he was lying on his back or his side?

– I'm not sure, but I think his side.

– What happened next?

– I was still kneeling over him when I heard someone enter the flat. Professor Borsódy was standing in the doorway. He said something about having come back for his coat. I told him that I'd killed Professor Kellner and that if he wanted to call the police I would wait for them to come.

He seemed stunned at first but said he didn't want to call the police, that I should go home and not talk to anyone, that he would handle things. I was too frightened and confused not to listen. The next day, I learned that two skinheads had been caught and were suspected of the crime.

– May I ask you when you decided to confess?

– At Professor Borsódy's funeral this
morning.
– And you're aware that he confessed to
the murder in his suicide note?
– I assumed as much when the police din't
release the contents of the note. I mean
if he had merely written that he was distraught over Professor Kellner's murder,
you would have reported that, right?
– Probably.
– I couldn't let him take the blame for
me, to dishonor himself and his own
memory for me.
– There's no other reason for your confession?
– What will happen to the boys you arrested? Will you drop the murder charges?
– As it happens, they've not been charged
with murder. Why do you ask?
– I don't want others blamed for my actions.
– I can understand that. But I'm surprised by your compassion for the skinheads. You saw how they worked over Mr.
Neumann.
– Can you turn off the machine now?
– As long as you're prepared to sign a
transcript of this statement. After you
read it over of course.
– I'll sign it.

"Well, Major," the Colonel said, pushing the document back across the desk toward Balogh. "What do
you make of this?"

"The status of the Borsódy's confession is un-
changed, since I always assumed he'd drawn it up to
protect the murderer. This doesn't mean he wasn't
involved. As for Hegedűs's confession, I don't know
what to make of it, sir. I just finished reading the

medical examiner's report on the cause of death." Balogh held up the other document. "Some of the details in her confession don't mesh with Korbács's findings."

"For example?"

"The injuries sustained by Kellner as a result of a blow to the head were serious, but the official cause of death is asphyxiation. Fibers from the flag were found in Kellner's mouth and nose. Korbács believes that someone rolled up Borsódy's raincoat in the flag and suffocated the still-breathing though unconscious Kellner with it."

"Go on."

"We knew that Kellner received some cuts to the base of the skull with shards from the smashed jug when he fell. It now seems that he sustained additional lacerations in an area a little higher on the back of the head when someone applied enough pressure to Kellner's face to asphyxiate him with the flag and raincoat. The scattering pattern made by the smashed jug around his head further suggests Kellner was rolled onto his back."

"So Éva Hegedűs is either lying or she's just wrong when she says that Kellner was dead when Borsódy arrived. But let's say she wanted to protect Borsódy's good name by lying about his involvement: how does that change the fact that she's guilty of murder by her own admission? Even if Borsódy finished Kellner off, she's still guilty of manslaughter with intent to kill. Did she say anything when you turned off the recorder?"

"Only that the skinhead Zoltán might be the son she gave up for adoption twenty years ago."

"I knew there was another reason why you seemed lukewarm about her confession. You think her confession is mainly an effort to clear her child."

"The thought had crossed my mind. We both know the skins didn't kill Kellner, but she doesn't know we know that."

"Did she say why she thought Zoltán was her son?"

"She said a mother knows her own child."

"Do you believe her, Balogh?"

"I believe she believes Zoltán is her son."

Krebán spun his chair around to consult Laci Papp's image on the wall. When he spun back to face his chief detective, he said: "I'm sorry, Balogh. I understand your doubts, but we have to run with this. I talked to Budapest this morning and the message was clear: close this case in the next few hours or we'll send some of our people down there, and I don't have to tell you what that means other than to say that Major Prickhead likes his coffee black with lots of sugar."

"I'll charge her, sir," Balogh said.

"No argument?" Krebán said. "I rather like our little skirmishes."

"No, sir. We're not in the business of resolving every last little contradiction that arises during a murder investigation even if the public seems to be of that opinion from reading police procedurals. Éva Hegedűs has supplied us with a motive: a broken promise; and, with the exception of the points I just mentioned, her confession agrees with most of what we know about Kellner's murder.

"Besides, it will actually help matters if we let it out that the case has been closed. Petri disappeared from his conference yesterday, though I doubt there's been foul play. His wife won't admit it, but I think he's been in touch with her."

"So he's flown the coop. Maybe he's shacked up with an attractive Old Church Slavonic specialist in her Buda Hills love nest? Am I right to suspect you have other reasons for wanting to flush him out of hiding?"

"We've good reason to believe that Petri hired the two skinheads to dissuade Kellner from publishing his memoirs. In fact, he seems to have choreographed the whole night of terror just to intimidate Kellner; he'd even arranged to have his own and Borsódy's residences hit to make it look as if the publication of the memoirs might not only endanger Kellner, but those close to him. The second Arrow Cross was intended for Borsódy but there was a mix-up with the addresses."

"You've skimmed the draft of the memoirs by now," Krebán said. "Do they mention Petri?"

"Not by name. It's a case of guilt by association. Even though he doesn't name names, Kellner offers a blanket indictment of his profession, both under socialism and now. Petri's up for a ministry post and I can understand why he, who unlike Borsódy wasn't merely trying to protect Kellner from the extremists, would be nervous about the publication of a work that questions, if only indirectly, his integrity as a scholar and administrator."

"Why wouldn't he express his fears directly to Kellner, who was, after all, his benefactor?"

"He wasn't supposed to have seen the manuscript. Only Éva, who typed it up, and Borsódy, who returned it to Kellner on the evening of the murder, would have read it with the author's consent. But Petri seems to have read parts of it on Éva Hegedűs's pc without her knowledge, and Borsódy might have expressed his concerns to Petri about the memoir as well."

"If Petri hired the skinheads in advance of the date of Kellner's murder, and I assume he did since this sort of exploit takes planning, it's going to be tough making the case that he's the murderer…"

"…Because," Balogh continued the Colonel's line of thought, "he only hired them to scare Kellner into altering or suppressing his memoirs. I've considered that, sir, but I've also considered the possibility that something might have compelled him to pursue more extreme ends between the time he hired the skinheads and the day they came down here."

"You're wondering whether Petri read the contents of the typescript that Éva Hegedűs returned to Kellner on the evening of the fifteenth and why reading them may have provoked him to take more serious measures."

"I'm positive he read them, sir. On the office pc again. Incidentally, someone, probably Petri, doesn't want us to read those pages, because when Éva Hegedűs came to work Wednesday morning, someone had removed her pc's hard drive. As for what they said, we may never know, since Éva Hegedűs confessed to getting rid of both the original and the copy and the most she would tell me was that reading them indicated to her that Kellner had broken his promise to her."

"Petri felt threatened by what he read."

"Once again, sir, I'm not saying that he ever thought about killing Kellner, but things could not have been set up any better if he wanted to insure that the skinheads would take the blame if someone decided to off Kellner that night. On the other hand, he may have finished the job that someone else began."

"You think *Petri* may have suffocated Kellner with the flag and finished framing the skinheads, and then for good measure, set up a second frame by dropping Borsódy's coat in the park. What makes you think Petri wasn't home asleep as he claims?"

"Officer Dániel checked out his story about going right to sleep after he and Officer Horváth left the Petri residence on the night of Kellner's murder. We thought he might have made a phone call to the skinheads from the railroad station later that evening.

"We couldn't find any witnesses at the station, but a girl in the *cukrászda* across the way thinks she saw Petri twice that night. She's certain about the first time. He bought some *pogácsa* a little before nine and complimented her on her nose-ring. She's pretty sure she saw him leaving the station an hour later when she locked up for the night."

"In that case, we'd better track him down, Balogh. Anything else?"

"Seems that little number who played footsie with young Zoltán on the train ride down here last week would like to bring him some homemade cakes, some magazines, and some fresh underwear."

"And you want me to approve the visit."

"She's not family, sir, but she did come forward for questioning. I don't see any harm in letting her see her beau."

"You might ask the prisoner how he feels about it, though if she's as pretty as you say she is, I doubt he'll object. I'm fine with it as long as there's no sex involved. Why should that bald prick get more than I do?"

"Yes, sir."

"Now I've a small favor to ask of you, Balogh. I'd take care of it myself but I get sick just thinking about that shyster Uborka. The fat bastard has just served us because he hasn't been reimbursed for the flag the skinheads stole from Bartók Square. Just pay the prick and have him drop the suit."

"Shall I have the business office send him a check, sir?"

"Why don't you have one of the boys run it over to his office during lunch hour. Call one of your buddies over at the fire department while you're at it. Uborka's office is in an old building. I'd hate to see him fried like a piece of fatback over an open fire because his wiring doesn't come up to code. Due to a peculiarity in his rental agreement, Mr. Uborka gets fined for any fire code violations. Then again, laying down a few hundred thousand forints to modernize one's electrical system is nothing compared to ending one's days as a toasted marshmallow. Don't you agree, Balogh?"

Saturday, 24 June

CHAPTER FIFTY-SIX

"Why have you taken me to Karcag?" Kati said as the bus that had moments earlier let them off at the town's main square and pulled away in a cloud of exhaust.

"Can't a man take his lady friend on a pleasant jaunt to Karcag without arousing suspicion?" Pál said.

"I'm just curious, Pál," Kati said without a hint of suspicion.

"I'm doing a favor for Balogh," Pál said, relenting.

Karcag, he reflected upon completing a visual tour of the square, possessed no more provincial bleakness, no less backwater shabbiness than his own hometown. And he supposed that those who'd put similar distances between themselves and Karcag could likewise be expected to harbor feelings for the old town that grew warmer or cooler in direct proportion to the lesser or greater likelihood of having to return to live there.

When Balogh had asked him to travel to Karcag in search of birth records, he'd refused at first. But the refusal had sounded half-hearted even to Pál: his compassion for Éva and his sadness over István

Borsódy's suicide had won out, though by no means easily, over his desire to stay out of the Kellner case. He'd decided to help Balogh even though his fear was great, fear of learning the truth, not about who killed his once-mentor or why, but the truth that he'd been trying, with great mental and emotional exertion, to keep from surfacing in his consciousness like some long-submerged branch loosed by a violent current from the river bottom.

Until he learned of Borsódy's suicide, Pál hadn't even been aware of the strength of his own desire to avoid the truth. It was only at the poor man's funeral yesterday that he'd considered the possibility that Borsódy killed himself because he'd never been able to confront the real reasons for her leaving, because he lived so long avoiding them that he couldn't live with them when they all came home at once.

Pál gazed south across the square toward the town hall. A blinking bride and groom emerged from the Maria-Theresa yellow building into the bright morning sun while members of the wedding party nudged the squinting newlyweds toward a photographer. Another bride and groom with *their* wedding party waited for the first party to clear the entrance. Though it was a Saturday, Pál bargained that he could persuade the clerk in charge of the civic nuptials to check the birth records. Balogh had provided Pál with a letter for just this purpose.

"Did you get what you came for?" she asked when Pál sat down beside her under an ancient plane tree twenty minutes later.

"Éva gave birth to a boy, but there's no father listed," Pál said. "The child was put up for adoption."

The Angelus began to chime. Pál stood and turned in the direction of the bells. He said: "Shall we visit the priest while we're here?"

"Why, Pál. Are you asking me to marry you?"

Pál led Kati to the church across the square.

Hunched over the engine of an old Wartburg in the dusty shade of black locust trees, the man with broad, sun-burned shoulders—they first mistook him for the janitor—turned out to be Father Tivadar. Wiping engine grease from his hands with a rag, the priest explained that he'd heard of the Hegedűs family, but both mother and father had died years before his installation in this parish and their daughter, an only child, had moved away.

Pál asked about baptismal records, and the priest invited him and Kati into the church, going around back in order to let them in the front. Father Tivadar met them at the church doors wearing his collar and guided them to the small vestry, where in addition to priestly garb, two thick ledgers—one for marriages, one for births and baptisms—were kept. Pál told the priest the date of birth. The ledger revealed that Éva Hegedűs had indeed baptized her child three days after his birth. The church records agreed with those Pál read in the hospital, adding only the name of the father after whom the child was named.

CHAPTER FIFTY-SEVEN

Erzsi tugged at the bow and tore away the blue wrapping paper.

"They won't take it back," Pál said. "So you'd better like it or say you do."

"Thank you, *Apu*," Erzsi said as she studied the Plexiglas and aluminum box with a lamp attached to what looked like a reflecting hood. "What is it?!"

"You said you wanted me to surprise you."

"I am surprised. I just don't know what it is."

"Don't ask me," Pál said, waving his hands. "Some man thrust the contraption into my hands and ran away without telling me."

"Pál, don't torment the child," Ágnes said, smiling. "Just tell Erzsi what it does."

"Why, it's an incubator," Pál said. "You put the eggs in there, turn on the heat lamp, and wait for them to hatch."

Erzsi clapped her hands together. As did Ágnes, from whom, after all, she'd learned the gesture: "That's a wonderful gift, Erzsi. I used to watch the chicks hatch at my grandparents' farm."

"It's for chicks and ducklings and goslings," Pál said. "But the man at the farm across the river said you can hatch whatever you like in there. Ostriches. Auto mechanics. Gorillas. Even dinosaurs."

Erzsi looked at her father in a way she'd also learned from her mother.

"Well, he's got all different kinds of eggs in any event. We can go over there this week and pick out an assortment if you like," Pál said. "I forgot to give you your birthday message."

Erzsi opened a large card in the shape of an egg and read aloud:

Drága Erzsike,

May all your counted chickens hatch!
May all your ducks stay lined up!
May all your geese be silly!

All my love,
Apu

Erzsi threw her arms around her father as he bent down to kiss her.

"It's a wonderful gift, Pál," Ágnes said. "Though she'd love anything that came from you."

"Where are the other guests, Ági?" Pál said.

"Your parents went out for a walk five minutes before you arrived. I'm surprised you didn't pass them on your way here. My brother and Ildikó and the children are on their way." Ágnes paused to address her daughter: "Erzsi, why don't you go down to the lobby to wait for your cousins."

When Erzsi had gone, she said: "Bertalan wanted to wait until he heard from me."

"Don't be foolish. Call him. Tell him to come right over."

"Are you sure it's OK, Pál?"

285

"You act as if I hate the man."

"You pushed him in front of a tram last month," Ágnes said. "I know it was an accident, but—"

"Ági, I offered him my hand in friendship and tripped. The tram was still ten meters away. Didn't I help pull him off the rails?"

Ágnes said nothing.

"He doesn't think that I…"

"No. He just doesn't want to intrude. When we heard you weren't bringing Katalin, we thought—"

Pal's mother and father appeared in the doorway carrying several cartons of strawberries and a loaf of bread. "Call him now, Ágnes," Pál said and walked over to greet his parents.

Balogh arrived with his family just as Pál's father finished relating his triumph over the slugs that had invaded his patch of cucumbers and tomatoes. He moved onto other topics: "I read that your old professor died, Pál. Professor Kellner."

"I attended his funeral on Tuesday," Pál said.

"That's too bad. I'd always wanted to thank him for saving you from the Party." Pál's father's ice-blue eyes still held their glimmer under cumulus white eyebrows that floated up and down, as if by their own will, the wide expanse of his forehead. "I did the best I could to stop you, but if it hadn't been for your professor, I'm not sure you'd have escaped joining. He deserves a father's gratitude for that."

"It's not as if he acted intentionally," Pál said, making his last stand.

"Are you sure?" Pál's father asked without calculation though the effect on Pál was profound.

The possibility that Kellner had meant to force his student's decision had never once occurred to Pál and he wasn't about to entertain it now. Still, he could feel doubt taking hold of the most defining conviction of his life and giving it a good shake.

"And now I'm going to have some more of Ágnes's stuffed cabbage," the old doctor concluded. "It's the main reason I've never forgiven you for leaving her. Because of you, I can only get Ágnes's cooking on special occasions."

Balogh approached and his sister's former father-in-law placed both hands on the detective's shoulders. "Ah, Balogh," he said. "It's good to see you. I'm just going for another roll of your sister's stuffed cabbage. It's good, though not, as I was just telling Pál here, up to her usual high standards." Here, he eyed Pál, who looked back at his father confused. Undaunted at having been caught in a harmless lie aimed at attaining mere animal pleasure, the old man continued: "Well, in any case, Pál, make sure you and Balogh see to it that I get a full five-minute head start before the two of you lay into Ági's stuffed cabbage like Komodo dragons into a goat."

Balogh looked at Pál and raised an eyebrow.

"He's afraid we'll eat it all," Pál said after his father walked away.

"I got that part," Balogh said. "It's the bit about the Komodo dragons that took me by surprise. As comparison go, we couldn't have done much worse."

"I shouldn't worry about it."

"I'm not worried about it," Balogh countered, "It's just that I've been watching nature shows with the kids and these Komodo dragons are repellent. They don't have teeth so they just sort of pull the goat apart but only after they've sickened the poor beast with their bacteria-ridden spit. You see, the Komodos first infect their victim and stalk it until it's too weak to run or defend itself. Many days might pass between first contact and meal time. The victim is in agony most of that stretch."

"You know a lot about these creatures, Balogh. But so does my father. Have you and he been sneaking off to meetings of the naturalist society? What's all this about goats?"

"I just know what I see on TV, but that's enough. Since it's rather difficult to get the dragons on film otherwise, the filmmaker tied a live goat to a stake and let the dragons have at it. Grisly stuff."

"That's why you didn't like my father's comparison. But a stuffed cabbage roll is hardly a live goat. I mean it's already dead by the time we get to it, isn't it? I doubt a stuffed cabbage roll feels anything at all by that point." Pál paused to examine Balogh's gaze. "I don't like the way you're looking at me, Balogh. You're feeling more carnivorous than usual, aren't you? I know because I've begun empathize with that dismembered goat. I'm afraid I must ask you to kindly refrain from gumming any part of my body or showering me with your rancid saliva."

"It's funny, Pál, the whole time I was watching that goat being ripped apart I was thinking how good it is that the human animal is seldom reduced to measures as disgusting as these."

"I'm afraid we do something far worse than what the Kimonos do."

"Komodos, but what's that, Pál?"

"When these Komodos run into a goat on some jungle track, they just think, 'yum, lunch.' They don't even *think*, 'yum, lunch.' We're the ones who find their idea of lunch disgusting and there are some people who feel better about themselves because at least one other creature is more disgusting than we are."

"I cannot imagine that anyone could take consolation from that way of putting things," Balogh said.

"No, but one that did wouldn't enjoy the smallest shaft of illumination from your parable of the Kimono, the goat, and the filmmaker" Pál said.

"It seems that I've taught you something this afternoon, Pál," Balogh said. "Now hurry up and tell me what it is."

"In your parable, Balogh-san, the only genuinely despicable act is the filmmaker's decision to tie up the goat. Nobody forced him to offer up a living thing to the gods of educational programming. The goat is the victim of our evil machinations. The Kimonos no more than ignorantly assist us in our wickedness."

"That's it, Pál," Balogh cried. "I'll never eat stuffed cabbage again."

"Or try to learn anything from educational television," Pál said.

"Next question: what did you learn in Karcag?"

"Éva gave birth to a son and had him baptized before putting him up for adoption."

"And she's got into her head that the skinhead Zoltán is the child she gave up. She thinks she's protecting her own son with her confession."

"Is it possible?"

"Sure, no one outside of my section and the Colonel knows that Zoltán and Zsolt are no longer suspects in the murder case. You're not supposed to know that either."

"I meant is it possible that Zoltán's her son?"

"I don't know how it could be, but there might be a way of proving that he isn't without arousing anyone's suspicions. I've another favor to ask you, Pál. I need you to go to Budapest for me tomorrow."

"Why can't you go yourself?"

"It has to look as if murder case is closed now that we have Éva Hegedűs's confession. If she or Borsódy didn't kill Kellner, we want the murderer to think he's in the clear."

"And you think that you know who the real murderer is." Pál couldn't believe that Sándor could kill anybody, let alone his mentor, but Balogh clearly felt he had cause to suspect him.

"I'm not sure, but he disappeared from a Slavic Studies conference on Thursday. He didn't show up for Borsódy's funeral."

"That surprised me. Maybe something's happened to him."

"I've a hunch he's fine." Balogh looked him straight in the eye: "Pál, I need your help. All you have to do is drop in on Zoltán's parents and find out if he's adopted. See if they know anything about the mother, about where he was born. I'll put you up in a clean hotel and you can travel to Budapest and back in a first-class carriage."

"What if I don't go? What will you do then?"

"What will you do if I don't send you to Budapest tomorrow?"

"Start looking for another bargain excursion to Dalmatia. I've already put Kati off once because of this case."

"What's one more week, Pál?" Balogh tried another tack: "Besides, I know how much you love those Mickey Spillane stories with that trigger-happy private detective of his. What's his name, anyway? Mallet?"

"Hammer."

"Well, here's your big chance, Pál. You get to be Mal— Hammer for a day."

"You think I'd enjoy being shot at?"

"You think Zoltán's elderly adoptive mother is packing heat?"

"I need an hour to think about it. But I have a question for you: did Borsódy think he was protecting Éva and his son by confessing?"

"Do you think she would have told him she'd had a child by him after all these years?"

"If she thought it might save the child's life."

"I thought about that, but if she'd told him the child was still alive, wouldn't she have given him a reason to live? A man doesn't learn he has a son and off himself," Balogh said. "But a man who learns that his one great love had gotten pregnant by him and that she had an abortion rather than tie herself to him might. It wasn't Éva Hegedűs who told him that. Petri left for Budapest right after the funeral last Tuesday, but we think he slipped back into Szeged for a few hours before slipping away again."

"So you think he may have told Borsódy that Borsódy himself had gotten Éva with child all those years ago?"

"And that the pregnancy had been terminated on Kellner's insistence. But in that case, Kellner must have thought that Petri was the father."

"Maybe he was, maybe he is," Pál said. "All right, Balogh, I'll go."

SUNDAY, 25 JUNE

CHAPTER FIFTY-EIGHT

I stood at the middle of Margit Bridge, at the point where the span breaks upriver thirty degrees to make a right angle with the Buda shore. To my right, the sleepy eastern slope of Rózsadomb rose above the Duna's foggy banks, its villas dozing beneath a white blanket of mist. I stood at the middle of the bridge and smoked half a deck of Benson & Hedges 100's. I flicked the butts over the hand rail and followed their descent into the river.

No one else was on the bridge. The mustard yellow Number 6 tram rattled by again, blurred faces looked out from behind fogged-up windows beaded with rain. Cold and wet, I tugged on the lapels of my raincoat, trying to make up my mind. I smoked another cigarette and stared long and hard at the river. I saw a streak on the water and knew by the look of it that there was a snag in the current. Mist curled up off the water.

To my left, on the Pest side, loomed the bleak, dingy White House, the former Party headquarters from which Kádár ruled the People's Republic. At his desk, beneath a painting of Lenin playing chess, the First Secretary played chess for thirty-two years.

Then, Comrade János died. The painting vanished. The state coat of arms that adorned the White House, like the big, red five-pointed star that topped Parliament's great dome, disappeared. Behind me, the wind began to rise, bearing the wet-clay tang of the leafy oak and walnut trees that guard Margit Island. A cold, insinuating rain began to fall. The past never seemed more past.

It was ten o'clock, too early to call on Zoltán's parents. The next train back to Szeged would pull out of Nyugati Station in less than an hour. I couldn't think of a reason why I shouldn't be on it. An old saying ran through my head: *Ez nem az én asztalom.* This is not my table. None of my concern. The dark particulars of Zoltán's birth and adoption by a couple who, even now, were no doubt waiting to learn whether their only child would the leave world of light for years of prison night saddened me.

Sad too, and bewildering, the impossible and impossibly obscure string of accidents that had lead the child back to Szeged, the city of his maculate conception, charged with dire purpose. Had he begun to sense the dire purpose of the one who'd charged him only once the cell door slammed shut, enclosing the deceived youth within thick walls, damp and rimed with mold?

Ez nem az én asztalom. Zoltán is not my child. Poor Éva killed Kellner out of rage and grief for her lost son. Dear Borsódy killed himself out of grief for his lost love—I prayed he'd not been led to believe he'd lost a son as well. Then, Éva confessed to clear her son of murder. The wretched circle was complete. Balogh had even closed the case. Why couldn't he leave the past alone?

I understood the official reasons why Balogh couldn't come to Budapest himself, why he'd asked me to travel here instead, to search for answers, which, if found, would neither bring two dead scholars back to life nor lessen the pain of those whose lives had been changed forever by their deaths. The case file may have been closed, but so many questions turned up like so many old bones by the investigation's harrow refused to be plowed under again. I even understood Balogh's "unofficial" desire to uncover the sequence of visible and invisible actions that led to Kellner's death, even if that meant going back two decades to Kellner's original counsel to a distraught young Eva. In short, I understood Balogh's yearning to know the whole truth. I simply didn't share it.

For I was haunted by the presence of other "unofficial," unspoken reasons for keeping the investigation alive, grounds unimagined by Balogh, who, surely, meant me no harm. Something like fate must have brought Zoltán back to Szeged to help bring about the death of the man who twenty years ago had insisted that Éva terminate her pregnancy. Something like fate might be guiding Balogh's desires and my own actions now, but to what terrible end. Unlike Balogh, I could not imagine how this search might yield knowledge that could heal those who received it rather than wound them even more. *Ez nem az én asztalom.*

So I don't know what carried me the wrong way across Margit Bridge to the Király Baths on Fő Street in Buda's Viziváros district. Perhaps the thought of riding back to Szeged soaked to the skin had sent me in search of thermal waters and an hour or so during which my clothes might dry. I passed through a low door into the steamy embrace of the Turkish bath, fragrant with chamomile and crisscrossed by ghostly beams of colored light born of apertures in the Ottoman dome above.

I slipped into the octagonal pool and closed my eyes. I opened them again and saw a tanned, bald man smiling at me through the scented mist hovering just above the surface of the water.

"*Mellick vadjuke*," he said in barely intelligible Hungarian and wiped his brow with a moist hand adorned with many rings, some with stones.

I responded in English: "I think you mean to say *melegem van*: 'I'm warm'. *Meleg vagyok* translates: 'I'm a homosexual'."

"*Mellick vadjuke*," he said, continuing to flash his teeth at me.

"How nice for you."

"You wanna go back to my hotel room?"

"Not really."

His smile showed no sign of giving out. I put him down for an American. He seemed to be having trouble with his vision, widening and narrowing his eyes several times and then began to blink uncontrollably.

I was explaining that each pool boasted different healing properties and that he might ask one of the staff to recommend the best one for eye ailments when he grew impatient and said: "Don't you know a come-hither look when you see one?"

"Apparently not."

"Aren't you gay?"

"No."

"You know, where I'm from, the baths are gay."

"I didn't know there was such a thing as gay water."

The man burst into shrieking laughter.

"You are *too* funny. I'm just saying you'd never find a straight male at a Manhattan bathhouse."

"Where do straight men go to wash?"

Bewildered, the American wrinkled his nose, regarded me for a moment and once again erupted in screams of mirth. "O my Gawd! You're a riot. I'm taking you back to New York with me. I'm Artie Needleman. And you are?"

"Pál,"

"Pawhl."

"Pál."

"Pa-a-ahl."

"Perfect," I lied.

"Can I ask you a question, Pohl?"

"By all means," I said, wondering why Americans always asked if they could ask a question before they asked one.

"I've heard that you Hungarians are the wildmen of Europe, but please!" He held up the little cotton apron provided for the bather's modest passage to and from the heated pools. "I mean, what is this? Tarzan's loincloth? Do these come in leopard-skin?"

Before I could figure out which of these questions he expected me to answer, he'd asked another.

"What else do you want to know about me?"

"You've told me so much about you already, Mr. Needleman."

"Artie. Just humor me. I want to feel exotic. I never feel exotic."

"Of that you need not worry. Is this your first trip to Budapest?"

"Landed at Hairy Fairy Airport last night."

"Ferihegy, but close enough."

"There must be something else you want to know about me?"

"Do you like your work?"

"I buy women's sportswear for a large discount chain in America. What's to like? Next question."

"Who do you love, Artie?"

"Well, *this* is getting rather intimate."

"We're very direct, we Magyars."

"I like that. Let's see. There's my mother, Mrs. Naomi Feldman of Pompano Beach, Florida. There's my dachshund, Mr. DeMille. I loved a man named Rey. And I loved a man named Sol. The last two are dead."

"I'm sorry, Artie."

"Rey was my lover for twenty years. I lost him to cancer a year ago."

"I'm sorry."

"Sol was my father. Stepfather actually. I never met my real father. Sol survived Auschwitz and found his way to New York where he got a job in a candy factory working for next to nothing. Ten years later, he had his own men's shop. He was sixty when he married my mother. She was in her late twenties. I was a rather precocious nine-year-old whose chiefest joy was dressing up our kitty-cat in satin gowns and tiaras."

"Did Sol know you were *meleg*?"

"I'll say. I worked at his store after school and in the summer. When I was fifteen, he caught me in the stockroom with a Puerto Rican boy my own age. He just said 'excuse me' and closed the door."

"What did you do?"

"I let my friend out the back and went looking for Sol. He was folding shirts out front, acting as if nothing happened. I didn't know what to say so I starting folding shirts too. When we ran out of shirts, he said, 'To your mother I will say nothing. But you should maybe tell her about these feelings you have. She will understand.' I asked him if he understood. He said, 'What's to understand? There's not so much love in this world, Arthur. When it finds you, you don't push it away.' He told me that when his little son died of typhus in the camps, he swore to God that he would never love a child like that again. Then he looked right at me—he had the kindest eyes I've ever seen—and said he was glad God hadn't listened to him. I cried for a month when he died."

"You were fortunate to be loved by a man like that."

"Did you have a Sol in your life?"

"My father. He'll be seventy-nine next month. Perhaps one other."

"Is he dead?"

"Yes, he is dead."

"I'm sorry."

"We hadn't spoken in years."

"Did you forgive him?"

"No, I didn't forgive him."

"Did he forgive you?"

"I don't know."

"I bet he did."

"Thank you, Artie."

Ez nem az én asztalom. This is not my table. Zoltán is not my son. László Kellner was not my father. I was determined to walk back to Nyugati Station and board the next train back to Szeged, but I turned the wrong way off Margit Boulevard and found myself climbing Rózsadomb instead.

They lived off Rómer Flóris Street in what had once been a summer cottage, a whitewashed one-story with a red-tiled roof. She was tending to her roses in the front yard. He was on the side of the house threading the tendrils of cucumber vines through the often-mended cross-strips of an ancient trellis. They were old.

I told myself that I would stand at their front gate for ten more seconds and if they didn't notice me, I'd leave. I was about to turn and go when she saw me. She called to her husband with no more concern than if she'd spotted the letter carrier.

"Can we help you, *uram*?" he said, walking over to stand beside his wife.

"I'm here about your son."

Monday, 26 June

CHAPTER FIFTY-NINE

I couldn't breathe. The air reeked as if every man, woman and child in Pest had lit up—this was by no means a statistical impossibility here in the land of the wheeze and the home of the asthmatic—and simultaneously exhaled the acrid inhalations of several hundred thousand noisome Russian cigarettes. Guided by a smoky logic only a fellow tobacco user could appreciate, I did what any rational partaker of that fragrant weed would do: I lit up too.

The rank river fog had worked its way into every corner of this gray Pest morning, lingering over iridescent pools and sliding through the bars of rusted factory-yard gates. This fog wasn't like Mr. Eliot's feline mist yellowly rubbing its muzzle on windowpanes, rubbing its back upon windowpanes. This fog liked the sound of breaking glass and, having, in its day, smashed more than a few panes and set off more than a few half-hearted alarms itself, would gladly convey shattering news over a row of office buildings to another street.

Angyalföld. Angel's Land. Right away. Somewhere someone must've been having a good laugh at this former "Red" district's expense. I'd not slept well last night, so I wasn't in a laughing mood. Besides, a quick look round one of the largest and last of old Budapest's breeding grounds of working-class agitation and unrest would convince even the most nostalgic prole romantic that the district had been christened by the same perverse naming-spirit that had led a lusty Leif or ruddy Erik to dub that god-forsaken Arctic waste "Greenland." Angel's Land. Nothing doing.

A hundred years ago, this angelic ground was Budapest's answer to Old Chicago's ironbound district. Then, the capital's drumming factories and humming plants burgeoned on either side of the Váci Road, resembling, with their smokestacks, so many inverted toadstools fashioned of iron and brick. Now, car showrooms and shopping malls lined the ancient way to Vác. And though the workers had held on as long as they could even after the last of the factories closed, there couldn't have been more than a few flats left in the district that hadn't been swallowed up by the prefab monstrosities of late state socialism.

I checked the address on the envelope that Zoltán's parents gave me. The man who lived there had faithfully sent money for the boy's care, on behalf of the biological father, each month for more than twenty years.

I turned onto Klapka Street, found the pre-war apartment building where he lived, and made my way inside. Fodor answered the door in a shabby woolen robe and corduroy slippers. Age had lent all of them—the man, the robe, the slippers—an indeterminate color. He was tired-looking, bald, and short, but mostly just old. His teeth were bad. A strange combination of amusement and malice flashed in his sharp black eyes. I thought the gaze might signal the survival of ancient training in the arts of menace and tried not to hold it against him.

I introduced myself and told him why I'd come. He waved for me to follow him through the cheerless flat to a drab kitchen. Fodor sat down at the kitchen table and began cutting up a fried egg with his fork. A bright green ring of pepper lay half-on, half-off the plate.

"Sit down, Professor Berkesi. You don't mind if I have my breakfast while we talk?" Without waiting for an answer, he folded a slice of white bread and dipped it in a puddle of greasy yolk. The dripping yellow mass more or less made its way past his lips. But as the crumbs and daubs of yolk gathered in the corners of his mouth and on his chin, I began to wonder if the old man's refusal to make use of the napkin that lay folded beside his plate was part of an effort to establish psychological advantage. Why else would one about to be questioned adopt the techniques of one who questioned others for a living? Perhaps Fodor was not an adoption lawyer after all.

"Professor Berkesi," he said, pushing aside his plate, "You want information about a young man in trouble. What makes you think I can supply you with this information?"

"I'm told by this young man's parents that you may have been responsible for his adoption and that you continue to serve as an agent for the biological father."

"The arrangement is an informal one. I'd already known the father for many years when he got a woman who wasn't his wife with child and he requested my assistance in placing the child in a good home."

"When you say the arrangement is informal, do you mean that you're neither an attorney nor affiliated with the state adoption services?"

"You flatter me by using the present tense, Professor Berkesi. I've been retired for many years. But no, I was neither of these. I'll save you some time and tell you I served the former regime in several capacities, which placed me in a unique position to help my friends.

"Had the father gone through the usual channels, he would have had no further contact with his son, unless the child himself, reaching his majority, sought a relationship with either or both of his biological parents. The father found this condition unacceptable since his marriage had failed to produce a boy, though he has two healthy girls."

I considered how Hungary's tribal past sometimes still asserted itself in shaping her people's attitudes concerning sons and daughters. Even now, parents often spoke only of the boys in a family as children, so that was customary in some quarters for a father of, say, two sons and a daughter to say he had two children and a girl. As the father of Erzsi this way of thinking was alien to me.

I'd rarely encountered Fodor's brand of quiet self-assurance and cool authority among the bureaucrats with whom I'd been obliged to deal all my life. Many civil servants made a show of exercising largely nonexistent power. Such shows were grand in inverse proportion to the bureaucrat's actual authority. Judging from Fodor's blasé manner and tone, I guessed that this enfeebled man had once wielded real power while shunning such displays.

Fodor said: "Professor Berkesi, you have the information you came for. You may have more questions, but I am not inclined to answer them."

"I was hoping to learn the name of Zoltán's biological father."

"I've told you as much as I want to, and, may I suggest, as much as you need to know." Fodor rose to his feet. I remained seated. He began to clear the table.

I felt chill as it dawned on me that this decrepit little man washing dishes might have been an *ávós*, a former operative of the State Security Department, and, then, after the sinister ÁVO was "dissolved" following First Secretary Rákosi's fall, an agent of the special III./3 division of the secret police.

For a moment, I even imagined that Fodor was none other than the squat, bald, and ill-favored Rákosi himself, the Muscovite Magyars still called "Stalin's dog." That vile politician still suffered the indignity of having the marble cube containing his ashes smeared with all manner of shit during informal rites of desecration conducted fortnightly within the walls of Farkasréti cemetery.

If I was right about Fodor's avocation, by what means might I get him to say more than he already had? I knew what Mike Hammer would have done. How many times had I read scenes in which Spillane's shamus worked over unwilling informants or likely suspects?

In the closing pages of *One Lonely Night*, Hammer squeezed the life out of "the greatest Commie louse of them all," even as he explained to the dying man that he'd be to blame for the death of his Party. Hammer had laughed a little as he watched Oscar

Deamer's face turn ten shades of black. The avenger's laugh was the only sound on a snowy winter's night in New York City.

Yet watching Fodor shuffle around in his ill-lit kitchen was enough to persuade me that I didn't have the stomach to deal with commie agents the way Hammer did. Besides, I needed a way to get Fodor talking again, not to turn him into a slobbering fool.

Fodor hadn't exactly asked me to leave. If he'd been an *ávós*, he might not have many friends: a few former contacts, one or two fellow agents as old and frail as he. It was just possible that Fodor was enjoying my company, that he was lonely and that he wouldn't mind if I stuck around.

"I'll be going now, Mr. Fodor." I rose and turned to leave.

"I was just going to make coffee," Fodor called after me. "Won't you have a cup?"

"I don't think so," I said and continued walking toward the door.

"A shame," he said. "You know, Berkesi, we might have met long ago had circumstances been different. You let down old Kellner terribly when you refused to join the Party."

I turned around to look at Fodor: "How do you know about that?"

"I don't have to tell you."

I turned the knob and pulled the door open wide.

"Did I say I wouldn't tell you?"

I closed the door halfway.

"I was active at the universities at one time," Fodor said. "Come back inside."

I kicked the door shut: "You knew Professor Kellner?"

"Of him." He set two cups on the table. "We never met."

"How do you know he was angry with me for not joining the Party."

Fodor smiled. "How do you drink your coffee?"

"Black. Did Kellner know about your activities?"

"He may have sensed our presence within the University, but he knew little of our operations. He wasn't someone we could trust. We never approached him."

"It's strange to hear you speak of trust."

"Why? Because we didn't trust Kellner? He'd been with Nagy."

"Only because your type never trusted the people."

"You're not that naïve. Our interest in ordinary people's lives had nothing to do with trust."

"What did it have to do with then?"

Fodor bared his cracked and yellow teeth in lieu of a smile: "Why, love. What else. Didn't you know that?" He laughed a little. "Who could have loved them more than the secret police? Who else, with unflagging interest, listened while they talked about their lives? Who else wanted to learn everything about them?"

"Now you're being perverse."

"Really? Can you come up with a better definition of love than constant attention and earnest care?"

"Your love killed many in the interrogation rooms of Andrássy, No. 60," I said as I recalled how this elegant address had housed successively Horthy's secret police, the Arrow Cross, and after the communist *coup d'etat* of 1948, the ÁVO.

"If some died there as you say, Berkesi, it was only because they rejected our love. But let's not argue. For there's another kind of love in which we excelled. Our actions expressed without reservation what every man who loves his country wishes in his heart of hearts: the subjugation of all but a few of his fellow citizens."

"Not every man," I said.

"That's easy for you to say now, thirty years *after* you lost your chance to run with the wolves. We had our eye on you for years. You showed great promise."

"I don't know what you're talking about."

Fodor ignored my objection: "We were just waiting for Kellner to invite you to join the Party so we could approach you through the usual channels. He chased you off and offered us Petri instead. His timing couldn't have been worse for us or for you."

"What do you mean?"

"'68 was a difficult year for the secret police, here, and in Czechoslovakia. And to think, we nearly had you then. You've no idea how close we were to having you in Prague."

I fought off the temptation to sound him out further on Prague, on Jan, on Zdena. I had to believe he knew nothing about what happened to the Hodeks in the days after the Russian invasion. Our secret police had enough to do here putting out fires wherever anyone fanned the newly glowing embers of Magyar liberty.

Even though I'd never beat Fodor at his game, I thought of how I might put him on the defensive by stating as a fact the question I'd most wanted him to answer: "So, you recruited Sándor. You recruited Sándor as an informer and, years later, his son as a neo-Nazi thug."

He glared at me. "I think you'd better go now, Professor Berkesi."

"I'll go. Just tell me this: have you told Sándor Petri why you sent his only son to be framed for László Kellner's murder? Does Sándor know that the boy sitting in Szeged jail is his son?"

I made for the door again. This time, I walked right through it.

CHAPTER SIXTY

"Is that a *pork* cutlet?" I pointed to a grayish patty on a roll. I'd ducked into a sandwich joint across the street from Fodor's building in case the retired secret policeman stepped out for some air.

"If you like," the counterman said, and laughed a vaguely mocking and trailing-off sort of laugh that made me want to put my fist in his mouth.

"Are these fresh?" I pointed to a tray of sandwiches corseted in plastic wrap. The counterman said nothing but his expression told me that I must be very crazy and slow-witted to ask such a question. "Just give me a black coffee and some sunflower seeds," I barked at him.

I had it figured for a long wait. I ordered a second cup of coffee and surrendered to the sagging charms of a ham sandwich sweating in its cellophane wrapper. Back at my window seat, I folded back the top slice of bread and sniffed at an infinitesimally thin pinkish transparency draped over a flaccid lettuce leaf and a withered slice of tomato. Not enough animal flesh there to sustain the heartiest germs for long. I wolfed it down, following it with two more.

When I finished my third coffee, I tried calling Balogh at his office, but only got his answering machine. I didn't leave a message.

"Do me a favor, buddy," I said to the counterman who was now smiling at me in this terribly benign way that made me want to throttle him. Instead,

I threw down a thousand forint note. "See that building over there? Keep an eye on the entrance and see if an old man comes out while I go for a leak."

His expression didn't change. I took that for a yes and stepped out back.

He was wearing the same smile when I returned a few minutes later.

"You can pour me another," I said. He reached for the coffee pot and refilled my cup. "I guess no one left the building while I was gone."

"I thought I was looking for an old guy."

"That's right."

"One left ten seconds after you went out back," he said, then pointing out the window and to his left: "He turned up that street."

I took off after Fodor, sure I'd lost him. Somewhere up ahead a car started and I saw a black Pobeda pull out of an alley and head up the block away from me until it took a right at the next corner. I was relieved when it vanished; it had been a favorite with the authorities and when people dreamed, as they still did, of knocks on the door before dawn, it was usually a Pobeda in which they were driven away. I was still walking, thinking about my next move when the Pobeda, having circled the block, screeched to a halt beside me.

"Get in, Professor Berkesi," Fodor said.

"Thank you, but I'd rather walk."

"I said get in."

"I said I'd rather walk."

Fodor continued to watch me as he addressed the massive skinhead who'd emerged from the driver's seat and was now hastening toward me around the car: "Ferkó, help the professor into the trunk since he refuses to ride with us in the cabin."

Ferkó—the name filled me with dread—reached inside my jacket and relieved me of my cell phone. Then, the ape lifted me with one hand and, folding me under his arm like a newspaper, opened the trunk with the other, dropped me into it, and slammed it shut. While my skills as a "tail" had just been shown to be sorely lacking, any embarrassment I might have felt was overshadowed by the knowledge that I was being escorted to an unknown destination by a sadistic *ávós* and his bone-crushing giant. I drew what consolation I could that I'd been spared the sight of traffic rushing toward us.

The Pobeda came to rest fifteen minutes later. Through the good offices of Ferkó, I was lifted out of the trunk and marched into a disused factory. It occurred to me that we'd not even left Angyalföld or if we had we'd only driven a few kilometers up the Váci Road.

Once inside, I was jostled into a janitor's closet. I heard a click and a hanging bulb revealed a stool, a tin washbasin, and a wooden box of empty blue siphon bottles. The room smelled of disinfectant.

"You're gonna have to wait here till he's ready for you," Ferkó said. "I cleaned it up a bit. There're some goose fat and onion sandwiches and a few cans of diet grape soda on the ledge over the sink. It's all I could do on short notice."

Having surprised me with his delicacy, Ferkó closed the metal door behind him. I heard the key turn in the lock.

On the ledge with the sandwiches and the soda cans, three dog-eared paperbacks lay. I glanced at the first title, then at the second and third, and set them down again. Georges Simenon wrote more than two hundred novels, seventy-five of which feature Inspector Maigret and his swollen liver. What were the odds that the janitor's library would consist exclusively of *Maigret chez le Dentiste*?

By the time Ferkó came back for me, I'd read through the *policier* twice and was in the midst of adding up the liters of wine, plus aperitifs and beers, quaffed by Maigret from the time he finds the lifeless body of the attractive hygienist strapped to the dentist's chair, a hapless victim of Dr. Nox's brand-new, high-speed drill, until he wrings a confession out of an odd little Belgian from whom Nox purchased dentures made from ordinary household items.

Ferkó took me to a large space feebly illuminated by moonlight shining through dirty windows overhead. The space was filled with shadows of the size Ferkó's frame might cast against a high wall. But shadows were seldom free-standing, nor did they possess the dimensionality of great forms.

Someone pulled a switch and I found myself surrounded by giant cast bronze or carved and polished stone figures of Lenin, of Stalin, of brawny industrial workers joining hands with able-bodied farmers. It occurred to me that this is where the surplus agitprop had ended up once Statue Park was full. Just beyond the city limits, that post-Soviet sculpture garden, resembling an outsize miniature golf course for Marxist ideologues, served as the final resting place for much of Budapest's demoted statuary after the changes of '89.

"Where did all these statues come from?" I asked Ferkó as he pushed me down into a chair and made short work of binding me to it.

Yet it was Fodor, wearing a blue artist's smock over a shirt and tie, who answered me: "I thought you might enjoy seeing my work."

On the base of the nearest statue, an out-of-place sculpture of the Romanian fascist Ion Antonescu, the carved inscription read: **CSORBA '97**. I checked two or three other signatures, all identical to the first though the dates differed. My mind not only balked at making sense of Fodor's claim that he'd created these works when they were signed by Csorba, a name I dimly recognized; it couldn't get itself around another recognition: that these figures were not the mass-reproductions that survived the change of regime eleven years ago but recently carved or newly cast originals.

"None of these works bears your name," I said.

"They do. They just don't bear the name 'Fodor'," he said. "Csorba is my anti-Bolshevik tag. In Bolshevik circles, I go by Fodor."

"But the statues are all signed Csorba," I said. "You don't extend that distinction to them based on subject."

"Only Csorba, alas, is a sculptor. But I take your point: since Csorba heads the *Anti-Bolshevik League*, you're not surprised to find a fascist like Ion here. You can't see him but General Franco is just over there behind Marshal Tito. It's the presence of the communists that troubles you." Fodor-Csorba smiled in a way that was meant to reassure me he wasn't crazy. "But fascist, communist: these distinctions are meaningless to me. Mere ideology. I honor these men not for their political affiliations but for their knowledge of the human heart and the love they bore their people."

I'd heard about a kind of love that sometimes grew between torturer and victim, terrorist and hostage, guard and prisoner. But Fodor had another kind of love in mind, one that began in the fiercely held conviction that the heart demands complete submission and that only the tyrant understands our most secret longing for cruelty and repression. If Stalin once called writers "the engineers of the soul," in this view who but Stalin and his fellow despots merited the designation "the sculptors of the heart?" It dawned on me that Fodor had brought me here to die as an expression of such love.

Out from behind the enormous statue of a exultant worker of the world who'd lost nothing but his chains, Ferkó wheeled an enormous auto battery of improbably high voltage from whose terminals ran cables with copper alligator clamps on both ends.

"Are you sure you charged it properly this time, Ferkó?" Fodor-Csorba said. "I don't have to remind you how embarrassed we all were the other day when we ran out of juice in the middle of a sensitive line of questioning."

"She's been charging all morning."

"I hope so, Ferkó," Fodor-Csorba said, his tone admonitory. "Now, would you kindly unbuckle our guest and get him out of those trousers. I doubt he'll be able to do so unassisted."

I teetered on the brink of consciousness as Ferkó approached gripping and releasing the alligator clamps, looking rather like a hardened veteran of the late shellfish wars, whose valor had earned him both gratitude and a pair of prosthetic claws from his arthropod brothers and sisters.

"I'm afraid that's not what I had in mind, Fodor úr," Sándor Petri said. I hadn't seen him come in, having been overly preoccupied with the first clamp about to find a tender mark below my waist.

"Please have Ferkó put that apparatus away and send him home," Sándor continued. "I don't think Pál will need much persuading to tell us what we want to know."

Fodor-Csorba said: "Ferkó, unclip our guest and then why don't you take the rest of the evening off."

Ferkó must have shrugged like a child and removed only the first clamp for, much to the relief of the pain centers placed at regular intervals around my brain, he hadn't yet applied the second, and sulked off with the battery in tow. I say "must have" because I'd swooned as the nose of first clamp was tucked snugly into place. Otherwise, I'm sure I would have experienced something akin to my nervous system's newly restored peace of neuron.

I revived to find myself back in pants, short and long, and Sándor wallowing a half-tumbler of good whiskey under my nose.

"Have a snort of this, Pál," he said, lowering the rim of the glass to my lips. "I'm sorry about that crude display of intelligence-gathering methods. No one will be subjected to torture on my—say, Pál, you're looking better already."

"Thank you, Sándor. Under the circumstances–"

"Don't say another word," Sándor said and then, turning to speak to Fodor-Csorba: "By the way, Pál is just as curious as I am."

"Curious about what?" the old sculptor said.

"About when you were going to tell me that you recruited my only son for the frame-up in Szeged,"

Sándor said. He drew a pistol from his sport coat and aimed it at Fodor-Csorba.

"What are you complaining about? You told me to send you two skinheads to make some criminal mischief," Fodor-Csorba said, and, without waiting for an answer, sprang, if an arthritic old man may be said to spring, out of the line of fire.

The first shot hit V. I. Lenin in the right hip.

The second shot winged Josef Stalin.

The third shot entered Fodor-Csorba's skull near its base and, meeting little resistance from brain wall and brain during its gradual ascent, easily shattered the cheekbone just below the left eye socket, punctured the bloodless flesh of the upper cheek, and, breaking free from Fodor-Csorba's orbit, lodged itself in Friedrich Engels's groin.

Agent Fodor-Csorba of the defunct ÁVO died, one might say, in mid-flight, though his body, sensible only of its own forward momentum and thus unaware that its animating principle had flown, carried him forth in two or three more mechanical strides before he crumpled like a trampled paper lantern at the great stone feet of Karl Marx.

CHAPTER SIXTY-ONE

"*Ja*!, Sándor said, marveling at his own marksman-ship. "I haven't fired a pistol since National Service." I marveled at his casual tone. He'd just killed a man, after all, even if the man he killed had wanted to kill me. "I guess all those hours on the firing range served me well, Pál. And to think, I hated shooting practice even more than marching."

"How did you know?" I said.

"That he'd set me up?" Sándor said, "How do you think these ÁVO types get their kicks? First commandment: Come up with something on every-one. The only thing he had on me is my son. I knew what I was getting into when I asked Fodor to act as go-between in the adoption. With these guys, it's all about control."

"And it's not about control with you?" I said, re-alizing at once that I'd forgotten the second com-mandment: Never antagonize a man with a gun.

Sándor exhibited the restraint of one with an in-surmountable advantage: "I can understand why you might think so, Pál, but I'm just trying to hold on to what I have."

He untied me from the chair, unbinding my an-kles and knees so I could stand.

I turned around and offered him my bound wrists.

"That's enough for now, I think," he balked, and changed the subject back to Fodor: "I knew he'd try to place himself in an even stronger position someday by recruiting my son for the *Anti-Bolshevik League* as Csorba. Six months ago, through various channels, I learned he'd succeeded."

"Weren't you worried for the boy's safety?"

"I'd been able to keep an eye on Zoltán indirectly for all these years without Fodor knowing. Had I intervened in any way, he would've have found out. My son would have been in even greater danger."

"I don't see how, Sándor. The boy's in trouble."

"That was inevitable, I'm afraid. I figured the chances were good that Fodor would send Zoltán to Szeged as one of the boys I'd requested. It was high time he tested me to see if I knew anything about my son's activity within the *League*. So there wasn't much I could do to save the boy from jail if he was caught."

The nonchalant manner in which Sándor explained everything was getting to me. He'd given a hostage not to Fortune, who at least occasionally smiled on her captives, but to a man who was the human face of absolute injustice. If most people didn't visualize someone like Fodor when they imagined what evil might look like, that just showed how treacherous the dead agent had really been. That Sándor could remain so unmoved while recounting Fodor's one-man assault on human decency showed how there was nothing another human being could do, no matter how wicked or vile, that Sándor hadn't considered and, possibly, wouldn't consider doing himself.

"He's facing murder charges, Sándor!"

"He'll be cleared."

"You sound confident about that."

"My son has nothing to do with Kellner's murder." Sándor said, as much to reassure himself that he hadn't further endangered his child as to assert his claim's truth.

"I don't know how you can sound so sure of that, unless you know who the murderer is. Did Éva intend to kill Kellner?"

A long pause. "Yes."

I hadn't expected Sándor to cop to Kellner's murder, but I hadn't expected the answer I'd gotten either. Or maybe I had and just wasn't prepared to accept it.

"Did you know that she confessed, Sándor?"

"I thought she might, especially after István killed himself."

"She insists she killed László, then István made it look like another Szolnok."

"That's essentially what happened."

"What do you mean 'essentially'?"

"I mean except for one or two details, her account is accurate."

"László wasn't dead when you got to the flat, was he?"

I instantly regretted saying this. Instead of letting sleeping adverbs lie, I'd surprised myself by insisting on the whole truth. Someone was right after all. There *was* a first time for everything, though I'd guess that few first timers had ever felt as painfully aware as I did that my first time would probably be my last.

"No. He wasn't."

"But you're content to let Éva rot in jail for his murder?"

"You see, Pál. There you go too far. You insist on ignoring two facts. First, Éva is convinced that she killed László. She needs to believe that she killed him. For taking her happiness from her. Second, she thinks her confession has spared the young man she thinks may be her son a long stay in prison. I just don't see how disabusing her of either notion could be seen as an act of compassion."

A smile crept across Sándor's face.

"I have to admit, Pál, this exchange strikes me as little absurd. I mean, here I am, pointing this loaded gun at you and you accuse me of murder. The fact that I'm still armed seems to carry no weight with you."

"I wouldn't say that," I said, trying to make Sándor feel more menacing. "I'm actually quite terrified."

Which was true, though I was too paralyzed with fear to appear frightened.

"Come off it, Pál. I'd understand if you thought I wanted to keep you alive when I shot Fodor, but my action wasn't motivated by any desire to save your life. Leaving you tied up can't be good. If I were in your shoes, Pál, I'd take things more seriously."

A quick glance at my decrepit oxfords nearly prompted me to object that no serious person would be caught dead in my shoes. The likelihood of *my* being caught dead in them was increasing moment by moment.

"I'm sorry, Sándor," I offered instead. I *was* sorry, for more reasons than I could enumerate.

"I'm the one who's sorry, Pál," Sándor said. "But with you gone, there'll be no one else who knows that Zoltán is my son."

"Balogh will put the pieces together. He'll figure out your role in this."

"He's got no physical evidence on me. What he does have are signed confessions from both István and Éva. All most policemen want is a neat story."

"You don't know Balogh. He's wants the truth."

"We should get going."

"Where are you taking me?"

"Not far."

"Are you going to shoot me when we get there?"

"Not unless you give me cause." He sounded as if he meant it. "Actually, I was hoping I could encourage you to take your own life."

"With the same sort of encouragement you offered István?" I stared at the pistol.

"I felt terrible when I heard that István swallowed those pills. It was never my intention that he kill himself. I merely led him to see for himself that by confessing he could save Éva from spending the rest of her life in jail."

"That's all it took?"

"I may have said something about Éva's reasons for leaving him."

"Don't be so modest, Sándor. You obviously played István like a gypsy plays his violin. I'm surprised he didn't slip you a few forints."

"Pál," Sándor said, "if I I'd known going in that my efforts at persuasion would turn out to be so effective, I never would have planted the flag evidence. Now come on. Ferkó's out back with the car."

"Ferkó's with you?"

"Ferkó's with me. Do you think I would've allowed Fodor to torture you?"

Ferkó opened the door of the Pobeda's rear compartment.

321

"You wouldn't have a blindfold by any chance?" I said.

Sándor said: "Do you think I'd go through the trouble of getting together a firing squad at this time of night?"

"It's just so I won't have to see the traffic, because if you want me to sit up straight and watch the oncoming headlights, you may as well shoot me."

"In that case, we're both in luck. Just stretch out in the back seat, face down. You won't have to stare into the headlights like some wide-eyed roe-deer and I won't have to waste a bullet."

The interior of the Pobeda was nicer than the trunk if only because it had seats. I'd never been in one before but I assumed that the leather upholstery, plush black carpeting, subdued lighting, and radio-telephone were all standard. The only option was the manacles ring-bolted to the floor. Door handles must have been optional also because there didn't seem to be any.

After twenty minutes or so, I felt the Pobeda begin to climb and I assumed we were somewhere in the Buda Hills. The smallish peaks that passed for mountains in Hungary were still half an hour's drive north. Ten more minutes passed and I heard the crunch of gravel under the tires. The Pobeda glided to a halt.

"Keep the motor running, Ferkó," Sándor said. "I'll be right back."

The effect of Sándor's words on me was less chilling than, well, humiliating. Not only did he know I was listening, but he spoke to Ferkó in the same casual tone that a chess master might use when, in the midst of a match with a touted challenger, he turns to a friend and says: "Lunch in five?"

Any sane person would have been terrified, and, no doubt, somewhere inside me there was a sane and terrified person padlocked away in my mind's equivalent of a root cellar by the impostor whose words these are and whose absurd sense of honor had been gravely affronted by Sándor's offhandedness—as if the threat of imminent death were less ruffling than a condescending remark.

Through the cellar door, the real me, gnawing on a raw potato to calm his nerves, heard the impostor think: "I might be dead within the quarter-hour, but I'll be damned if Sándor's going to treat my death as casually as if he were taking out the trash."

Real me tried to think of something to say in response like, "Hey! Idiot! Spare me the feigned outrage. My life's at stake, not your pride," but decided against it, only to find that this hearing of thoughts business went both ways.

Sham me: "Our honor's at stake, not my pride."

"Honor, Schmonor!" was all real me could manage.

Sham me thought: "How do you look yourself in the mirror each morning?"

"Why do you think I wear a beard?" real me thought back.

"Do you think you might like to get out of the car, Pál?" This question belonged to Sándor, who was propping open the rear door with one hand, while lackadaisically waving the pistol at me with the other.

Ferkó had parked the Pobeda at the base of the stone lookout on János-hegy standing 529 meters, at its highest point, over Budapest. The tower itself, a splendid example of the brief late nineteenth-century vogue called the neo-Romanesque style, wasn't nearly that tall and anyone falling from its crenellated parapets or one of the observation decks that ringed its walls would not have much time to take in the finer points of its construction.

Sándor had recovered enough of his tact not to offer any of the gruesome jests about being squashed like a grape upon the ground's rising up to meet you. But that couldn't have mattered less to me, since it turned out that my impostor shared my fear of heights: unpadlocking the root cellar door and handing me back the deed to myself, he wished me no hard feelings and dissolved in a liquid flash of neurochemical fire.

My vertigo kicked in just as Sándor and I arrived at the base of the dark tower looming above us. Jánoshegy set to spinning in one direction, the tower in the other. My entire being convulsed and seemed to say: "There's no way you're getting me up there." I'm translating, of course. The language of entire being doesn't sound anything like this. To Sándor's ears, it must have sounded something like this: a longish wail that rose and fell unpredictably within the sonic range defined, at one end, by a train whistle's low moan and the owl's hoot at the other, followed by the thud of my body as it hit the whirling ground.

I was still clutching the grass, trying to make myself as low as possible, when the vertiginous feelings that had welled up in head subsided long enough to let some of Sándor's words pass into my understanding.

"I'd forgotten you were afraid of heights, Pál"

"I'm not afraid of heights so much as falling," I said, rising to my feet.

"Do you think it would help things if we covered your face with my jacket and I led you up the stairs like a blinkered mule?"

"I might be able to make it as far as the first rampart by that means."

"But that's only a few meters high, Pál. You won't even bruise yourself jumping from that height."

"I'd be happy to adjust the rate of my descent accordingly."

Sándor shed his coat and draped it over my bowed head much as a hangman pulls the black hood over the eyes of the condemned. He took my hand and led me up the tower in silence.

I refused to take the stairs less than one at a time and, like a small and stubborn child, would set my lagging and my leading foot down beside each other on the same tread before I would resume my sluggish ascent. Rising thus by modest increments, I drew the grimmest satisfaction from imagining Ferkó in the car below, checking his watch, lighting yet another cigarette, growing impatient with his master who'd predicted that this wouldn't take too long.

Upon arriving at a fatal altitude, Sándor backed me up against a wall and drew his coat from off my head. A swift night wind lightly slapped my face and brushed my hair. And I heard Sándor say: "Now, keep your eyes closed. I don't want you to fall down like before. Not yet anyway."

His slip was bad enough. I resented his recovery even more. If I had to die, it was probably a good thing that the one responsible was an insensitive boor like Sándor. I tried to draw comfort from the fact that each time I'd been ready to succumb to self-pity and fear, Sándor, as if on cue, had managed to say something to annoy or offend me. Though it had never before occurred to me that I might, in the midst of a fit of pique, set off to meet to my maker, as emotions associated with death go, anger seemed preferable to terror.

Sándor placed his hands under my arms and prepared to raise me with my help into a sitting position on the top of the wall. From that position I'd make it to my knees easily enough, before standing up and turning around to face the void.

"Shall we get this over with, Pál? Anna's waiting for me in a villa not far from here. She'll swear I was there all evening should anyone ask."

"But no one will believe I took my own life," I said. "I haven't any reason to kill myself."

"Of course they will, Pál, and, if you don't mind me saying so: yes, you do. Why, you're a textbook candidate. You've been such a disappointment to yourself and others. It's true you had a great career ahead of you in Slavic Studies before Kellner threw you out of the department, but then you transferred, in disgrace, to a struggling program with little or no prestige. Then there's your failed marriage. I'll bet you're still filled with remorse for cheating on Ágnes."

"Ágnes didn't want me to leave. *I* thought it would be best if I moved out."

"That was gallant of you," Sándor said, "But even as a student, you were a moody bastard. *Istenem*. You were so morose. You would mope about so absorbed in self-pity that no one could get so much as a *megvagyok* out of you. And you're legend for your creepy twilight rambles through the cemetery. I bet you know all of the caretakers and gardeners and gravediggers by name."

"There's a new man operating the back-hoe whose acquaintance I haven't made yet."

"See?" Sándor said. "You've always struck me as someone too much in love with death. Nobody's going to be that surprised you jumped."

"Perhaps, you're right," I said. "I just don't think I can bring myself to throw myself off this tower."

"I can't just shoot you."

"Then don't." I played my last card. "Tell me what you told István to send him over the top. Maybe it will work a second time."

"I don't see how. Your situation is entirely different from his."

"Nothing else has worked so far."

"I told István that Éva had been with child by him but that she had terminated the pregnancy on László's advice. I thought that might provide him with enough after-the-fact motivation to make his confession seem credible. I lied about everything, but it did the trick."

"Did you ever consider that you didn't *need* to lie about everything?"

"What are you asking me?"

"Did you ever consider that you weren't lying to István about everything?"

"Did I ever consider not lying to István about everything? No. I probably told István some lies I didn't need to tell to make him confess, but I never considered *not* telling any of them. To be honest, I didn't give much thought to what I was going to say in advance. I just improvised."

"I'm still not making myself clear."

"That's not my fault, Pál. I find your way of posing a question irritating."

"Let me put it in the form of a statement then: You didn't need to lie about everything, Sándor. You didn't need to lie about everything because not everything you told István was a lie. István *was* the father of the child. You weren't lying when you told him that."

"What are you saying? The boy's mine."

"Éva needed you to believe that. You might not have helped her had you'd known the truth."

"You don't know what you're talking about."

"When Éva learned she was pregnant, she didn't know what to do. Though she was certain the child was István's, she was terrified that István might not believe her if he found out that she'd been with you around the same time."

"I'm the father of that child."

"She went to Kellner for advice but there was some miscommunication because he assumed the child was yours. He needed to protect you from scandal, so he insisted that Éva terminate the pregnancy. She didn't understand why Kellner would want her to abort the child she was going to have by István. Still, she would've obeyed Kellner had she not run into you. You offered her a way to save her baby, to find it a good home. All she had to do was let you think that you were the father. It never occurred to István that Éva had been pregnant by him until you told him."

"But she wasn't pregnant by him. I've already told you. I lied to István so he'd confess to doing what I did."

"You only thought you were lying."

"How do I know you're not lying?"

"I've seen the birth and baptism records. I'm sorry to have to tell you this, Sándor, but you don't have a son. Zoltán is István's boy. He was baptized István

Borsódy."

"I don't believe you."

"Did you ever think about why Kellner was so anxious to protect you? He wasn't worried that you'd be exposed for cheating on your wife. He was worried that the exposure itself might lead the Interior Ministry to drop you as one of their informers. Perhaps he mentioned something like this in the pages you read on Éva's pc."

"He was trying to help me get ahead."

"He was trying to keep you in place as an informer for as long as possible because he knew he could manipulate you."

A long silence followed.

"Sándor?" I said finally.

"Why did he hate me?" Sándor said, his voice filled with despair.

"He didn't even hate you, Sándor. He used you."

"Why did he save you?" he cried.

An immeasurable distance opened up between us. Sándor had been damned all along. Kellner had marked him from the start just as—it was terrible to arrive at this knowledge only now, now as death approached—just as Kellner had marked me for a life less damnable.

I thought I heard someone running up the steps of the tower, but I kept my eyes closed tight. Then I heard Balogh yell at Sándor to drop his gun. I heard a shot. I heard a body collapse against the rampart wall and slide roughly down to its base. Balogh shouted at me not to move. I opened my eyes and watched him approach Sándor, who was doubled over, his legs folded awkwardly under him. Blood flowed down Sándor's back and over his sides, blackening his shirt in the shadow of the rampart. A piece of his skull had been shot away. Balogh uncurled Sándor's lifeless fingers to release the still-smoking pistol and ejected the empty cartridge from its clip.

Two more officers arrived. One called for an ambulance, the other helped me down off the battlement.

"Where did you come from?" I said to Balogh. He looked bigger somehow.

"We got a call," he said. He gazed at the Pobeda below. Ferkó was lighting the cigarette of a uniformed policeman.

"Ferkó's with you?" I said. "Just how long were you going to wait before showing yourself, Balogh?"

"I'm sorry, Pál. We cut it a little close, but we had to come in on foot so Petri wouldn't hear us," Balogh said. "Are you all right?"

"I'm not all right. I was seconds away from being forced off this tower. I wouldn't have imagined that you would place my life at risk. You're much tougher and more cunning than I thought, Balogh."

"I couldn't tell you that we were keeping an eye on you, Pál. People who know they're being looked out for can't help but act as if they know it. Fodor and Petri would have picked that up and killed you." Balogh paused as if chastened by his own words. "Let's just say we were lucky to have had Ferkó in deep cover all this time so he could make sure nothing happened to you."

"I'm feeling rather like that poor goat devoured by the Kimonos just now."

"You've every right to be upset with me for not telling you everything before I sent you on this errand. I never expected that you'd track down this

Fodor or Csorba character and then try to tail him. But I hope you're not implying that I've begun to resemble a certain filmmaker or, even worse, that Petri played the part of the Komodo in this episode, because, unlike the dragon, he *knew* he was doing wrong."

"I wonder if there wasn't something of the goat about Sándor. At least when he was still a young student. I wonder if he wasn't guided toward a role he'd never asked to play by someone who knew that once he was cast in that role, he'd never be able to relinquish it."

"I thought Kellner looked after him all those years."

"I'd thought so too. It's no matter. It's just the way Sándor sounded just before you arrived. Something he said before he pulled the trigger."

"You might give Kati a call," Balogh said, handing me my phone. "I think she's been trying to reach you."

I took a step in the direction of the stairs, but I lost my balance and would have fallen had Balogh not steadied me.

"I'll need help getting down from here, Balogh. I can't make it by myself."

"None of us can make it by ourselves, Pál. Haven't you learned that by now?"

WEDNESDAY, 28 JUNE

CHAPTER SIXTY-TWO

"Kellner must have been shocked to find Sándor's reports at the archives," the soft-spoken Tamás said over the half-hissing, half-screeching brakes of the 12:47 from Budapest. Pál had chosen the dingy restaurant at railway station for today's fish special: the snowy-fleshed pike-perch caught only in the cloudy waters of Lake Balaton.

Pál speared another piece of *fogas* and told himself that Tamás would arrive at the truth more quickly if he said nothing. He watched his old friend's pale thin face color slightly as his tone shifted from one of bland curiosity to more than casual interest mixed with notes of confusion. The station's PA blared with news of the incoming Makó train.

"Kellner *was* shocked to discover Sándor's reports?" Tamás said again, chewing on the question as if it were a gristly chunk of stew meat.

"How's your *pörkölt*?" Pál said. Tamás's plate glistened with beef and paprika gravy smelling of onions and fat.

Tamás smiled the way he always did when experience confirmed his darkest intuitions. "Find what you seek," With his fork, he steered a square of meat through its sauce and into a bank of bright yellow pearl-shaped noodles. "Kellner knew what he'd find even before he gained access to the Secret Police archives. That's why you're not saying anything. He knew about Sándor's informing."

Pál ate the last of his fish.

Tamás laid his fork down. "When do you think Kellner first suspected Sándor?"

"I think he suspected Sándor would turn all along."

"You speak as if Kellner distrusted him *before* Sándor joined the Party."

"That's what I think. Kellner thought Sándor was the kind to turn informer long before Sándor joined the Party and that's why Kellner encouraged him to join."

"Why would he do that? He encouraged both of us to join. Did he think that we'd turn informers too?"

"He was sure we wouldn't. In that respect, Sándor showed far more promise than either of us. I'd even bet that Kellner was reasonably sure we wouldn't join the Party, though now it seems he needed to make sure by forcing the question at the worst time."

"Are you saying that Kellner wanted Sándor to join the Party *because* he was unprincipled and ambitious, and thus more likely to inform on the department than we were?" Tamás shook his head as if he couldn't believe what he'd just said. "Pál, Kellner had just been appointed department chairman. He'd only been rehabilitated a few years earlier. His own position was by no means secure. Why would he encourage Sándor to join the Party if he suspected Sándor might inform against him and everyone else?"

"He considered Sándor an insurance policy. He represented Kellner's best hope of minimizing the harm done by informants to the Slavic Studies faculty and its students. To the extent that Sándor was un-principled, he wouldn't think twice about informing on anyone in the department, but neither would he feel obliged to report everything that occurred nor even what he chose to report *as* it occurred."

Tamás continued for Pál: "But to the extent that Sándor was ambitious, Kellner must have gambled that Sándor would be careful not to portray the de-partment in too harsh a light for fear of implicating himself by association with counter-revolutionary atti-tudes and practices."

"That's it. Sándor was a known evil. That's why Kellner had to protect him even after Sándor raped Éva, even at the expense of Éva's and István's future happiness—if only he'd known the child was István's. It was a gamble he felt he had to take. Had it paid off? Perhaps Kellner felt it hadn't in the end. Perhaps that's why he died with so many regrets, why he felt so compelled to set the record straight in his mem-oirs."

"Wouldn't you think that placing the young Sán-dor, who was innocent enough before he joined the Party, in a position to compromise himself might be a source of regret for Kellner?"

"I'm sure Kellner agonized over his decision, but he didn't coerce Sándor to inform. Sándor just struck Kellner as the sort that might." For the first time since he'd stood on the battlements waiting to die, Pál remembered the despair, the terrible tone of betrayal he'd heard in Sándor's voice moments before he killed himself. Generous tears filled Pál Berkesi's eyes. He was crying for László Kellner.

"What's the matter, Pál?"

"I'm ashamed, Tamás. I hated him for years. I would duck into doorways whenever I saw him coming. What must he have thought?"

"Guilt has great powers of seduction, Pál. You mustn't give into to it. If all you say is true, you never had to ask for his forgiveness, though you finally seem to be offering him yours."

"It's taken me so long to figure out that he was trying to protect us when he forced me to leave the department. He knew what a loyal friend I had in you. So he knew you would leave with me. He knew because he had a friend like István Borsódy. He saved us, Tamás."

"Kellner was never the ogre he was made out to be, not by any means, but don't go to the other extreme and turn him into our patron saint."

"Borsódy said something at Kellner's funeral that I didn't understand at the time. You remember when he spoke of how he'd fought with Kellner over the fate of a student only to conclude much later that Kellner had been right. I took it the wrong way. I thought he meant that he'd come to believe that Kellner had been right to let us walk out of the department without making the slightest effort to bring us back as if we weren't worth the trouble."

"At the time, Pál, it was hard *not* to feel that way."

"Borsódy was trying to tell me that he'd once thought he could keep students like us safe from harm by having us join the Party. Kellner thought that the best way to keep us safe, which for him meant free from compromise, was to make sure we would never join it."

"You know, Pál, you may be right about their looking out for us. Just before he retired, our first chairman in the English Department hinted to me that two of his University colleagues had approached him separately. Seems they wanted to smooth our path a bit, dispel any doubts that old Bessenyei might have had about us after we appeared like pariahs on his doorstep."

"Did he specifically say that Kellner and Borsódy had approached to him?"

"He wouldn't reveal their names, but who else would have acted on our behalf?"

For a long time, Pál and Tamás look at each other in silence, only beginning to sense the enormity of their loss. They thought of their fathers and their mothers, of all those who had gone before them through a treacherous world. But most of all, they thought about their teachers, of the sacrifices they'd made so that their students might continue to grow in the understanding that would shine within them, protected, until fresh words might freely answer a stifled people's captive words.

László Kellner and István Borsódy must have believed that time was still far off, since the present, of all the shapes it might have assumed during their final days on earth, had come to resemble nothing so much as the dishonest past they'd known. It had made little difference that one had set to wrestling with that past while the other had tried to make his peace with it. In the end, both men had arrived at the same grim conclusion.

Once, in youth, they'd glimpsed a better two-weeks world of their own and a free people's making.

In age, they'd tried to shore up the remnants of that shattered world if only to make life in this counterfeit one more bearable. In the end, they'd been unable to sustain even the faintest image of that lost world and they'd seen enough of this one. Merciful death came to both cloaked in oblivion.

A line from an old play inscribed itself on a page in Pál's mind. He read it: *"The oldest hath borne most; we that are young shall never see so much, nor live so long."*

"I've got news for you, kid," Tamás said. "We ain't so young anymore."

EPILOGUE

Saturday, 16 June 2001

Balogh was late to the cemetery. The large crowd gathered at the busy end of Széchenyi Square for this year's Life and Freedom Party rally had spilled out onto Bridge Street and blocked traffic in both directions. Stranded, Balogh could only watch from his car as canned polka music gave way to the thunderous applause that overwhelmed the retiring party chief Ferenc Gyufa the moment he stepped up to the microphone. Balogh thought he could make out, underlying the great man's every gesture and inflection, a distinct "passing of the torch" leitmotif. Gyufa introduced today's main speaker, the newly elected president of the Life and Freedom Party, Szeged chapter: Mr. Viktor Uborka, Esq.

The even-more thunderous applause that greeted that fleshy eminence died down just as bridge traffic began to move again, though not so quickly that Balogh missed Uborka's entrance. Clad in a robin's-egg blue suit, as bright as his own and his party's future, and a regal-looking sash borrowed, no doubt, from a touring company of *The Prisoner of Zenda*, Uborka spread his arms wide as if to gather up his audience in his life-giving embrace.

Balogh was the tenth and final member to join the much smaller party assembled in a quiet corner of Újszeged cemetery. Two in the party had already been there for some time. A pair of recently unveiled head-stones marked where László Kellner and István Borsódy lay, one beside the other.

Among the living, Tamás Garay stood farthest to the left before László Kellner's grave. To his right stood Pál Berkesi. Both held advance copies of Kellner's soon-to-be-published memoirs. The last-known draft of the complete manuscript had never been found and Éva Hegedűs had destroyed the only two typescripts of the appendix. But early last July an unclaimed hard drive with the same serial number as that stolen from Éva's pc had turned up in little tech repair shop on Vas Street in Budapest. The missing texts were retrieved, edited with a light hand by an esteemed committee, and published with the minimal scholarly commentary and notes best suited for works aimed at the general reader.

To the right of Tamás and Pál, and before the grave of István Borsódy stood a red-headed young man in his early twenties with his mother, Éva Hegedűs. Since his release from prison, Zoltán had visited Éva every day, first at the women's house of correction, and now at the small house she shared on Bokor Street with five other female offenders as part of her work-release program. Having been forced to abandon her position in Slavic Studies when her pris-on sentence began, Éva had recently filled a similar position when Tamás's secretary of many years took early retirement.

To be near his mother, Zoltán had moved to Szeged. His adoptive parents encouraged him in his decision to relocate, convinced that he'd be wise to put some distance between him and the skinhead gang to which he'd once belonged. Zoli lived with Gabi Varga at her Galamb Street flat. They were saving up to buy their own place.

Gabi stood right behind Zoli and Éva, holding hands with Balogh's niece Erzsi, who was looking forward to her eleventh birthday this week, and who, in turn, held hands with Kati. After this morning's informal service, Kati and Pál had a date to look for last-minute offers for week-long excursions to Dalmatia. For luck, they would begin their search at the window of the Oroszlán Street agency where Pál had been creamed by a thundering herd of one distracted Uborka.

Last week, Zoli, finding himself not far from Bartók Square walked to Hajnóczy to remind himself of what a thug he'd been. He passed Oszkár Neumann just meters away from where they'd met the previous year. Mr. Neumann didn't recognize Zoli, who'd long since grown his hair back. For a moment, Zoli considered introducing himself and apologizing but was afraid of scaring the old man. Instead, he silently requested Mr. Neumann's forgiveness for the hundredth time. Not everything, he often told himself, can be made right.

He's not seen Zsolt since prison, but Zsolt, like his friend, seemed disinclined to return to the movement, especially once his guru Csorba the sculptor was exposed as a former communist and a member of the secret police. Zsolt thought he might like to move out of vandalism and into more licit graphic arts.

Csorba's sculptures were auctioned off in a single lot to the enterprising German owner of Worker's

Paradise, a postmodern theme park outside Berlin built to cash in on growing nostalgia for life under the Soviets. The fascists in the lot initially posed a problem whose solution entailed nothing more complicated than renaming Romanian fascist dictator Antonescu after the Romanian communist dictator Ceaușescu. Franco was rechristened after a head of the Polish secret police. Pinochet was transformed in name only into a Slovak minister of agriculture.

The statues of higher-profile fascists such as Hitler and Mussolini presented a more difficult challenge for the buyer. Hitler was auctioned off on eBay. American neo-Nazi groups initiated a bidding war, but the winning bid came from a Jewish youth group from Temple Beth Shalom in Merrick, Long Island.

Mussolini met a more ignoble fate and now hangs upside-down, a counterweight at a large industrial plant in Sarajevo. Workers use the dictator for spitting contests during lunch breaks.

No one knows where Sándor Petri lies buried. Word has it that Anna requested he be interred in an anonymous grave. She sold the Mátyás Square house last October and is said to be living with her children at her parents' house near Balaton.

Pál and Zoli lay wreaths on the graves of their dead. Éva watches the son she thought she had lost forever as he honors a father lost at birth. Pál smoothes the earth over László Kellner as he honors a father gained through death. Heads bowed, Pál and Zoli began to work out their respective salvations.

THE END

AFTERWORD

Hungary, and Szeged in particular, was Jack Roberts'
second homeland. His first visit to Szeged as a Fulbright professor lasted a full academic year, from Sep-
tember 2002 through July 28, 2003. He returned for
his next visit in May 2004 (the poem "Margitszigeten"
is dated May 28, 2004 and he held a poetry reading in
Classroom 3). Next he arrived on December 17, 2005
and stayed till January 12 conducting a round of visits.
In 2006 the fourth visit was connected to the 50th
anniversary of 1956, he could be invited officially to
take part in the celebrations by reading from this novel in the Fall. He also found the time for a poetry
reading (his translations of Radnóti's poems) in mid
October, and we also visited the police HQ then. The
lecture on detective fiction he gave that Fall was part
of his work on this novel. His next visit started in
May 2008 and he stayed through August, he gave a
talk on Hammett, on the Flitcraft episode in *The Mal-
tese Falcon,* on June 16. He even visited Kübekháza
and Révfülöp. In 2010 he had his sabbatical from
home and he stayed from March 30–July 18, teaching
and supervising theses, including PhD level, maintain-
ing friendships and making friends as the basis of it
all.

His research, when he arrived in 2002, was concerned with versions of American Pragmatism. He
taught a series of courses connected to this and also

lectured on American literature. Then he shifted his attention to aethetics and terror. He had a basic humility—a willingness to learn, not only academically. Part of this was his growing interest in detective fiction. We visited the police HQ at Szeged together to catch an impression and learn about the hierarchy. He got interested in events of 1956, and I suspect wrote a *roman de clef* [a novel in which actual persons and events are disguised as fictional characters] about 1956 and its aftermath in a university context.

Writing detective fiction did not come naturally to Jack. Writing poetry did. Just look at his piece "Margitszigeten," which he wrote in 2004:

> The stones of the ruined monastery
> tremble with a childishly insipid
> and, no doubt, immensely popular
> television theme launched heavenwards
> from a psychedelic mobile phone
> whose besotted owner croons his love
> to his third last love this week.
>
>   Some might call
> this profanation, but what's profane
> about love and faith. If not his faith,
> why not then that of the duskrunners
> steps away on the island-ringing path.
> Quiet as monks, surely as austere,
> these too would home before dark.
> Here, on this island, in this double city,
> in this behorded, kinged, and sainted country,
> all is reconciled.
>   And I am reconciled.

Forty years it's taken me to learn what I need
what another knew in youth and youthful death.
Sándor, your language defies me, denies my own.
And so with you I say: Szabadság, szerelem!
E kettő kell nekem. And love's still love
And freedom just another name for faith.

I am not saying he did not work on poems, he did, it took him two years to do this one. But it came out as if easily, a graceful gesture to himself and to his second homeland, to which he had become so attached a few years before.

Neither did he keep detective fiction in the focus of his attention. The fact that he came prepared, when he first arrived on his tour of duty as a Fulbright Professor, carrying The Library of America volumes by Hammett and Chandler as gifts to me, an as yet unknown colleague, attests to his good graces and good taste not trying to impose his own favourites on others even as presents (he could have brought me a tome by William James!).

It is so unfair to have other people, strangers writing about something that you yourself ought to explain. Like me here, trying to say something about Jon Roberts and his novel.

"Not how he died, not what he died of, even less why he died, are of concern, to me, only the fact that he did die, he is dead, is important: the loss to me, to us" (B.S. Johnson)

György Novák